Piper Jea

FALLING FOR KOREA

Vaniker Press

ISBN: 979-8-9864577-0-3 (eBook)
ISBN: 979-8-9864577-1-0 (Paperback)
ISBN: 979-8-9864577-2-7 (Audiobook)
www.piperjean.com

For my darling girls
Find your Gilbert.
And for Pauline
I miss you, cuz.

1

SYDNEY

Our plane shuddered and dipped, waking the baby that had finally stopped screaming. The elderly lady next to me jerked with a gasp and clutched at her arm rests.

"*Halmeoni*, are you okay?" I asked, using the Korean title for grandmother. She wasn't *my* grandma, but she had been my seatmate for the fourteen-hour flight to Seoul. A formal title would be expected. She looked pale and even more nervous than when we had taken off.

"I'm fine, dear," she said but slumped lower in the seat next to me. Her petite frame seemed to disappear in the silky ruffles of her dress.

I took her hand in alarm. It was cool and clammy. Was this just motion sickness or something worse? I waved at the flight attendant in first class with quick movements.

She walked to us, bent close to the older woman, and spoke gently. "Halmeoni, how can I help you? Would you like some water?" She pulled a bottle from the apron at her waist.

"My pills." Halmeoni reached for the leather purse next to her on the seat. I took it and unzipped the main compartment. A silver case sat on top, and I opened it to a neat row of blue capsules. Her voice came out paper-thin. "Those are the ones."

I pressed a single pill into her hand and watched as she brought it to her mouth. The flight attendant held the water to her lips and Halmeoni swallowed. She took a shaky breath.

"I'm okay. Just give me a minute and the medicine will help."

The flight attendant stood up, her poised demeanor reassuring me more than Halmeoni's still weak smile. "Press the call button if you need anything at all."

Halmeoni gave a polite nod as the woman moved down the aisle, but leaned closer to whisper, "They'll come running because they don't want an old lady like me dying on their flight."

I stared at her, heavy lines creasing my forehead. "No one wants that." Least of all me, I thought. I was afraid of so many things, but death topped the list. Not my own, just a general dislike of the idea. My uncle Greg, who was the world's worst psychiatrist, said I had crippling PTSD. He was wrong. And the word crippling was total overkill. My high school GPA remained Ivy worthy, and I'd held down a part-time job since I was twelve. It was true that I slept with the light on. And I'd rather bleed to death than step inside a hospital, but then I'd only been ten when I watched my mom almost die. Could anyone blame me if I was a little clingy after months of watching Mom fade, chemo-thin, while dodging social workers and getting myself to school on time? I'd like to see Uncle Greg live that childhood and walk away normal.

Halmeoni chuckled next to me. "No need to look so serious. I'm too stubborn to die."

I tried to smile, but she still looked pale.

"Really, I feel fine now. Tell me your name, dear. We've sat together this whole flight, and I've been too rude, not talking to you. I didn't realize you spoke Korean."

"That's okay. I should have introduced myself earlier. I'm Sydney Moore."

"Well, Sydney. You don't need to fuss over me. I'm more worried about you flying into Seoul all alone. You can't be older than my grandson. How old are you, child?"

"Seventeen," I said.

"I guess you're old enough, but be careful of strangers. You'll light up the airport with all that blonde hair and your blue eyes." She tsked. "Such a pretty thing to fly alone."

"I'll be careful," I said.

Halmeoni looked pleased and leaned closer. "Tell me your secret. How do you speak Korean so well? You must have been raised in South Korea. Maybe your parents are diplomats?"

Not in this life. I wondered what she would think if she knew my dad had died before I could walk, and Mom and I were dirt-poor. "Nothing so interesting," I said. "My grandpa was military and stationed in South Korea when my mom was born. They stayed eight years and then when she was fourteen, she moved back with a host family, even finished high school there. After that she swore her kids would learn Korean." I shrugged. "I guess it's a little eccentric, but it wasn't until I went to kindergarten that I learned English."

"Well, you speak better than my grandson. His slang and K-pop words don't make sense."

I couldn't hide my grin. "Thank you, Halmeoni."

"Are you here as a tourist, then?"

"No." I swallowed the hot lump in the back of my throat and blinked hard. I hadn't cried when I left, and I wouldn't do it now. "My godmother lives here and she's been depressed, so I came to keep her company. She and my mom are best friends, so I couldn't really say no." I actually had said no, even pleaded and begged, but my mom wasn't having it.

"You don't seem happy. Do you not like your godmother?"

"Oh, she's great. Her family was my mom's host family when she came here for school. I just don't like leaving my mom."

Halmeoni frowned. "You've never left your home?"

I nodded my head, embarrassed. Uncle Greg would love hearing our conversation. His nickname for me was "Superglue." I knew I wasn't normal on this. No one my age wanted to hang out with her mom on Friday night. I did.

"How long will you stay?"

"I'm not sure. My godmother bought just the one-way ticket, but I have to be back home in a few weeks to start school."

"So your godmother is wealthy, and you are not. This is why you are flying first class and also why you don't look like these other girls." Halmeoni nodded like she'd solved some great mystery.

"Other girls?" It should have sounded rude, but Halmeoni said it like I was special for being different.

She waved her hand in a dismissive fashion. "You know, the ones with Princess Disease."

I laughed. I'd never heard the term, but I knew a princess or two back home. I glanced down at my faded jeans— not designer faded but Goodwill faded. They were too big, cinched around my waist with a scarf and then rolled high at the hem. I'd paired my fashion-forward attire with a fitted white shirt, an extra from my mom's housekeeping uniform. "I guess I don't look rich if that's what you mean?"

"I mean you look kind, Sydney. Your sunshine spirit will be sure to brighten your godmother's life. She is lucky to get a visit from you."

"I hope so. I'm good at cheering up my mom."

She patted my hand in agreement and nodded, then pointed out the window. "Look." I turned as the clouds parted with the afternoon sun. Seoul appeared below us, spread out in miniature. Tiny high rises and roads wove and intersected with more buildings and roads. The city was beautiful and the sky, a flawless blue. The kind of sky that comes when summer is almost over, but you hope for one more perfect day. All good omens.

I sat back in my seat. It would be okay. I could do a few weeks without Mom. She'd been in full remission for almost six years, and I hadn't had a panic attack in two. Nothing to worry about. The only nagging thought was that she would be alone while I was gone. Unless you counted the visits from Uncle Greg, and I never counted him. Mom turned a blind eye, but Uncle Greg's counseling sessions made my life miserable. At least in Korea I wouldn't have to see him for a while.

"Is someone picking you up? Incheon is a large airport. If you want, I can have my driver take you home."

"My godmother is picking me up. I guess I should start calling her Suni, or Mrs. Kim. Or, I know you guys say names different here—the last name first—so Kim Suni."

Halmeoni's eyes got large. "Did you say Suni?"

I nodded.

"Is Kim Suni your godmother?"

"Yes. Do you know her?"

"I wish I did." Halmeoni sat up straighter and smoothed the silk of her skirt like the queen of England might stroll down the aisle at any moment. "I've seen her at charity events, but I've never sat at her table."

I wrinkled my brow. The leather bag nestled in Halmeoni's lap was clearly expensive, and the diamond ring on her manicured finger was far from small. I knew my godmother wasn't poor, but she wasn't stupid-rich either. At least my mom had never said she was.

Halmeoni patted my hand. "If we run into each other again, I hope you will introduce me to Madam Kim. You are a favored child."

Before I could respond, a heavy thud rolled through the cabin and my jet-lagged brain registered that we'd landed. I leaned closer to the window and watched the runway fly below us before we slowed and shuddered to a stop at our gate. The seat belt sign turned off, and weary passengers stood, some eager and some slow. Everyone wanted off the plane. Everyone but me.

I made myself stand. The sooner I could cheer up Suni, the sooner I could go home. Halmeoni gathered her purse, then stood slowly and wobbled a bit on her feet.

"Do you need help getting to customs?" I asked. My mom had explained how long it took to get to baggage claim, and I worried that Halmeoni wouldn't be able to walk that far.

"My personal assistant will be waiting with a wheelchair. But you are welcome to follow us."

"Okay," I said, happy not to be alone.

Halmeoni paused. "But I do wonder something. Are you familiar with the Kim's son? I read he was quite the leader in an article they did about his school. I believe he is a senior this year, so probably close to your age."

I blinked. Suni didn't have a son. I mean, I didn't think she did. I'd never asked or even wondered if she had children. I covered my unease with a polite smile. "What's his name?"

Halmeoni furrowed her brow. "I don't remember, but he was very handsome."

Stupid of me that I'd never asked detailed questions about Suni's life before. I took Halmeoni's hand to steady her, then chewed my lip as we moved down the aisle. Other than the gifts and occasional brief phone call, when I said thank you, I knew next to nothing about my godmother. I didn't even know if she was married. Or maybe this *very handsome son* was one of many children.

After shuffles and waiting, we were off the plane and a woman in a smart black pantsuit waited for Halmeoni with a wheelchair. "Madam." She spoke softly as she helped her employer sit. It took forever to clear customs, and then finally we were to baggage claim and the assistant began the scramble to retrieve luggage.

Halmeoni gave my hand a final squeeze. "This is goodbye, then."

I didn't see Suni anywhere, but I put on a brave face. "It was so nice to meet you," I said.

Halmeoni stared past me. "I think this will be a good visit for you," she said, pointing.

I turned and followed the line of her finger. A guy leaned against the wall across from the spinning carousel of suitcases. He stood out, tall and broad but with a face that said boy more than man. He wore his black hair longer in the front and short on the sides. Shadows played below cinnamon-dark eyes, giving him a mysterious, if not sleep-deprived, look. He glanced down at his phone and back up, scanning the crowd. Good thing *he* wasn't my ride. His eyes met mine and stopped, then quickly jerked away. It didn't mean anything. A lot of people had stared at me since getting off the plane.

I turned back to Halmeoni. "Do you know him?"

She gave me a funny smile. "It was so nice to meet you, dear." And then her assistant was pushing her towards the glass doors along with a cart of suitcases.

I looked back to where the boy had stood, but he was gone. Instead, a middle-aged man stopped in front of me. He was dressed in a dark suit and tie with salt-and-pepper gray hair. He spoke, out of breath and in English. "Excuse me, miss. Are you Sydney Moore?"

I took a step back and answered him in English. "Um, and you are?" That's when I noticed he held an electronic tablet with Sydney Moore scrawled across it. "Yes, I'm Sydney," I said feeling slow and thick in the head. Lack of sleep and too much recycled air were catching up.

He gave me a quick stiff bow. "I'm Hyun, your driver. If you will direct me, I can collect your luggage and escort you to the car."

The man spoke perfect English, but slowly. I wasn't sure if the slow part was because English was hard for him, so I answered in Korean. "I only have one bag. It's the blue one with duct tape on the wheel." I could see it moving on the belt, as beat up and alone as I felt. "But where is Suni?" I asked, disappointed to not have been greeted by someone more familiar.

Hyun gave another stiff bow. "Madam Kim is working in Canada at the moment."

2

CHUL

My mother's text came with no warning.

> **Sydney Moore**
> **ICN International**
> **United 893**
> **3:12pm Sun Aug 6th**
>
> **Please pick up Shannon Moore's daughter. Sydney will be attending Daeshim Academy with you for her senior year. They have her schedule in the office. Your father will be here another few weeks, but I'll find a way to fly home tonight and check on her before I go back for work.**

What was my mother trying to do now? It wasn't lost on me that both my parents were spending more time away from home than normal. I got the message. They were still mad. But why have me pick up this girl? Hyun would be better. She texted me again.

Are you there, son?

I texted back.

I'm here, even though you never are.

I tried putting in my headphones and maxing the volume with ARENA-Z, but she just kept on.

The Canada deal is taking longer than we thought. You are responsible for getting her to school and watching over her. Make sure you sit together at lunch. I had the yellow guest room on the third floor prepared.

I responded with a thumbs up emoji and then drove to the airport. I'd pick her up, but then she was on her own. I could barely handle my own problems without babysitting some girl who would be struggling all year. I doubted she even spoke Korean.

As far as I knew, Sydney was poor. I knew her dad had

died when she was a baby, and her mom worked as a maid at a hotel. But if she needed a private school, why fly her all the way out here? My mother could pay for any prep school in the states.

I sighed and leaned against the wall. The airport was crowded, but I scanned the throng of tired passengers. My phone pinged, and I pulled it out of my jeans pocket. It was a photo from my mother.

When I was growing up, she'd talked a lot about Shannon's perfect daughter. I think somewhere around twelve-years-old I got sick of hearing about how wonderful Sydney was and tuned it all out. I never bothered to wonder what she looked like. But the universe, or karma, or whatever you want to call it got the last laugh on this one, because Sydney really was perfect.

I couldn't help but stare— sun-kissed skin, easy smile, silky blonde hair, and all those curves. In the photo, she wore a blue swimsuit and had her arms wrapped tightly around her mom, the California coast blurred in the background.

So that's what this was. My mother was trying to play matchmaker. Why else would she send *me* a picture like *this*? Whatever my mother was up to couldn't be good, and if this girl was stupid enough to get involved, I wasn't. My finger hovered over the delete button and then, like an idiot, I pressed save. Not that it meant anything. I still wasn't getting anywhere near Sydney. A girl like that wouldn't just cut ties with her old life to come eat kimchi. My mother had to have promised her something.

So I did what I always do when I can't handle my parents. I called Hyun. It rang and he sent me to voicemail. Twice. I tried a third time. He picked up on the last ring.

"Yes, Chul?"

"I can't do this. Mother just texted me a picture, and I'm out."

"How can you be *out* from a picture?"

"I should text it to you."

"Please don't. Just man up and give the girl a ride. You own three cars."

"It's not that." I sighed, running my hands through my hair. "I just need to stay away from her. It's better if we never meet."

"Why? No, don't tell me. I'm too old for this. It will be something angsty and dramatic that I can't listen to—"

I interrupted his rant. "Doesn't it seem odd that she would agree to come here for her senior year? What does Sydney want out of it? And more importantly, what does my mother want?"

Hyun sighed. "Why are you being paranoid again? Your parents love you."

"If they love me so much, why don't they ever come home? My father acts like he can't even be in the same room as me."

"Your father isn't the expressive type. That doesn't mean he doesn't care," Hyun said.

"I know what he's like, but it's been worse since . . . you know, last year."

"If you're referring to the one incident, then you're wrong."

"See," I snapped. "Even you can't say it. I got arrested. They covered it up with money and connections, but that doesn't mean I'm forgiven."

Hyun went silent on the other end, then raised his voice, something he rarely did with me. "Your parents made it go away because you're a good kid. You made one bad choice, and the only reason you got arrested was because that college jerk dumped the blame on you."

I cleared my throat. I didn't know Hyun thought of it that way. I doubted my parents did. Hyun was more willing to give me the benefit of the doubt. But like always, that had to be enough. "Okay, I'm sorry."

"I don't want to hear any more about getting arrested," he said.

"Got it."

Hyun sighed heavily. "Good."

"But will you help me with Sydney?"

"Why is picking her up a problem? You normally don't mind helping people."

"She's being paraded in front of me like bait. Everything Mother's asking me to do is stuff she normally assigns to you. I'm sure she's up to something, and you probably know what it is."

"I don't know any more about Sydney than you do, but I doubt she's coming here to ruin your life. Your mother may be manipulative at times, but she's trying to make your future better."

I snorted. "You try being on the receiving end, and then see if you still feel the same way."

Hyun laughed. "I've known Suni since before you were born. Do you think she hasn't meddled in my life before?"

"Either way, I'm not getting anywhere near Sydney Moore. She lands in forty-five minutes. So unless you want some American girl wandering around Incheon alone, you'd better move it." I hung up before he could argue and then walked to baggage claim. He'd come. I knew he would, but I'd stay long enough to see her in person.

3

SYDNEY

How could Suni be in Canada? I numbly followed Hyun out the glass doors but stopped when the humidity hit me. He didn't notice, just continued on with my suitcase to a black town car with tinted windows parked just a few yards down.

Mom had specifically said Suni would pick me up, and even though Hyun looked legit, I couldn't just drive off with a complete stranger. "Hey, Hyun, can you call Suni for me before we head out?"

Hyun paused but then nodded. "I understand. You don't know me. Of course, I can call her, but I don't know if she will pick up. Meetings have been keeping her longer these days."

Sweat started to run down my neck, and I wasn't sure if it was from the smothering hot air, or because I'd just flown halfway around the world for no good reason. Hyun pulled out his phone, tapped on the screen, and handed it to me. "It's ringing."

I nodded and took it with a smile. It went to voicemail, but I did hear the silvery chime of Suni's familiar voice. I didn't leave a message. "Do you mind if I call my mom? It will be international, so I can pay you back."

"Yes, you may certainly call your mom, and there is no need to pay me back."

Thankful that Hyun wasn't asking me why I didn't have my own phone, I quickly dialed Mom's number. Mom had said she would be disconnecting the phone we both shared to save money, but I hoped she hadn't had time yet. A recorded message said it was no longer a working number. I chewed my bottom lip. I had no choice. I could either wait here with no phone and no idea where Suni lived or go with Hyun, who honestly seemed like a really nice guy. Still, I hoped I wouldn't wake up with only one kidney or something.

I handed the phone back to Hyun after he closed the trunk on my suitcase. He opened the back door for me. I got in and waited until he was driving before I spoke up. "Do you know when Suni plans to be home?"

"I'm not sure. I know she changed her return flight when she found out you were coming, so it should be soon."

"Oh," I said, relieved. "Is there stuff she wants me to help with around the house? I was planning to do whatever she needed, and maybe when she gets back from Canada, we could do some sightseeing to cheer her up."

Hyun's eyebrows raised in the rear-view mirror, and he frowned. "Suni doesn't like sightseeing."

"What about walks? Does she have a favorite park, or does she like to go hiking? Sunshine is very helpful for depression."

"Suni has a personal trainer, but I don't think they walk. Are you in need of walking for depression?"

"No," I said, embarrassed. Suni probably didn't speak to her driver about her health. Guilt settled over me like yesterday's makeup. I needed to just keep my mouth shut until I could talk to her. I leaned back into the leather seat and tried to remember exactly what Mom had said about this trip. It had been sudden and weird, the way she'd hustled me to the airport without even letting me pack for myself. It had all seemed like an emergency when I got home that afternoon.

She waited for me just inside the door with keys in hand. "Syd, you won't believe what happened today."

"What?" I asked.

Mom was usually so chill, but she fidgeted with her keys and rocked from foot to foot nervously. "I'll explain in the car." She took my arm and walked me right back out the front door. "We need to hurry. The plane leaves in three hours, and traffic is bad."

"What plane? Are we going on vacation? Shouldn't we pack?"

Mom marched me to our old beat-up Nissan. "No need. I have your suitcase and stuff all ready. Hurry and get in."

"Wait. Where are we going?"

"Syd!" Mom raised her voice, and my eyes went big. She never acted this worked up. "Get in. We can't be late."

"Okay, okay." I climbed in the front seat and put on my seat belt. "Did we win a vacation or something?" Mom liked to call into radio shows when they ran promotions and contests. One time we won concert tickets to Riot Cardia. I'd never heard of the band, but we went, and it was cool to see her smiling and swaying to the beat, even if the music was old-people-weird.

"No, you might as well have, though. Suni bought you a first-class ticket to Seoul. I know you've always wanted to meet her, and now you get the chance. Your flight leaves in a few hours."

"You mean us, right? I wouldn't go to Korea alone."

Mom frowned. "I can't go. I have to work."

The first tide of panic stirred in my stomach. "Did you really tell her you had to work? You have lots of vacation saved. I'm not going without you. Let's reschedule the trip so you can come, too."

"Sweetie, I really can't go. This is still the busy season at the hotel, and Suni needs you now. I think she has some pretty severe depression. She needs you to cheer her up. And just think, you can see all the places I've told you about. There's the Blue House, and Namsan Tower. Oh, and make sure you visit Lotte World."

"What about my job?" I said. "I can't get fired any more than you can."

Mom glanced at me sideways. "I called your boss this morning and told her we have a family emergency. She agreed to let you take whatever time off you needed."

"Mom!" The desperate feeling I knew so well fixed itself under my ribcage. "I'm not leaving you," I said through gritted teeth.

She flipped on her blinker and jerked the wheel to change lanes.

"Whoa, slow down," I said.

"I'm just so mad at you, Sydney. When are you going to grow up?"

"What?" I opened my mouth, then closed it hard.

Mom's voice gentled. "I'm sorry."

I took a breath and tried to stamp down my confusion and hurt. Suni was Mom's closest and oldest friend. She was worried, and here I was complaining that I couldn't leave home. I didn't want to admit it, but I knew I was being selfish.

"I didn't mean to snap at you." Mom's eyes had gone all shiny. She couldn't cry. I'd do anything to keep her from crying. I swallowed hard and forced myself to say the words. "You're right. Suni has done a lot for me. I can go and help her."

Mom visibly relaxed. "You will?"

"Of course," I said, trying to keep my voice calm and even for Mom's sake.

"Promise me that no matter how hard it is, you will stick it out. I need you to promise me this."

Hopefully Suni wasn't so bad that she was languishing in bed. If she was, I could make her soup and read to her. I was fast at cleaning, and I could make sure plenty of natural light filled the house. "I promise, Mom. Don't worry. You're only a phone call away, and I can give you daily updates on how Suni is feeling."

"No. That would be too expensive. I've decided to shut down our phone for a few months to save money." She snatched it out of the cupholder where I'd put it to charge.

"We can't go without a phone. It's bad enough that we share one," I said.

"Suni says she has a phone that you can borrow there. Just send me emails. I've put some Korean bills, the laptop and your passport in your backpack."

"I can't even call you? But what if you don't feel good? Or what if I have an emergency?"

"I'll check my email every morning. It will be just like we're together."

"It really won't."

"Sweetheart, you need to learn that you can't always be right next to me."

I turned to look behind me. Our giant suitcase, the one that could fit a small elephant inside, crowded the backseat. My school backpack sat on top. Both had seen better days. "You packed a lot. What day do I fly home?"

"Suni didn't buy a return flight. You can come home when she feels better."

"School starts on the 20th so make sure she gets my ticket before then."

"You can work all of your schooling out after you get there. Now, I'm trying to drive. You need to let me focus on the road."

Hyun's car hit a pothole and jarred me from my thoughts. I sat up straighter.

"We are almost there, Miss Moore," Hyun said.

Flashes of dense green trees, and glimpses of the occasional house that looked more like the mansions in Bel-Air flew past the window. The car continued to climb and wind into the hills, then turned. Hyun stopped, and all I could think was that maybe we'd gotten lost. A three-story mansion with Greek pillars—and a fountain big enough to wash a car—was built onto the highest bench of the hillside. I turned and looked out the back window. Below the drive, Seoul stretched as far as I could see.

"This is where Suni lives?" My voice wavered. "Are you sure?"

Hyun turned around in the driver's seat with reassuring eyes. It should have soothed me. Who cared if Suni was over-the-top rich? She was my godmother, and I was here to help her, but despite knowing that, my jaw quivered. I started to laugh. My whole situation was ridiculous. I probably would've been okay and not scared Hyun, except without warning, my laughing turned to tears.

I needed Mom. I needed to know she was okay. An image

of her lying in the hospital bed flashed through my mind. I shook it off. Mom was fine. My trip here would be short. I found a used tissue in my backpack and wiped my face. Hyun had gotten out. He paced in front of the car and spoke rapidly on his phone.

This was just great. The first time I leave Mom and I'm crying like that ten-year-old again. I got out of the car and faced Hyun. "Sorry. I'm okay now."

Hyun said a few harsh words to whomever he was talking to, then hung up. He smiled at me, but it was tight. I'm sure he didn't appreciate having some teenaged girl melt down in his car. "I don't normally cry like that," I said. It was lame, but true. "I'm probably just tired and homesick."

"That is perfectly acceptable if you cry, Miss Moore."

"Just call me Sydney."

"Sydney, then. Come with me, and we will get you settled."

Hyun carried my suitcase, but I insisted on bringing in my own backpack. We entered through the front door, and the blessedly cool air smelled like fresh flowers and furniture polish. A double staircase of dark wood loomed over us like two reaching arms. Despite the bright lighting and gleaming marble floors, the house felt empty. Lonely.

I followed Hyun up not one but two flights of stairs. The second opened onto a large landing staged with antique wooden chairs, benches, artwork, and a glass case displaying what I thought to be old Korean battle gear. It all looked so strange and out of place, more like a museum than a home.

"Jae-ho, Suni's husband, collects antiquities," Hyun said.

So Suni *was* married. I was beginning to see more and more that Suni, despite being my godmother, had shared next to nothing about her personal life. She would ask me questions on the phone and sometimes offered her advice, but that had been the extent of our relationship.

There were two hallways off the landing. Hyun led me

down the second but pointed back to the first that remained dark. "That leads to the young Master Kim's rooms. He will come find you later and make sure you have everything you need for tomorrow."

The young Master, huh? I tried to keep a straight face, but—really? Did the staff actually call him that? I definitely wouldn't need anything, but I nodded to be agreeable.

Even with secondhand furniture and shabby carpet, Mom kept our apartment cozy. Soft lamps and music welcomed me home along with her smiles. The deserted mood at the Kims left even the air feeling heavy. If this was what their son had to come home to every day, I felt sorry for him.

After a few turns, Hyun finally stopped at a bedroom. The door stood open, and a maid moved around the room turning on lamps.

I only saw the bed. It was round, bigger than a king, and in the center of the room. I was hours past tired and just wanted to crash. The maid turned down fluffy white bedding that called to me. Another maid entered the room and took my suitcase from Hyun, then began unpacking it into a massive armoire that took up one whole wall.

I ran over and closed the suitcase before she could do something embarrassing, like unpack my bras. "Oh, thank you so much, but I prefer to do that myself."

The woman quickly bowed, then looked at Hyun, a little confused. He nodded, and both maids hurried out. "Would you like to dine now, Sydney? I can have whatever food you would like brought to your room."

At home I always ate dinner with Mom while we talked over our day. I shrugged. I guess meals at the Kims' would be with me, myself, and I.

Loud knocking broke through my heavy haze of fuzzy warmth. Mom was probably getting ready for work. I should make her breakfast. I stretched and smiled, then bolted upright.

I wasn't home. I rubbed my eyes and remembered. I'd

collapsed in the massive guest bed after a shower with the hope that I'd sleep for the next twenty-four hours. I looked at the clock by the bed, 10:22 pm. Who would knock on my door this late?

The knocking got louder. I rolled out of bed, fumbled for the light, and staggered forward to open the door. A petite woman with sleek black hair, cut short to her jaw, beamed at me. I knew this woman from the many pictures Mom had in our photo album. The careful makeup, the white pantsuit, the heels—this was Suni. And she looked no less elegant in person. I gasped, surprised, when she pulled me close and wrapped her arms tight around my shoulders. She must have known I needed the hug.

She stepped past me, and the smell of peppermint and flowers followed her into the room. "Sydney, I'm so glad you made it to us safely. I want to apologize for not coming to personally greet you at the airport. You must have been upset, not even knowing who the driver was."

I opened my mouth to explain that I wasn't upset about that, but she rushed her words past mine.

"My son was supposed to be there, but he got held up. Really though, Hyun, is more like family than staff. You can ask him for anything, and he'll be happy to help you."

I ran my fingers through my tangled blonde locks. I knew my eyes were probably still red and puffy from both jetlag and my little crying fit. "I'm okay. Sorry to worry everyone."

Suni laughed. It sounded so much like my mom's laugh. Mom said they were rare kindred spirits and remained connected despite living oceans apart.

"I'm so happy you're here. School starts tomorrow, so my son will take you in the morning and show you around. I work long hours, but if you need anything, he's here to help you."

"School?"

"Yes, it's an amazing school. You're going to love it."

"I'm not going to school here. My school back home starts in a few weeks. I'm registered and everything."

"Your mom sent all of your records over. It's all arranged, and they have your schedule in the front office."

I blinked against the grit in my eyes. Maybe there'd been a massive miscommunication between Suni and Mom. "I'm just here to help you out for a few weeks. Mom said you would buy me a ticket home when you felt better."

Suni looked away and began twisting a big diamond ring on her left finger. "Well . . . yes, of course."

"Because I can, uh, keep you company. I've really wanted to meet you in person, and Mom said you've been a little down lately."

She took a step closer. "I appreciate that, but we can work out how you can help me later. I actually have to go to Japan early tomorrow, and then from there I go back to Canada. In the meantime, I want you to go to school. And can I give you a little tip on how to not feel homesick and beat jetlag?"

I could only gape, completely blown away by her whirlwind of information. Suni did not need my help, and if she was depressed, she hid it well.

She seemed to take my blank stare as a yes. "It's best to just jump right in. Starting school and making new friends will help occupy your mind. There are uniforms in your closet. I think I got the right sizes. Oh, and I almost forgot." She reached into her pocket and pulled out a brand new phone. "This is for you. Shannon said you can read and write Korean well, but this model may still take some getting used to."

I took the phone, a little overwhelmed. "Thank you."

"If you need help with any of it, ask my son. He's good with all the tech stuff." Suni smiled. "You're like a daughter to me so I want you to make yourself completely at home." Before I could argue or even say thank you, she gave me another quick hug and left as quickly as she'd come.

I walked to the bed and flopped back down. A giant dumpster fire had just dropped from the sky to burn down my life. But I was too tired to cry or even think.

My new phone pinged. I realized I still held it tight in my hand. It took me a minute to figure out how to use it. Everything really was different in Korean, but I opened the text app to see a new number.

> **I heard you freaked out when I wasn't there to get you. Hyun will help you with whatever, so don't expect me to always be around. And apparently you speak perfect Korean. That will make this easier. I'm supposed to take you to school tomorrow. Be ready at 8. I don't like waiting.**

Freaked out? You don't like waiting? It must be Suni's son. What a jerk. He couldn't even come talk to me in person? I texted back, double-checking my Korean before pushing send.

> **What's the name of the school?**

He replied right away.

> **Daeshim Academy**

I quickly did a search and found the school on my new phone. If this guy thought he was driving me, he was crazy. I'd take the bus. I texted back.

> **I didn't mind Hyun picking me up. Just got a little homesick when I arrived is all. I can take care of myself tomorrow and ride the bus.**

His reply came immediately.

> **Don't be ridiculous. The nearest bus stop from here is 5km away.**

I texted back.

> **Great, that's an easy walk for me, and you don't like waiting.**

I pushed send, then saved his number in my new phone under the name "Loser." Honestly, who tells someone they've never even met that they don't like waiting? My phone pinged again.

> **Loser:**
> **Fine by me.**

4

CHUL

It was late, but I knocked on Hyun's door anyway. He was one of those insane early risers, so when he opened, giving me a dirty look, I wasn't surprised.

"You realize it's after one in the morning," he said.

I pushed my way in and flopped down on the sofa next to his bed. "Can't sleep. My insomnia is back." Hyun stared blankly at me, and I felt a twinge of guilt. He was here for me, no matter what it cost him. I should at least let the man sleep. But I couldn't, not yet. "She's refusing to go to school with me," I said.

He pulled up the chair from his desk and sat, leaning his forearms on his knees. "I thought you said—let me quote you here—*it's better if we never meet.* Why do you care if she doesn't go with you?"

"Because you'll call and yell at me when I don't drive her," I said.

"I'll yell at you because it's your fault that she won't go with you."

"Why do you assume it's my fault?" I asked.

Hyun quirked an eyebrow. "Isn't it?"

"Well . . . yes, but it might not have been."

"I've met Sydney. I was her ride home, remember? She's a sweet girl." Hyun smirked, clearly amused. "Why would I think any of this is her fault?"

I sighed. "Fine. You're right."

"Did you go talk to her with that scowl of yours?"

"No. I texted her."

"Brilliant. And I bet you said something rude."

"I might have come off as . . . impatient."

Hyun shrugged. "That's what you get when you treat a girl poorly. Now she won't ride with you, and you don't want my wrath."

I grinned at him. "None of us want that. Can you drive her?"

"No," Hyun said flatly.

"She'll get lost."

Hyun shrugged. "Not my problem."

"So you just expect me to go beg her forgiveness or something?"

"I'm sure she won't forgive you that easily. It's a pity, too." Hyun narrowed his eyes, and a smile tugged at the corner of his mouth. "She's pretty. I would pin her as your ideal type, even. It's probably good that you don't plan on meeting her. You can't handle a girl like her."

I groaned and raked my fingers through my hair. "Hyun, you're not helping. She can't be all alone. We both know it. Just give her a ride."

"Why don't you track her?"

I jerked my head up. "What do you mean?"

Hyun leaned closer. "I was the one who bought her a new phone. And, of course, installed an app to track her location." He pulled out his own phone and tapped at the screen. "There. I just sent you a link with a password. You have access to her phone's location now. Is that enough to put your mind at ease?"

It wasn't. If I had my own computer, I could look deeper into her life. Just knowing her location wasn't going to be enough if she attended Daeshim. There was too much risk at a school like mine for a girl with no connections. "I'm also going to need a new computer for my first day back," I said.

Hyun stood and walked to his closet. He returned and

placed a sleek silver box in my lap. "It's the newest model."

I grinned, my fingers itching to touch it.

"I don't think I need to remind you to be careful. Nothing illegal, or you'll regret it."

Taking a peek into Sydney's digital world wouldn't be that big of a deal. She was living under my parents' roof now. I could argue ethics, but Hyun would agree that Sydney needed to be safe. I would need to monitor her phone *and* her computer.

Hyun eyed me closely, and I did my best to look innocent. "I hope I don't need to remind you that losing your spot with the CTF team right before the international competition was a big blow to your father. He bragged a lot about your abilities at work. He's hoping you can still join cybersecurity at Kim Corp when you graduate."

"I didn't know that," I said, soberly. With every CTF competition, and all the cash prizes I'd won, my father had given me no more than a nod. I had no idea he even cared—or that he intended for me to work for him. "I thought he wanted me to study business and get my MBA in the States."

"He did, until he realized how good you are. Your father knows the only defense against outside hackers is to beat them at their own game. Just make sure you don't screw up again."

What I'd done my junior year hadn't just been me. It had been a dare for the whole CTF team from a rival group. None of us were into the darker stuff, malicious hacking, or stealing money. But I'd be lying if I didn't say that we were all curious to know if we could. The dare was stupid, but we took it. I still remembered the cold feeling of the steel handcuffs when the officers walked me into their precinct. Our team's *Sunbae* had been there when they released me, but he couldn't look me in the eye.

The fluorescent light flickered above my cell as an officer in a blue uniform swung the door open. He bowed respectfully to my father and Hyun, then walked away, leaving us alone.

"Why are none of the rest of the team here?" I asked. My

father stared at me, grinding his teeth, but didn't answer.

"We all did it," I said. "We were just messing around to see if we were good enough to pull it off."

Hyun's eyes flicked nervously between my father and me.

"We are leaving. Right now," my father said. "We'll talk when we get home."

I lowered my eyes and nodded then followed close on my father's heels. Hyun brought up the rear. We exited the cell hall to a large intake room crowded with desks and overflowing shelves. Sunbae sat in one of the chairs, laughing with a few of the off-duty officers. He went quiet when he saw us and looked down at his hands. I stopped next to him. He was the leader of this group. Why was he here chatting it up when I'd been sitting in a cell for the last few hours?

"Where is everyone? Why weren't you in there with me?"

My father turned around and watched us but didn't interfere. Sunbae stood slowly and took a step closer so he could whisper in my ear. "We can't go down for this, Chul. You're the youngest. You'll only get a slap on the wrist, but we'd do time. Besides, you're loaded, so your family got you off. No harm done. You didn't even spend the night here."

I walked out of the precinct that night certain of one thing. I'd never join a team again. Anything I learned or accomplished from here on out, I'd do on my own.

Hyun tried to act casual when he gave me the computer, but I knew him too well to not see it, the tightness around his eyes, the way he tapped his foot. He wanted me to be able to use my talents, but he was scared of them, too. He didn't need to be.

"What if my father finds out you gave me a computer?"

"I'm going to tell him tomorrow."

I envisioned Father getting a text in the middle of a meeting. Hyun liked to spring things on my parents. He enjoyed saying that it was his job to keep them on their toes. But this time, it might not end well. "What if he gets mad?"

He laughed. "I'll tell him you stole it."

"Hyun."

"Relax. Last time we played golf together, he asked me to buy you new equipment."

"You're lying," I said.

"Okay, I'm lying."

"You are, so don't act like that," I said. "You saw him smash all my computers."

Hyun sobered. "He regrets that. I've never seen your father as afraid as he was when we drove to the police station that night."

I snorted. "And I wasn't afraid?"

Hyun leveled me with a hard stare. "If you're afraid, it should be for Sydney. This girl isn't ready for tomorrow, and you're still crying because your father can't say he's proud of you. He is proud, and he's not going to say it. Get over yourself and take care of Sydney."

I was out the door with the laptop under my arm before he could say more.

5

SYDNEY

I sat on the bench alone. Loser hadn't been kidding. The stop really was five kilometers away, five point two, to be exact. It wouldn't have been such a bad walk, but the humidity mixed with the wool skirt of the school uniform was torture. The weather reminded me of the rundown laundromats in L.A. where there was no A/C and the washers always leaked—sticky and hot. I longed for flip-flops and a tee shirt instead of the itchy uniform Suni had left in the closet.

The other commuters at the stop looked like they were going to work, and there wasn't a single student in the group. I turned on my phone and reread the email that I'd sent Mom before I left. She hadn't emailed back, but then she might be in bed already. There was a sixteen-hour time difference.

Hey Mom,

I don't really know how to be mad at you. But I'm really mad. You pretty much conned me into coming to Korea and starting school. If Suni is depressed, it's because she works too much. I can't do anything to help her since she's spending most of her time in Canada. Seriously, what gives? Is it this stupid elite school you want for me? I'm sure Daeshim Academy is great, but my old school back home is fine. I'll play nice and go to school here for a few weeks because Suni asked me to, but I want to start my senior year in California. Please talk to her and ask her to buy my ticket.

And not to worry you, but I'm going to starve here. For breakfast, a maid—yes, an actual maid in a white apron—came to my room with a tray. It smelled like death, but I smiled and took it. She said it was abalone porridge. I didn't eat it. You know I'm a picky eater. I don't even like most *American* food.

So Suni. She's lovely. I am glad that I took this trip—this *short* trip—and got to meet her. I can see how you two would be forever friends. They have a driver, Hyun, who I guess is more like family. He's super nice and picked me up from the airport because Suni was in Canada. Suni's son, however, is a spoiled jerk. He sent me a rude text acting like I got him in trouble because I cried a little after I got here. I guess he was supposed to pick me up, but that isn't why I cried. Anyway, I don't see us being friends anytime soon. Like ever. Lucky for me this house is so big we probably won't bump into each other. Seriously, I could get lost here. It's like a museum. I'm almost afraid to touch a light switch because I don't want to leave a smudge.

Make sure Suni gets my ticket home. Next week would be great.

Love you,
Syd

The bus came. It was a little early, but I wasn't sure about how firm the schedules were, so I got on. I tried to pay in the *won* Mom had given me, but the driver wouldn't accept it. Finally, a guy behind me scanned his card twice. I offered to pay him back, but he just leered, so I moved to the back of the bus. My phone pinged in my bag, and I pulled it out to see a text from Loser himself.

> **Loser:**
> **You are on the**
> **wrong bus. Get off**

at the next stop.

I texted back.

> **How do you know
> I'm on the wrong
> bus?**

> **Loser:
> I just drove past
> your stop and saw
> you get on the
> A line bus. That
> won't take you to
> school. You need
> to get off and then
> wait for the C line.
> It will be red, not
> green.**

I looked out the window, and sure enough, this bus was green. I texted.

> **Once I get on the
> C line do I still
> get off on Payong
> Street?**

> **Loser:
> Yes, and then you
> take the 7 line
> eastbound high-
> speed train. That
> station is 8 blocks
> away, so if you
> run, maybe you'll**

make it on time.

I swear, I could almost feel his sneer through the phone. I sent one more text.

I've got it. Thanks.

Loser:
Do you though?

Could he be any more of a jerk? I texted back.

Yes!

Loser:
You know about
East station, then?

I tapped out my answer on my phone so hard that I was getting strange looks from the other passengers.

What about it?

Loser:
You have to get
off the 7 line train
at East Station,
and then take the
South City line,
where you get
off at Dalgong
street. You can
practically see the
school from that
stop, so even you
won't get lost.

When I'd looked up the route last night, it hadn't seemed this complicated. I couldn't believe I'd messed it up this much.

The bus started to slow. I realized this was where I needed to get off if I wanted to catch the red line. "Excuse me, I need to get off," I said. The bus seemed more crowded than when I'd gotten on, the aisle completely full. I got a glare from an older man when I tried to squeeze by, but the bus was stopping. I moved faster, and my foot stepped on something that went squish. My balance teetered, and I slid forward, careening into the passengers in front of me. Someone pushed back. I landed on my knees with a painful thud.

Before I could catch my breath, an elderly lady was shaking a bag of what looked like smashed boiled eggs in my face. "Do you see this?" She yelled. "This was dinner for my family. What are we to eat now?" She shook the bag harder, and bits of broken up egg white flew at my face. "You stepped on my eggs. Don't come to my country if you have no manners."

I fumbled in my backpack for my wallet, and with a mumbled apology, I offered the lady 10,000 *won* for her trouble.

She snatched the money from my hand just as the bus began moving again. I struggled to stand. "Wait," I called, but no one even looked at me. I didn't blame them. The whole bus smelled like eggs now. Gross.

My knee throbbed, and I winced when I reached down and felt a sticky wet scrape. Great, my knee was bleeding too. My phone pinged again.

Loser:
Did you get off the
bus?

Miserable now, I texted back.

No.

Loser:
Because???

I tried not to come off as pitiful as I answered.

I tried. It was
crowded.

I don't know what I expected after that. More instructions? A kind word? Any of that would have been great, but he didn't bother texting me back. I tried to ask an old man sitting closest to where I stood when the next stop would be, but he just made a "*tsking*" noise and glared at me. I stared hard at my phone, willing the screen to light up. Please text. Please text. Like magic, it pinged again.

Loser:
Get off at the next
stop. Hyun is on
his way. Don't
get on any more
buses. Just wait
for him.

Relief that he'd texted warred with my desire to tell him to shove off. But at the same time, I knew I wouldn't make it to school without his help. I texted back.

Thank you. I will
figure out the
route better for
tomorrow.

> **Loser:**
> **I heard you were a smart girl. I guess my mother was wrong.**

I gritted my teeth and texted back.

> **I heard you were a gentleman. I guess my mom was wrong too.**

> **Loser:**
> **Maybe I should tell Hyun not to pick you up?**

I texted back.

> **Maybe I should call your mom for a ride?**

> **Loser:**
> **You don't belong here. You should just go home.**

I laughed out loud. For once we agreed.

6

CHUL

I wasn't getting out of my car until the green moving dot on my phone showed that Sydney had actually made it to Daeshim. The school's underground parking lot hummed with lights and air conditioning. It was peaceful compared to my morning. Combing through Sydney's different accounts had kept me busy. Now I had full access to anything electronic she'd ever touched. Probably not what Mother or Hyun had in mind when they'd told me to take care of her, but this was the safest way. Most of what I'd found just confirmed how sheltered her life had been.

After watching her at the bus stop, I'd started to wonder if she wouldn't be better off skipping the first day of school, at least until someone could take her shopping. She just didn't have the look. Her makeup, hair, nails—none of it would pass at my school. Money opened the doors of Daeshim, and that's what the first day was all about. Glamour was our god, and everyone looked forward to the parade of cars, jewelry, shoes, and bags. All of that was just as important as our grades.

I opened the ridiculous email she'd sent her mom and read it again. What's so bad about abalone porridge? At least she'd caught on that Suni wasn't depressed. My mother probably hadn't cried since she was a kid herself. Both our parents wanted her here, and I had no idea why. She didn't either, from what I'd read.

But by far the worst part about this whole mess of a

morning was Sydney's texts. She was right. I wasn't being a gentleman. I never spoke to girls the way I had with her. My phone vibrated in my car's cup holder. I picked it up.

> **Min:**
> **Where are you?**
> **The Dean is**
> **out here, and**
> **everyone is**
> **almost inside. I**
> **thought we could**
> **go to first period**
> **together.**

I texted her right back.

I'm running late.

Min was another problem. She'd been a problem since sixth grade, when I told her I didn't want to be her boyfriend. The girl had a conquering complex, like Bonaparte or Alexander the Great. But it wasn't land she wanted. It was me. And Min demanded full and complete devotion.

Most of the privileged class followed her on social media. I did too, but only to keep her from messing up my life. When I was hacking, I could shut things down or delete her accounts. But since I'd lost my equipment, the scales tipped to her side in our private little war.

She'd hung out all summer on her yacht with two French style influencers. In her last post, she'd hinted that her mystery man couldn't wait for her to return home. The next day, two more posts from her friends said she was heading back to Seoul to see her much-missed boyfriend, Kim Chul, the promising heir of Kim Corp.

It was never gonna happen. I'd called her that same day.

"Hello, Chul." Min's voice purred velvet smooth, even when she was mad.

"Hi," I said. "I read you're coming home soon."

"Did you miss me? How did you like the post from Barcelona?"

"You looked nice." I could tell she'd had a professional photographer. Min strolling along a beach in her bikini, Min laughing in the waves, Min reading, her book carefully placed to hide that she was sunbathing topless. In every picture she tried to look classy and tasteful while still showing off as much of her body as possible. And Min did have a great body.

But all sirens do . . . until they eat you.

If you looked closely at her pictures, you could see it in her eyes. Mean and shallow followed in her wake.

"Is that all?" she asked. "I looked nice?

I cleared my throat, refusing to say more. "About you coming home. You don't want everyone to get the wrong idea about us. Maybe you could clear it up before you get back. Didn't you find a weekend boyfriend in Paris? What about a good-bye series with him? Your followers would eat it up."

Min laughed. It was the perfect chime of feminine and sexy. "A few of my friends thought it would be fun to speculate. They even have bets going. Don't worry. I let them post that about us because it's just a joke."

I swallowed, all nerves. Every time I tried to make Min give up, she dug in deeper.

"But, you do know, lots of people think we should go out," she said.

"I don't," I said.

"Why?"

"We're just different. I'm not into the same things you are."

"What are you into, Chul?"

"Um . . . school. I've got to focus for college exams."

"Funny," she breathed. "I've got to focus too. I only have this last year to get what I want."

I leaned my forehead against my steering wheel. I hated

thinking about that call, how I'd completely lost my nerve. Min wouldn't give up. She didn't understand failure because she'd never experienced it. I was the first person in her life to ever tell the girl no. If Min ever found out that Sydney was living in my house—she couldn't find out. My phone pinged.

> **Min:**
> **I'll see you second**
> **period, then. I**
> **need to talk to you**
> **about something.**
> **We can go to the**
> **Museum Teashop**
> **after school. You**
> **drive. My driver**
> **is off for the day,**
> **so I'll be stranded**
> **otherwise.**

I texted her back.

I'm leaving early.

I checked Sydney's location again. She'd be here in thirty minutes or less. We would both miss first period, but I would see her in person for second. So far, I'd only watched from a distance. But I had to admit, I wanted to talk to her up close, see her reaction to me. I knew I shouldn't want it, but I did. And funny thing—I really hated that she saved my contact as Loser.

7

SYDNEY

I liked Hyun. When I got off the bus, there he stood, patiently waiting with the black town car. No judgment, no lecture, just a semi-familiar face.

"Thanks for coming to get me on such short notice," I said, more than a little embarrassed.

Hyun bowed. "I'm happy to drive you anytime, Sydney." He held the door open for me. "Please get in."

I climbed in the back seat. The bus was a fail but despite that, I'd make today a good day. I had to. And it wasn't like I couldn't cope with a new school for a few weeks. Mom and I had moved so many times that it'd gotten easy. I'd always figured school out fast—who to avoid, who to avoid at all costs, and who would be a friend. I knew to watch for the unspoken language that floats on the currents of snark and attitude. And most of the time I found my place just fine.

We arrived late. Hyun insisted on stopping to buy a bandage and ointment for my knee. Nice of him but unnecessary. When we pulled up to the circular driveway in the front of Daeshim, he hurried to open my door. "Your second period is just starting," he said.

I got out and stared. The school wasn't large, the building no bigger than a small department store, but it shimmered, pride and honor in every sleek line. Polished steel accents along the roofline reflected the morning sun. If anyone doubted the exclusivity of Daeshim, they couldn't miss the statue of Socrates that towered over the stone steps leading to the front doors. "This place is nice," I said.

Hyun chuckled. "That it is. They will have your schedule in the front office. I sincerely hope you have a wonderful first day here."

"Thank you, Hyun." I headed up the steps without looking back. I pictured kind ladies in the office, impressed with my perfect pronunciation of their language. They'd gladly walk me through the halls and show me my classes.

That's not how it went when I introduced myself to the woman in the front office. She grabbed a folder and shoved it at me along with a hard plastic name tag. "Don't expect any special treatment just because you work for the Kims. Here's your schedule. You've already missed first period, so get to second."

She thought I worked for Suni? I shrugged. It didn't matter to me if the lady was a grump. My name tag was printed in the typical standard for Korean with my last name first. "When in Rome," I mumbled as I pinned it on. I flipped through the folder. Second period was Advanced Math II room 318. "Excuse me," I glanced back up, but the office lady had already walked away. I tried catching her eye. She ignored me. I waved. "Um, hello. Can I get a map of your school, please?"

She grabbed a sheet from a file cabinet and then slammed it onto the counter with a look that said get lost. Maybe I should mention that I was Suni's goddaughter and not an indentured servant.

Room 318 was completely silent when I opened the door, but every head snapped to attention and zeroed in on me. I scanned faces for some hint of friendliness, but I was the flea under a microscope.

The teacher stood at the front of the room with a tablet in her hand. A math problem was lit up with a smart board on the wall, and most of the class seemed to be working on laptops. "Are you Moore?" she asked.

"Yes, but my first name is Sydney."

She didn't smile, not even a little. "Sydney, then. Please find a seat and open your Math curriculum on your laptop."

I hadn't brought my laptop. In California they just issued you one in class, and I had a feeling looking around at all the newer tech that my old HP wouldn't cut it here. "I don't have my laptop," I said.

The teacher went stiff. Her lips formed a hard line. "Why not?"

"I didn't think I would need it."

"What did you plan to use then, your imagination?" A few of the students snickered.

"I apologize." My brain scrambled for this teacher's name, Jang. And a title. I needed to use a title here. "Teacher Jang," I said. "I can bring it tomorrow." I shifted from foot to foot but then checked myself. *Don't fidget.*

A guy in the back of the room raised his hand. He had a big open smile and eyes that clearly said he was all about the fun. He wore his hair in long curly waves, with his tie loose about his neck.

"Yes, Lee Gun?"

The boy stood and gave a slight bow. "Teacher Jang, I can get a loaner from the office for Sydney."

Teacher Jang waved her hand at him like she was shooing a fly. "Fine then, go." She turned back to me. "Bring your own laptop by tomorrow. This school isn't a charity."

I nodded and walked to the back where there were still available seats. Lee Gun started down the same aisle, so I slowed and slid to the side to let him pass.

I don't know if I tripped him, or if he tripped me, but suddenly I pitched forward, and someone caught me. My face flamed as I realized that not only had I tripped and almost fallen, but Lee Gun held me upright. I pushed away and stepped back all in one motion. "Sorry, my bad," I said and hurried to an empty seat. I sat down and tried to calm myself.

I pulled out a notebook and pencil, then focused on the teacher instead of everyone staring at me. This was a really bad start.

I didn't recognize any of the formulas Teacher Jang wrote on the tablet. I just copied like crazy and figured I could work it out at home. Before too long, Lee Gun plopped down next to me and slid a laptop onto my desk. I dared a glance up.

He opened his own computer. "You're a new transfer?"

"What gave me away?" I said, with a toss of my blonde hair.

He laughed. "American?"

I nodded.

"You speak Korean well. When did you move here?"

"Yesterday," I whispered, sneaking a glance at Teacher Jang and the rest of the class. A lot of the students were talking quietly among themselves, so I figured we wouldn't get in trouble.

"You're kidding, right?"

"I still have jetlag and bags under my eyes to prove it," I said.

"Your eyes are beautiful."

Wow, this guy was a shameless flirt. "Thanks."

"Welcome to Daeshim Academy." He held out his hand. "I'm Lee Gun, but call me Gun since we'll be friends." What was supposed to be a handshake turned into a kind of hand holding squeeze. "I'll show you everything you'll need to know at Daeshim."

I pulled my hand back. Normally I would say I could just figure things out on my own. Except, I wasn't exactly sure I could. I had zero friends in this school, and so far, I felt like a solider involuntarily crossing into enemy territory. "Okay," I said.

"Great, let's start with your laptop." He opened it up and showed me the website that had basically all of their textbooks and classwork online. I found my password and student ID in my folder, and then I opened the work for Advanced Math II.

Miss Jang wasn't messing around—a weekly test and three online assignments daily. I glanced through some of the lessons and realized how much work this class would be compared to school back home. Good thing I was only here for a short time.

Gun opened my folder and plucked out my schedule. I reached to grab it, but he pulled away.

"You have some heavy classes here." He raised his eyebrows. "Harder than mine, even."

Determined to get it back, I reached farther, but he snapped a picture with his phone before I could.

"Hey," I said.

Gun looked up with innocent eyes and put my schedule back in my folder. "What? I said I would help you with school. We don't have another class together until fifth period, so I'll see you later." The bell rang, and he left before I could say goodbye.

I started to put my stuff away but got that tingly feeling, like an invisible hand had just walked up my spine. I glanced up and scanned the room. Teacher Jang was busy at her own desk, and most of the students were leaving. One boy I hadn't noticed before sat near the front. He glanced back at me, holding my gaze. He looked familiar, but I couldn't place from where. He was broad with nice features, full lips, a straight nose, and deep brown eyes. From the way he dwarfed his chair, I could tell he was tall. He didn't turn away, merely stared with an open, curious expression that pulled me in.

I broke first and looked at the floor. I quickly zipped up my bag and left to find my locker. I could feel his gaze follow me all the way out the door.

The halls were crowded with kids yelling and joking around. I guess high school was still high school, no matter what country you landed in. I found my locker and put my backpack inside, just to make it look less lonely.

Two girls stopped next to me. They were polished and beautiful and not here to share Skittles. I looked the tallest girl —clearly the leader—in the eye. She'd been in my last class and sneered when I'd said I didn't have a laptop. I tilted my head.

"Hey," I said, with a what-do-you-want look.

"We're here to welcome you to Daeshim. I'm Kang Min."

I nodded. "Thanks," I said and tried to turn back to my locker. The Min girl just kept talking.

"We don't get many transfers to our school. Mostly new kids get accepted here when their family reaches a certain *monetary* status." She smiled, but her eyes glittered with warning. "We never get foreigners. In fact, you're the only one."

"I'm just here for a short visit to help a family friend. I won't be at your school long," I said.

The girl next to Min barked with laughter. I glanced at her name tag—Park Ae-ri.

"Help? What kind of help?" Ae-ri asked. "Are you a maid or something?"

Min moved closer. "Are you here on a scholarship?"

"She must be. Look at her hair and that watch," Ae-ri said.

I gritted my teeth. I hated when people talked about someone like they weren't standing right there. "I'm not on a scholarship," I said.

Min's eyes narrowed. "Who's paying your tuition, then? One semester at our school costs more than people like you make in a year."

I tried to smile, but my face felt tight. "I can pay my own way." Learning tuition cost so much made me feel a little sick, especially since I knew Suni was covering the bill. I closed my locker and started to walk away, but Ae-ri grabbed my wrist. She had long polished nails, and their tips pressed against my skin. "Hey! Hands off." I jerked my arm down, hard, and then stepped back, putting some distance between us. Ae-Ri laughed and danced back, closer to Min.

Min watched me and noted my reaction. She wanted my weak spot. I'd met girls like her—smart, rich, and beautiful. You'd think they'd be happy. Some were, but the Mins of the world hid hard knots of mean deep in their cores.

I glared back at both of them.

Everyone else had gone to their next classes. Everyone except the guy who'd stared at me in math. He walked slowly towards us. Min turned to see who I was looking at.

Her sneer fell away, replaced with a soft smile. "Chul." She glided to his side and wrapped her arm through his as if they were practiced dancers.

His name was Chul, then. He was the only student I'd seen today without a name tag.

He looked down at her with cold eyes, but his tone was soft, and he didn't shake her arm off. "What are you doing, Min?"

I wondered if they were dating.

"Helping the new girl," Min said.

I hooked my thumb under my backpack. The strap was held on with a safety pin, and Chul's eyes landed on it. I told myself I didn't care.

"You should meet her. It's Moore, right?" She asked as I started to walk past.

"Sydney, actually."

Ae-ri laughed like they all shared a private joke.

I ignored Ae-ri and slowed long enough to lock eyes with Min. Something about the possessive way she held Chul's arm bothered me. I must be more tired than I realized. It wasn't like me to get so worked up over the gum-drop crowd. I didn't want anything to do with them so I continued past before things could escalate.

I glanced back to see the girls had moved closer to Chul. Min even leaned into him. I turned, telling myself it didn't matter. I saw the girl's bathroom and dashed in. Thankfully it was empty, so I went to the last stall and slammed the lid down for a seat. I wondered if Suni had been honest with my mom. If this school cost as much as Min was saying, my mom would never have agreed to let me attend here. I did a search for Daeshim and found their website, then scrolled through the menu until I found tuition. My hands shook as I opened a new email on my phone.

Mom,

You probably didn't know this, but tuition at Daeshim is 54K. That's more than Harvard! I won't state the obvious, but I will say I know neither one of us will be comfortable having Suni pay it. I'm hoping you get a chance to talk to her today and she buys my ticket home. It just doesn't make sense for me to stay here when I'm not helping and just being a mooch. I'll look for your email soon. I miss you—Syd

8

CHUL

It was weird how Sydney could be so feisty with Min in the hall and then such a wimp on the bus and at home. Her little crying fit that she'd glossed over in the email to her mom hadn't been so little, from what Hyun said.

And then there was Gun. That stupid move with tripping her and then taking a picture of her schedule—was he a stalker or something? I'd almost walked over and smashed the phone into his face. But I'm more civilized than that. So instead, I erased today's math work off his laptop. Now *that's* illegal, but worth it.

My mother wanted me to take care of Sydney, and that meant protecting her from guys she couldn't handle. And who was I kidding? That would be every guy in this school. Sydney was beautiful and vulnerable. That combination is hard for a lot of guys to leave alone.

Thankfully, she managed to lay low through chemistry and government. She even pretended to not understand Korean when another student asked her a question. We only had lunch, two more classes, and then we could go. If she could stay out of trouble until then, Hyun would pick her up.

I sent Sydney a text and watched as she read it under her desk.

**Hyun said you
made it to school**

**okay. He'll be
waiting for you
where he dropped
you off.**

I expected her to get mouthy and fight me on it, but she texted right back. Just one word.

Fine.

It was three minutes until lunch. I needed to get to her before Gun came sniffing around again. She was up and out the door as soon as the bell rang. I followed, giving lots of space, but kept her in sight. She walked straight to the bathroom. I sat down on the floor against the opposite wall outside and waited.

When Sydney came out, she saw me and stopped, just like I expected her to. I raised my head. We'd been staring at each other all day. It was time for us to meet.

"You ran away." I spoke soft enough that I would be hard to hear.

She frowned. "What?"

"You left too soon."

She took a step in my direction. "What did you say? I can't hear you."

"I said, I wanted to talk to you. Are you visiting from the States?"

"Yes." She looked apprehensive.

I opened my hands, let them hang on my knees, and tried to look harmless. Sydney took another hesitant step in my direction, and I gave her my warmest smile. "Where'd you learn to speak Korean so well?"

"My mom. It's the only language she'll speak at home."

"That's cool. I think you already know my name from your run-in with Min. I'm Chul."

"I remember," she said.

"You're in a few of my classes, too." She was actually in all of my classes. I guess my mother thought it would be funny to give us the exact same schedule. "And don't worry about Min. If she gives you a hard time, just come find me."

"I'm not worried."

Min didn't worry her, but for some reason, I did. "Have a seat. I don't bite." I tapped the floor next to me.

Sydney took a step back. "I have to get going."

I pulled out the packages of triangle *kimbap* I'd bought earlier. I knew Sydney hadn't had much to eat since she'd arrived, and if she couldn't handle porridge, then she'd never survive our cafeteria. "Have you had lunch?"

Sydney looked at the wrapper suspiciously. "What is it?"

"Just plain rice with seaweed."

She debated. I watched the play of emotions on her face. "You can throw it away if you don't like it."

She sat down next to me. I tried not to stare as her hair swung like a wall of gold silk when she moved. I really hated that I couldn't stop obsessing over her hair. It's not like I'd never seen a blonde before, but Sydney's hair was different, all sunshine. She smelled like summer.

I took a breath, then handed her the triangle of rice. I showed her how to open the package without tearing the seaweed. "If you're not big on Korean food, then this is about as safe as it gets." Up close, I noticed her blue eyes had gold around the iris.

Sydney swallowed hard and stared at the seaweed. "Do you mind if I take the seaweed off?"

I took it from her. "It's easy to peel." I flicked the last few bits away and handed her back the triangle of plain rice.

She sniffed it, and then took a tiny bite. "It tastes just like normal rice," she said with a happy sigh.

"What did you think it would taste like?"

"I wasn't sure. I'm just a really picky eater, and some of the food here scares me."

"Here, have another." I offered her mine, but she didn't

take it.

"Then what will you eat?"

"I can buy something else." I winked at her. "I don't think Korean food is scary." I took her free hand and placed the *kimbap* in her palm. Her skin was soft, and she blushed as our fingers touched. I pulled away quickly. "So why are you at Daeshim? Are your parents working here or something?"

Her eyes misted over. "My mom wanted to come with me, but she's busy at work."

"So then who are you here with?"

"I'm here visiting my godmother. She needed me to come help her for a while."

How could she still believe she was here to help my mother? She couldn't even take care of herself. "Is your godmother sick?"

"No, she just needs some company."

"Doesn't she have family?"

"Her son and husband are too busy with their own work."

I choked back a laugh. If she only knew. My mom was the busy one and rarely home. There was nothing she wouldn't sacrifice for her career. Still, this didn't explain why she'd brought Sydney here. "They sound awful," I said.

"Yeah, her son is a student here too."

"Really? What's his name?" I should have gotten an award for my acting abilities.

Sydney sighed, "I don't even know. He avoids me, but it doesn't matter anyway. I've been working on my mom to buy me a ticket home, so I won't be here long enough to worry about him."

It wasn't hard to let disappointment lace my words. "You're leaving soon, then?"

Sidney sighed. "My godmother will be okay without me. I need to get back to my own mom."

I nodded. I wished she could have stayed longer, but going home was the smart choice. If I had to put her on a plane myself, I would. "That's too bad," I said, bumping her knee with mine. "Daeshim doesn't have many girls as cute as you." She blushed again, and I looked away.

"Um . . ." She stumbled over her words. "It's a great school. Lots of cool people here, but not really for me."

I stood, and she stared up at me with her big blue eyes. "I've got to go. Enjoy your lunch," I said.

She held up the kimbap. "Thanks for this."

I nodded and gave her a smile before turning to walk away. I'd confirmed what I already knew. Sydney wasn't here because of her own scheming. She didn't want me or my money. Knowing this should have made me feel better. It didn't.

9

SYDNEY

So weird that Mom hadn't emailed me back. She would've had time to read it by now. She was probably still reeling over the cost of me going to Daeshim for even one day. I debated if I should text Suni and ask if she'd bought my ticket but thought better of it and closed my laptop. I needed to hurry and get my shower if I was going to make it to school. This week would most likely be my last, but I still had to look up the map and schedule for the bus if I didn't want a repeat of yesterday.

My phone pinged and I slid open my screen. Great it was Loser.

> **Loser:**
> **I just sent you an**
> **email. Don't screw**
> **it up this time.**

I dove for my laptop. What could that jerk have sent me now? There was one new message with an attachment, a detailed map. My route with times and stops were highlighted. I paused, shocked that he would take the time to help me like this. I'm sure he just didn't want me hassling Hyun again. Still, this was the first nice thing he'd done for me. I texted him back.

> **Thanks. I got it.**

That saved me a bunch of time. I jumped up and turned on the shower. Last night's zit cream had dried into flaky white smears all over my face, and I wore my Wonder Woman nightshirt with an attached cape. So tacky. I'd bought it on a dare from my friend, but only Mom had ever seen me in it. My phone pinged. It was Loser again.

> **My mother had Hyun buy you a laptop for school. It's on the table in the foyer.**

I peeked out of my room. None of the maids were up here yet, and the halls looked empty. I scrambled down both sets of stairs. There, next to a vase of flowers, sat a leather backpack. Could that be it? I looked around but didn't see anyone. The leather felt soft and buttery as I unzipped it. Inside, I found a brand-new laptop. I didn't know how Korean tech compared to American, but this looked top of the line. Suni had to know I couldn't afford something like this. She'd already bought me a phone. There was no way. I texted Loser.

> **Tell your mom thanks, but I already have a laptop.**

> **Loser:**
> **Are you trying to be rude?**

I texted back.

> **This is too expensive.**

**Loser:
Do you like
making
everything hard?
Accept it or my
mother will be
embarrassed.**

Why did he have to be like this? He blamed me for everything without trying to understand. To the Kims, a new laptop wasn't a big deal, but for me it was more than a month of Mom's salary. I stood there in a moment of indecision. Maybe he was right and I would offend Suni by not taking it. I put the laptop back inside and noticed a lunch bag. Did Suni ask the maids to pack me a lunch too? I unzipped the bag with one eye open, afraid of what I would find inside. Please, no more abalone. Three glass dishes each filled with something different were stacked neatly inside. Sliced cucumbers, oranges, and the last one had plain rice with a boiled egg on top. I grinned. Suni needed another hug. My phone pinged.

**Loser:
By the way, nice
pajamas!**

My head jerked up to the stairs above me. Could he see me? No one was there. I shoved the lunch back in the backpack and sprinted up the stairs to my room.

I arrived at Daeshim fifteen minutes early. A spot of shade out front called to me, so I sat down at a picnic table and waited. More than a few students stared in my direction as they walked to class. I'd never been good with attention. Uncle Greg said it was because I'd been neglected when my mom was in the hospital, but even Mom agreed that he was wrong on this one. Some people are just introverts.

Chul and another boy I vaguely remembered from yesterday walked over and sat at the picnic table next to mine. The other boy's name tag read Yun Jin-woo, but Chul still wasn't wearing one. He caught me watching them. I smiled and gave a wave but then pulled out my phone and pretended to be busy.

A long parade of black cars pulled through the circular drive. Drivers opened polished doors and students exited as new cars pulled in. One stood out from the others, a Rolls Royce. When the driver opened the door, Min and Ae-Ri tumbled out, laughing. They sauntered through the crowds that had begun gathering outside the school, and then, like a guided missile, Min walked straight to Chul. She hopped up and sat on the tabletop just above where he sat so her long legs were right at his eye level. He didn't notice how she crossed her legs, so ladylike, or wiggled closer until her hip almost touched his shoulder. Instead, he watched me with the same intense stare from yesterday.

My phone had never been more interesting. I opened my email again. Mom *still* hadn't responded yet. There were no new messages. Not even junk mail. When I looked up, Chul locked eyes with me and my stomach fluttered. I tried to look away, but he held my gaze. Then Min stood up, and the spell was broken. She whispered something to Ae-Ri, walked to me, and sat down. Min sighed dramatically while she fluffed her hair with long, gold-tipped nails.

I snorted. It was probably real gold.

"You're looking at Chul," she said.

"Yeah, to be fair, though, he looked first."

"You and those hips are hard to miss. If you don't want to stick out so bad, maybe try losing the blubber."

I sat up straighter. "Oh, you mean my American girl curves." I leaned in with one hand cupped over my mouth and whispered, "I'll tell you a little secret. Boys stare at what they like." I sounded way more confident than I felt, but no way was I going to sit here and let little miss-skinny-jeans call me fat.

Min stood abruptly. The gold of her nails glittered like daggers. "Leave it to a girl like you to think every boy wants her. It's so crass, Sydney. You don't even have a ghost of a chance with Chul." She strode off to the front doors without looking back, all confidence. Ae-Ri trotted after her.

I turned and faced away from the school, away from Chul and his friend who'd probably overheard Min's remark. My chest burned with each breath, and I could feel the flush of my face radiating waves of embarrassment. I wasn't as well-off as Min, and maybe I didn't have the perfect body she did. But I didn't want any of that. I didn't want to be here or have Chul staring at me. I wanted to go home.

Most of the students had gone inside before I dared get up. I started up the steps, and someone touched my shoulder. I spun back around, ready to yell or fight.

It was Chul. We stood toe to toe, so close. I could smell his aftershave, and some crazy part of my brain wanted to lean in.

"I'll walk you to class." Only a few students remained outside, but I could feel their stares as they moved past us. "I'm okay to go on my own," I barely whispered.

"The only way to get Min to leave you alone is if she knows you have friends who will stand up for you. You should hang out with me more, and she'll back down."

"I can handle Min," I said, taking a step away.

"I don't think you can."

"Who cares? I'm going home soon."

Chul looked down at his shoes. "Are you sure? Did your mom already buy your ticket home?"

I laughed. "We're not rich. Once she realizes how much this school costs, I'll be on the next plane out of Seoul." Just saying it out loud made me want to jump up and down, cheerleader-style. Mom couldn't argue the money.

Chul nodded, but his eyes looked desperate, almost

angry. "Do you have a plan B? You should always have a plan B."

"Thanks for the rice yesterday." It was lame, but I wanted him to stop looking at me like I was about to jump from an airplane without a parachute. "I've got to go to class." I hurried past him through the front doors and walked to History. I wasn't sure why Suni had signed me up for this class. I knew zero about Korean history, but since I was leaving soon, none of it mattered. I could lay my head on my desk if I wanted. Not that I would. If I did, I wouldn't be able to stop thinking about Chul.

I stepped inside the room, and Gun waved from the middle row. He tapped the empty desk next to his, and I sat down. Today he wore his shirt sleeves rolled to the elbow. Two thick silver bracelets with black onyx in the center stood out against the muscles in his forearms. If that wasn't enough to catch my eye, his dark hair flopped down around his eyes in a heavily styled look that said he spent big money to come off casual. Gun wanted to be noticed. Usually this would bug me, but he was also unassuming. Like he was just born to look good, so why hide it?

He pulled a folder from his binder and put it on my desk. "We were supposed to write a paper on the First Republic. I wrote yours since you missed first period yesterday. I figured you wouldn't get it."

I blinked in surprise. He'd written a paper for me? "That was nice of you."

Gun grinned.

I pulled my laptop out of the new backpack Suni bought me. "I wrote my own, though. I saw the assignment posted to the website you showed me yesterday."

Gun's face fell, but he recovered quickly. Leaning back and crossing both arms, he winked. "So you're the independent type."

Did guys still say that? "I thought it was just assumed that none of us girls needed knights in shining armor anymore."

"Don't get me wrong. I like a girl who can stand on her own. But Korean guys like to do things for pretty girls."

"Same with American guys."

"So . . . does that mean you have a boyfriend in America?"

I debated saying that I did. It might make the whole day easier. "No," I said.

Gun's eyes lit up. Clearly, he thought this was a good thing. "Do you want to hang out after school?"

A hush settled over the room, and I looked up. Chul walked in and looked from me to Gun with a scowl. He walked past us and sat somewhere behind me. Not a big deal to have him in this class, too. Except, ignoring Chul at my back would be like pretending it was dark on a sunny day.

"I have to catch my bus home. I'm not sure how late it runs."

"You ride a bus home?" Gun pursed his lips and frowned. "Where's your driver?"

"I don't mind the bus."

"You shouldn't ride a bus alone. Let me drive you. We can get food for our date, and I'll show you around Seoul on our way."

"Date?" I asked.

Gun raised his eyebrows. "You said you don't have a boyfriend, so it's okay if you date, right? Besides, I kinda grow on people. Who knows? Maybe *I* could be your boyfriend."

I wanted to cover my burning cheeks, but I was trying to act cool about the whole thing. A wadded-up paper ball bounced off my shoulder. I turned sharply, but all the students seemed absorbed in their own conversations. Chul was busy pulling out books and didn't look at me. I hoped no one had heard Gun ask me out and pitch the idea of being my boyfriend in the same breath.

I turned back to Gun. I'd go home soon, possibly as soon as tomorrow if my mom came through on the ticket. It'd be nice if I could tell her I'd done more than hang out in my room. And one date didn't mean anything. I wondered if I should text Suni to let her know or ask permission. I wasn't sure of the rules here. Gun placed one hand over his heart and smiled again. "I'm a complete gentleman. I'll get you home safely."

"Okay," I said. "But I don't really like Korean food." More like I'd rather eat my shoe, than have Korean food.

"I've got you covered. I know where to get American."

"Really, like a cheeseburger?" I asked, hopeful.

"Something better."

I couldn't blame someone who grew up eating abalone porridge for breakfast, but Gun didn't know what he was talking about. There's nothing on this planet better than a cheeseburger.

10

CHUL

I watched Sydney after school from a bench near the parking lot. Gun tried to carry her bag, but she declined. Smart, but then she wasn't smart enough not to get in his car. He even opened the door for her like he was some kind of gentleman. But I knew Gun.

Sydney's mom's email from this morning was unbelievable. I blocked it from her devices trying to buy myself some time, but Sydney was going to find out eventually. I opened my laptop and logged into her checking account. I cringed when I saw the balance.

Jin-woo sat down on the bench next to me and glanced at my screen. "What happened, did you get disinherited or something? Those are some scary numbers."

"It's not mine."

Jin-woo raised his eyebrows. "Whose account is it? I didn't know you were doing this again."

I shrugged. Jin-woo didn't hack, but we'd been friends a long time. He knew about my low point after my arrest. "Just one account," I said.

"Who?"

"Sydney Moore."

Jin-woo jerked. "That new girl Min wants to kill?"

I nodded.

"Why? Do you like her?" he asked.

"No." I tried to sound casual and not defensive.

He raised both eyebrows. "Sure."

"She's living at my house," I said.

He jumped up. "What? Since when?"

"Since both our mother's cooked up a plan to strand her in a foreign country."

"Lucky."

"Why's that?" I asked.

"Hot American girl living in your house. Tell me that's not lucky."

"She wants to go home," I said, annoyed.

"Are you going to send her?"

I scrolled through her account in disbelief. Sydney didn't even have enough for a one-way *economy* ticket. I could buy it myself and have her home before either of our mothers knew what I'd done. She'd be out of my hair. Of course, there would be hell to pay later, but it might be worth it. Her smile had been so happy this morning when she'd talked about going home. I logged out of her account. "No," I answered.

"You do like her, then."

I worried about Sydney, but that wasn't the same thing as liking her. I'd decided not to buy her a ticket because I didn't know all the details. But that didn't mean I was dumb enough to fall into my mother's trap. "If I do, then you better steer clear."

Jin-woo raised his hands in surrender. "I'm not touching Sydney. She's got more problems with Min than I can handle. I like my girls simple."

"Are we still on for basketball in the morning?" I asked.

Jin-Woo stretched and popped his neck. "Bright and early."

"I want you to invite Gun."

"I thought you guys hated each other."

"That's why *you're* doing the inviting." I checked Sydney's location one last time. She was at The Pancake House. I gritted my teeth. Gun didn't need to feed her. I'd already talked with the kitchen staff about how to change up her breakfasts and lunches.

I couldn't keep Sydney from the truth any longer or she would get suspicious. I unblocked her email account and watched as her messages began downloading.

11

SYDNEY

Of course Gun drove a Lamborghini. He strutted around the bright, flashy yellow car and opened the door for me, cool in his Cartier sunglasses. I wondered how many girls he'd managed to impress with this. Maybe it was common for the crowd at Daeshim, but money wasn't really my thing. Back home, some of the richest people I'd met could also be the cruelest. I climbed in with a polite smile, and he closed the door.

Within a few blocks the streets were packed with people and mopeds. Tiny shops and rows of red tents with vendors lined both sides of the road. This was the part of Seoul that seemed fun to explore.

"Oh, look," I said, pointing out the window. "Can we stop and try that?" A crowd of people milled about one particular food tent holding what looked like corn dogs.

Gun glanced in the direction I was pointing and made a face. "I don't eat street food."

"Why not?" I asked, surprised.

He shifted in his seat. "Why would I? I'm not poor, you know."

"Yeah, I figured, seeing what you're driving. Well, that and you go to Daeshim, but what does that have to do with anything? I don't expect you to take me somewhere expensive."

Gun shook his head. "Don't worry about it. I'm taking

you to a restaurant you'll like, very American."

I nodded, feeling optimistic. My mouth watered at the thought of cheese pizza or sub sandwiches. If it was something made from bread or cheese, preferably both, I was in. "I can't wait."

Gun grinned. "Good choice."

I smiled back at him, glad I'd decided to see Seoul at least once before going home.

"I noticed you talking outside with Chul this morning," Gun said. "You should probably avoid him."

"Why?" Chul had been nothing but nice. Maybe a little too forward, but he still didn't seem like a bad guy.

"Let's just say I've seen more than one student transfer out of Daeshim once Chul got involved in their life."

I shrugged. "He seems okay."

Gun's voice took on a bitter note. "He doesn't care who gets burned as long as he gets what he wants."

I kept silent.

"I guess you want to know what I'm talking about."

I really didn't. Most of the guys at Daeshim, Gun included, probably had egos that matched their bank accounts. Chul seemed different somehow. When I was with Chul, he wasn't looking at how much my clothes cost or who my parents were. He'd looked at me like he really cared.

Gun gave me a sidelong look and sighed. "You're new here, so you don't know, but last year my little sister, Ji-hee, entered Daeshim as a freshman. She did okay up until she met Chul. She crushed on him pretty hard. When Min got wind of things, the harassment started. If Chul had been serious about Ji-hee, he would have stopped it. Instead, he did nothing."

"Is Ji-hee okay?"

"She couldn't handle it. My parents sent her to a boarding school in England."

"I'm sorry," I said. "You must miss her."

"I do, but you don't need to be sorry. I just wanted you to know the kind of person he is." Gun sat up straighter in his seat and gave me a stern look. "It's important that you stay away from him."

Whatever happened could've been a misunderstanding. I wasn't sure, but I did know there were two sides to every story. "I really hope she comes home for a visit soon."

Gun nodded, but I got the impression he hadn't gotten the reaction he wanted. He smiled at me, and for the rest of the drive, he chatted about Seoul and pointed out a few places he thought I'd like to visit. We slowed near a small brick building with a yellow sign that read Pancake House. My stomach growled. "Is this for real? I love pancakes."

"I thought you might." Gun parked, and I was already out and walking. He laughed. "Hold up, they won't run out."

"Sorry, I'm just so excited to eat some *real* food, finally."

"I did good, then? You don't want to go back for the street food?"

I shook my head. "Pancakes are perfect."

The sweet smell of batter filled the air as soon as we walked in. A waitress got us seated right away and placed a menu in front of me. I didn't need one. I ordered plain pancakes with butter and syrup. Gun tacked on a couple of omelets, fresh squeezed orange juice, and fried potatoes to our order.

My first bite was perfect, fluffy and dripping with sugary maple goodness. I wanted to cry. I spoke around my second mouthful. "Thank you so much for bringing me here. You have no idea how hungry I've been."

Gun shrugged. "I can bring you here every day after school if you want. Where are you staying? I live pretty close to here, actually."

I didn't really know how to tell him that I was leaving. I still hadn't heard from my mom, but I was sure she would email soon with my flight info. "I'm staying in Pyeongchang, but it's just temporary," I said over another mouthful.

"Most people who go to Daeshim live there. What's the name of the family you're staying with?"

My phone vibrated and I pulled it out. One new text. It

was Suni.

> **Your mom called me. She said you're worried about tuition costs. Kim Corporation is one of the financial contributors to Daeshim, so your tuition is waived. Please don't concern yourself with money. I am happy to provide anything you may need.**

I choked on my orange juice.

"Are you okay?" Gun handed me a napkin.

I nodded. "Yeah, I'm good. Hang on. I need to check something." I opened my email, and it immediately started loading. Maybe there was something wrong with my phone, because I'd been checking for mail all day, but now there were at least twenty messages. I scrolled through and looked for anything from my mom. My finger stopped, and I hovered over her name. I opened it up with a feeling of dread.

Dear Syd,

Remember you promised me to stick it out no matter how hard things got. Sorry, you're staying for the year.

Love,
Mom

This had to be a mistake. I read it again, sure that my mom would never be this cruel. But the words didn't change. She didn't even explain, just a few short sentences.

"What's wrong?"

I blinked away tears and looked at my unfinished pancake. This couldn't be happening to me. I couldn't stay here for the year. "I need to go to the bathroom." I managed to choke out the words.

Gun pointed to a hallway behind me.

I bolted for the bathroom and made it to a toilet just in time. The pancakes didn't come up as nicely as they'd gone down.

My phone vibrated in my pocket, and I pulled it out to see two new texts.

> **Loser:**
> **Where are you?**

> **Loser:**
> **Hyun is worried**
> **that you haven't**
> **come home.**

The words blurred on the screen. I couldn't deal with this right now. I powered my phone off, went to the sink, and splashed my face with cool water. Chul's words from this morning came back to me. He wanted to know if I had a plan B. No. I didn't. I didn't have a clue what I was going to do now. I went back out. Gun stood at the window laughing on his phone. He saw me and got off.

"Did you have diarrhea?" He asked, like it was the most normal question in the world.

"Um, no," I said, a little horrified that he would ask that.

"Good," he said. "I'm glad you're not sick."

"I think I should head home," I said. What I wanted to do was beg him to drive me to the airport. But I knew, even if I emptied my checking and savings, I wouldn't have enough for a ticket home.

"What? You can't go yet. Besides, my friend just called. He's in a band, and they're opening at a concert tonight. Do you want to go?"

Gun started grinning before my brain could register that I'd said yes. Going for pancakes might be okay, but going to a concert without asking might be pushing it. Then the words of Mom's email repeated in my brain. *"Sorry, you're staying."* If dumping me in Korea was okay, then why would anyone care what I did?

We walked down a trash-filled alley that smelled like rotting fish and pee. I wrinkled my nose as we approached, careful where I stepped. The beat of muffled music escaped through a rusted steel door at the end of the alley. A short man in a rumpled army coat leaned against the wall. The red glow of his cigarette burned bright in the graying light. As we got closer, he puffed out his chest and gave Gun an expectant stare. Gun handed him a wad of rolled up *won* bills. He opened the door and waved us in with a smirk.

I hurried after Gun. "Why did you pay him so much?" I asked. "It's just a concert."

"We're underage."

"What does that mean? You have to be a certain age to go to a concert in Korea?"

Gun looked down at me and laughed. "You're joking, right? This is a bar."

"Oh." I stopped walking.

"What's wrong? I have a fake ID. I just figured you didn't."

"No, that's not it," I said, shaking my head. "I don't drink, like, ever. I want to go." I started to turn back, but Gun grabbed my hand.

"We don't need to drink. This band is way cool."

I shook my head.

"Look. They're only opening for another band, so if we don't hurry, we'll miss them. I promise, we're not here to drink."

I gave him a hard stare. "No drinking, or I'm leaving," I said.

He cocked his head and smirked. "Got it."

Music vibrated down the hallway lit only by a fluttering neon sign that said "TURN IT UP" in English. We came to a door that opened onto the main floor of the concert. The venue looked small, maybe less than a hundred people. Some were seated at tables on a balcony, but most of the crowd stood on the main floor in front of the stage. Everyone jumped and yelled to the music. The air was stale from smoke, and I coughed a few times, trying to adjust.

"Come on, let's get closer." Gun took my hand and pulled me through the crowd until we found a pocket where both of us could stand. "I'm glad we didn't miss them."

"What's the name of the band?" I had to yell. Gun leaned down so I could get close to his ear.

"*Diamond Interns.* The drummer used to be my neighbor until he moved out of his parent's house."

I nodded. "Cool." I had to admit they had the perfect vibe. A little punk, a little rock, and a whole lot of Korean. The lead singer had bleach-blond hair and wore it shaggy with a Yankees ball cap.

"Do you like it?"

"They're so awesome," I yelled.

Gun pulled out his phone and frowned. "Something's going on with my car. I need to go outside for just a minute. You'll be okay, right?"

The concert floor was packed full of strangers, and the only lighting came from the stage. No way was I staying here alone. I started to say I would go with him, but he didn't hear me.

"Stay here, and I'll be right back," he yelled and then disappeared in the blend of pumping arms.

One creepy looking guy with face tattoos stared hard in my direction. I looked away and hoped Gun would come back soon. The music ended, and the lead singer announced their last song of the night. Everything slowed with a ballad. The bass guitarist strummed in the background. People pushed in tighter as they swayed. Sweaty bodies crushed against me, and the hot smoky air became suffocating. I tried to stand on my tiptoes to see if I could find Gun. Someone shoved against me. I fought to keep my balance until arms steadied me from behind. A deep voice spoke in my ear. "Are you here by yourself, Sydney?"

I jerked and turned around as best I could in the tight space. Even in the dark with a cap pulled low over his face, there was no mistaking Chul. He rested his hands on my shoulders, creating a buffer from the crowd that let me breathe.

"I'm here with Gun," I said. I wasn't sure he could hear me. He didn't move away but seemed content to just stay and listen to the music.

The song finished with a soft progression of cords that bled emotion into the crowd. On the last note people rushed to get closer to the stage and Chul reached for my hand.

"I need to find Gun," I said, but Chul didn't stop or loosen his grip, only pulled me past people to a side exit.

I followed him out to the parking lot but stopped short when I saw Hyun. He stood rigid in his suit and tie and scanned for anyone leaving the concert. My stomach dropped. He couldn't possibly be here looking for me, could he?

Another hand clamped down hard on my wrist. I jerked around. "Gun," I said.

12

CHUL

Gun's eyes glared hard and flat in the lights of the parking lot. "I told you to wait there," he barked at Sydney.

I stepped closer to her and let an edge sharpen my words. "You left her alone. In a bar," I said.

Sydney tried to jerk her hands from both of ours, but I wasn't letting go, not with Gun still holding on.

"I didn't leave her alone," Gun said.

"She looked alone to me."

"Not as alone as you left Ji-hee," Gun spat.

"Hold up." Sydney forced a laugh. "Everything's fine. I didn't have any problems."

Neither of us broke to look at her.

Hyun approached at a near run. "Excuse me, Miss Moore."

Sydney let out a shaky breath and smiled adoringly, like he was an angel straight from heaven. Fitting. He'd saved her more than once now. Or I had, anyway.

Hyun bowed quickly. "I've been asked to bring you home . . . now." He glared at Gun, who dropped her arm like it was hot. Hyun wasn't big, but he moved like he could handle himself.

I gave her hand a gentle squeeze and stepped back so she could go with Hyun.

Gun finally looked at her. "My car got towed."

"Miss Moore," Hyun said sharply with another hard look

at Gun.

Sydney hesitated. I couldn't tell if it was leaving Gun that bothered her or just leaving us at each other's throats. One thing was sure. Sydney was oblivious to the kind of guy Gun was.

"Immediately," Hyun added, then gestured to his running car, double parked in the packed lot. Sydney followed him and got inside, her face a frown of confusion. She turned and watched us out the back window as Hyun drove away.

I faced Gun. "I'm glad you brought your sister up." I took a step closer. "I found out you hired that photographer. How much money did Min give you for the pictures? I bet it was a lot to sell out family."

Blood drained from Gun's face. "Shut your mouth. Those are lies."

"Do you think I would let something like that go? If Min had released those pictures, Ji-hee would have ended up worse off than living in the UK."

Gun's hands shook. "You have no proof."

"I have the video confession from the photographer you hired. He told me everything, even gave me the originals." I paused and let it sink in. I wanted Gun to understand how far I would go if he tried smearing my name. "I wonder what your father would say if he got a copy of that confession. The only reason I didn't do it sooner was to protect Ji-hee."

Gun stormed away without a word. But what could he say? He knew he'd lied, and now he knew that I knew. Hyun had the car, so I pulled out my phone and found a cab. When I finally climbed in, exhausted, the smell of sour soju and vomit wafted around me. I didn't care. Sydney was safe. I leaned my head back against the vinyl of the seat and let out a long breath. I couldn't believe that Gun had the audacity to accuse me of hurting his sister.

Ji-hee was a sweet girl with a bubbly and outgoing personality. Not really my type, but when she asked me in her shaky voice if I'd go to the mall with her, she'd been standing with

Min and some other girls from my class who would have laughed at her rejection. She wasn't as rich as most at Daeshim, and Min considered her the bottom of the food chain. Never mind that our chain was made of gold. Ji-hee was still at the bottom.

"Sure, Ji-hee. We can hang out," I said.

Ji-hee lowered her eyes and giggled. "I want to find a new dress for Min's party. It's this Friday. Are you going?" She didn't notice the way Min glared at her.

I shook my head. "Can't, I've got to train for my competition."

She frowned. "I was hoping we could go together."

"Why would Chul go with you?" Min's voice stayed smooth, but her upper lip twitched. I'd learned to read the tells of Min's more dangerous moods. She took Ji-hee by the arm, and to anyone watching, she would have seemed concerned for the girl. I knew better.

"Chul doesn't date freshman," Min said. "Why don't I set you up with someone? There will be a lot of new guys at my party. Interns are visiting my father's company this month."

Ji-hee had been too naive to read the threat behind the words. "That's okay. I don't want to go with anyone else," she said. "If you can't go, Chul, will you still take me shopping?"

I smiled kindly at Ji-hee and willed Min to let the slight go. "I'll take you tomorrow."

Gun stopped me in the hall the same day and grilled me, like I had malicious plans for his little sister or something.

I folded my arms and leaned against the locker. "What's this about, Gun? You and I have both been on plenty of dates, and I'm not the one with rumors floating around."

Gun flinched. There'd been more than one girl in this school complaining about Gun's less than gentlemanly treatment on dates. "Where are you taking Ji-hee? She's all excited, like she's got a date with a prince or something." His lip curled when he said the word prince.

The chip on his shoulder about my family's wealth was the reason we didn't get along. Well—that and Gun was a jerk. I snorted. "Dress shopping at La Monte."

Gun blinked. La Monte was out of his price range. I'd planned to take Ji-hee to the mall, but I couldn't pass up the sour look I got from him.

He looked down at his shoes. "What time will you be there?"

I couldn't exactly not tell him. Ji-hee was his sister. "Right after school. Maybe you plan to do some shopping yourself."

Gun laughed. "No need. I'm shopping in Paris over spring break."

"Sure you are."

Gun met my eyes with a glare. "You know you're not the only one with money. You act like you're better than everybody, but all of us have money."

I leaned closer. "Your dad's stock went down again this quarter." I immediately regretted saying that. I didn't use my wealth this way. Not even with Gun.

Spittle flew from Gun's mouth when he spoke. "I have my own ways of making money."

After his sister left, it took me awhile to piece it all together. Min wanted Ji-hee gone and Gun wanted money. Once he knew when and where I was taking Ji-hee, the only thing he needed was a sketchy photographer. There were pictures of me admiring a dress she wore, followed by pictures of her undressing. Never mind that she had been in the dressing room the whole time and I hadn't stepped a foot near her. Facts didn't matter when you had pictures, and that was all Min needed for a little blackmail.

I'd erased everything from Min's computer, but I was too late to save Ji-hee. I'd be a fool if I let it happen again. Gun wasn't getting anywhere near Sydney.

13

SYDNEY

Mom,

I don't understand. Why the whole year, and why lie to me? You can't force me to stay here.

I don't even want to email you. I'm that mad. I've done my best with every crappy situation thrown my way. But this is harsh. There's no reason for you to dump me here.

Syd.

My lips trembled as I stared at my inbox. I couldn't leave things like this. I loved Mom and this was probably just her desperate attempt to get me to not hang on so tight. It wouldn't work. I opened a second email and started typing.

Mom,

I'm sorry I got mad. I'm still mad. But I love you. And . . . I need advice.

You know how I've never really dated before? You wanted me to go out with that one guy, Steve, who kept on asking. He was cute. Maybe I should have said yes to at least one date. I'm regretting it now, because I have no idea what I'm doing.

This guy, Gun, asked me out to a concert. He's fun and makes me laugh. I can't tell for sure, but I think he might like me. The night ended early when he got into it with this other guy from school, Chul. Chul is different from Gun. He's intense, and when he's around, I'm hyper aware of him. He sat behind me in first period, and I had to force myself not to turn around and stare. I didn't think Chul was interested. I've talked to him a few times at school, and he's nice. But then at the concert when Gun left to check his car, Chul just showed up out of nowhere. I mean, did he happen to be there too—by himself—and then just decide to come hang out with me? He held my hand. I don't think my hand has recovered yet. Did he just do that because it was a crowded concert? I can't tell.

When I left, they were fighting. I don't know how to act normal now. What do I do?

Suni's son (AKA Loser) nags me a lot. But always over texts. I think he has severe social anxiety because I've never even met him. And so far, I've seen Suni only once. Other than Hyun, this house is a ghost town. I don't even see the staff because they all hang out in the kitchen.

Write me back. I miss you.

Love,
Syd

I bolted upright from the loud banging sound. Tingles, tight and numb, burned across my cheek. I groaned when I looked at the clock. It was only 9:00 PM, but I'd fallen asleep on my keyboard.

I opened the door. Hyun stood, there, frowning hard. I imagined it's what my dad would have looked like if he'd picked me up after curfew. Except, it hadn't been after curfew, and he wasn't my dad. "May I have a word with you, Miss Moore?"

I thought about saying no. Technically, Suni hadn't given

me any rules, and Hyun wasn't even supposed to pick me up from school. But he looked worn out standing in the hallway with a visible slump to his shoulders.

"Sure," I said.

He politely gestured towards the sitting area just down the hall that had two pristine white chairs. I followed him and sat down, rubbing the sleep from my face. Hyun sat across from me and leaned forward. His eyes, which usually stayed distant and passive, now held the shadows of concern.

"Miss Moore," he started, "I know this has been a shocking adjustment for you, but it's time to accept that you are here now."

I swallowed hard. "You don't understand what it's like."

"Don't I?" Hyun sighed. "I moved to California to go to Cal Tech. I was completely on my own, with no family or friends. I dreaded every day, and unlike you, I didn't have a firm grasp of the language. It wasn't until I met your mother that I started to enjoy living in the States."

"You know my mom?"

Hyun nodded. "She got me this job with the Kim family."

How could that be? Mom had never mentioned Hyun. I felt another stab of hurt. After just a few days here, it was like Mom had a secret life. A life before cancer, and a life before me. "How did you meet her?" I asked.

"We worked in the same food truck together. No one else could understand my English, but she spoke Korean, so they hired me."

"Did you know my dad?"

Hyun nodded. "Your father became a good friend to me as well. I was very happy for them when they got married."

Hearing Hyun talk about my dad made me almost jealous. I would never see who my parents had been together. I would never know my dad. "Were you there when he died?"

Hyun lowered his eyes and shook his head. "No, I had to go home before I graduated because of family issues. Before I left, Shannon arranged an interview for me with the Kims.

I had no idea that she'd been connected to such a powerful family. At the time, Suni was just six months pregnant. I served as her assistant and then also as her driver when she returned to work." Hyun smiled deeply, like he had good memories there. "I've been very happy living with the Kims. You will too, once you settle in and get to know them."

I shook my head. "I miss my mom too much. I worry about her."

Hyun patted my head, and I felt like a little kid. "Your mom wants you here. You show her disrespect by fighting her choices for you. Be a good daughter and trust her judgment on this."

I knew I should agree with him. I usually had no problem doing what my mom wanted, but I couldn't be this far away from her for a year. It was too long. I mumbled, "I'll try."

Hyun didn't look convinced and pursed his lips. "One more thing, Miss Moore."

I wiped at my eyes. "What?"

"Please don't turn your phone off or go to any illegal establishments. You were in a dangerous neighborhood, making it very difficult to find you."

I flushed with guilt. I knew I'd been stupid and irresponsible. "I'm sorry. Thank you for showing up when you did."

Hyun gave me a fatherly nod. "I'm glad you are home safe."

"Can I ask you something?"

"Of course."

"How did you find me?" I looked down sheepishly. "And did you have anything to do with my friend's car getting towed?"

Hyun's lips twitched, almost a smile. "I can't tell you that, but you should spend time and get to know everyone who lives in this house. Some people here might surprise you."

Whatever that was supposed to mean. Maybe they had a whole IT team working here that could track me down by hacking into traffic cameras. I laughed.

"I will be driving you to and from school from now on. You are not to take the bus or go with any friends without first getting permission from Master Kim. Understood?"

"Los—Suni's son? Why him?"

Hyun held up a hand. "Mrs. Kim's orders. You may know Korean, but you've proven you don't know this country. If you have an issue, take it up with her."

I nodded, miserable at the idea but knowing I was only getting what I deserved.

I puzzled over how Hyun had found me. I guess Suni could've assigned him to follow me. If he had, the guy deserved secret agent status, because I never once saw him. But would he really go so far as to get Gun's car towed? "Thanks for watching out for me, Hyun. I'll be more responsible in the future."

"Very good." Hyun stood and bowed slightly. "If there is nothing else, I hope you have a restful night."

I sighed. "You too."

After he left, I shuffled back to my room, feeling no better knowing that even Hyun expected me to stay here and be the dutiful daughter. I'd stay for now, but I needed to go home. Tomorrow would come and with it, school. I tried to think of that stupid plan B.

My phone buzzed as I entered my room and closed the door. I looked at the screen with a scowl. What did he want?

> **Loser:**
> **Hyun is supposed**
> **to drive you to**
> **school tomorrow.**
> **What happened?**

I texted back.

Nothing happened. I went out with a friend and then Hyun picked me up.

Loser:
That's not what I heard. If he brought you home, then something happened.

I texted back.

This isn't my home.

Loser:
You know what I mean.

I bit my lip as I texted him.

It could save us both some trouble if you bought me a ticket to California.

I got no response

I'll pay you back. When I get home, I plan on getting my old job back.

Loser:
Don't make me
laugh.

I quickly texted.

Seriously, I will.

Loser:
That's not why I
can't buy you a
ticket.

I texted.

What then?

Loser:
You've never seen my
mother angry. You should
plead your case with your
own mom.

I texted.

I've begged my
mom. She shot
it down. Can you
please help me out
here? I need to get
home.

How desperate was I to be begging Loser? But if he didn't come through, I was pretty much stuck.

I got no response for a long time. Maybe he was buying the ticket. My phone buzzed again. I grabbed it, hoping for a flight number.

Loser:
Not going to happen.

Defeated, I threw my phone on the bed. Who could blame him? I didn't like Loser, but I would probably do the same in his position. A timid knock sounded on the door. "Come in," I called out.

A maid opened the door, smiling politely behind a large cart of boxes. She wheeled it inside, followed by two more maids with their own carts.

I gasped. "What is this?"

"These were delivered for you today, Miss Moore." She kept her eyes low as she moved past me to the closet. "Please let us know if there is anything else you need. We can arrange for it."

"Wait. I didn't ask for this."

The last two maids exchanged a look. I followed them, but before I could protest more, they were lining the shelves with shoes, sweaters, bags, scarves, and hats. One of the maids started hanging up more school uniforms, then began with shirts and blouses. There were dresses, piles of jeans, jackets, leather purses, and boxes of tights and socks. Every clothing item I'd ever imagined seemed to be filling the closet as if by magic. Shoes arranged by color, jewelry on velvet trays.

This was stuff that happened in the movies, not in my crappy life. I laughed and stood there gaping like an idiot. Suni had lost her mind! She couldn't buy me all this stuff. I sat down on the floor of my closet and tried to compose the perfect text that said thanks, but no thanks. I really didn't want to offend Suni, but this had to stop.

Hi Suni,
Thank you for all
you've done for
me. You have been
so thoughtful
with everything.
New clothes are so
nice, but I really
don't need them.

Suni:
I'm in Tel Aviv and
near dead from lack
of sleep. Go ahead
and get whatever
new clothes you
want. Have Hyun
drive you to any
mall, and he will
charge it for you.
Don't worry about
the cost, just
have fun. I don't
know when I'll be
home, but I can
take you shopping
sometime.

Suni was in Tel Aviv? I thought she was in Canada. And apparently, she was working so hard that she couldn't even read my text right. Maybe I should have put the "don't need" in all caps. Or maybe Mom should have brought Suni home with us for the year. That would have done more good than dumping *me* here.

I debated texting back to clarify, but I already felt like an idiot for waking her up. Great, now she probably thought she hadn't sent enough to begin with. What kind of brat would ask for more than this?

"Excuse me," I said.

"Yes?" A maid looked up from the row of headbands and barrettes she was carefully arranging.

"I'm sorry, but can you box this all back up? I can't accept it," I said.

All three women froze. The first maid actually looked scared. "Is there some problem, Miss Moore?" She asked. "Do you not like the choices? Different colors or styles can be provided."

"Oh, no, everything looks perfect," I said, hurriedly. "I just can't accept it. Suni has been too generous. Please return the items and tell her I don't need any additions to my wardrobe."

"But Mrs. Kim didn't order any of this."

"She didn't?" I furrowed my brow. "Then who did?"

"The young Master Kim."

14

CHUL

I did another lay-up, gritting my teeth against the image of Gun holding Sydney by the wrist. Even basketball couldn't keep my mind off her. She thinks that idiot is fun? What was wrong with this girl? And intense didn't describe me. She just couldn't think of a way to say I'm hot and good at everything in her email.

Jin-woo took a step back. "Dude, why are you so mad?" His breath came out in hard pants as we both wiped the sweat from our faces. The morning air was already warm, and Daeshim's outdoor basketball court would be scorching in just a few hours.

"Where's Gun? Did you text him?" I asked.

"Yeah, he said he'd be here at seven."

"Great, where is he?"

"Uh . . . it's not even seven yet." Jin-woo looked at me like I'd lost it.

Maybe I had.

Jin-woo went to the other end of the court and shot baskets. I did ten more practice lay-ups before I stopped to check my phone. Sydney was still at the house. I could see the green dot of her phone on my map. She'd better get a move on if she was going to make it to school on time.

My phone buzzed with my mother's number lighting up the screen. I sighed and answered. "Hello."

"Good morning, son. Are you getting ready for school?"

"Yeah, kinda. I'm already ready."

"Good. I'm back in Tel Aviv. A supplier meeting got pushed out an extra day. I'm hoping your father and I will be home in a few days. How are things going with you and Sydney?"

"What do you mean?"

"Are you giving her rides?"

I sighed again. "Hyun is taking her today."

"Really? Why aren't you giving her a ride?"

"Don't worry. I make sure she gets to school."

"That's good. But spend some time with her. She's probably lonely."

I rubbed the back of my neck, which was starting to ache.

"That's not my problem."

My mother tsked. "Are you really so cold-hearted?"

"No, but I want you to stop pushing her on me."

She cleared her throat. "Is it too much to ask you to take proper care of Sydney? You know your father and I are busy."

And there it was—the story of my life. "Then she shouldn't be here. She wants to go home."

The silence on the other end extended until I felt twitchy.

"She's here to stay for the year." Her voice softened. "Maybe longer."

"This school isn't right for her. Korea isn't right for her."

"Shannon has some problems right now. You're just going to have to make the best of things and help her." There was pain in her voice.

"What problems?" I asked.

"You don't need to worry about it. Just do your best to help her fit in. Look, I need to go but . . ."

"What?"

"I love you," she said.

I paused. She almost never said that. "Me too." I hung up with a sigh. The truth was I wanted Sydney to stay. I even wanted to take care of her. Buying all that stuff had been fun. But when my mother talked like we should be together, I couldn't help myself. I always pushed back.

I shoved my phone back in my bag. It didn't matter what the big secret with Shannon was. I didn't need to know. But I wanted to. What would make a mother send her only daughter to another country for an entire school year?

"Hey, here comes Gun," Jin-woo said.

I looked up to see Gun walking our way. He stopped when he saw me. I motioned him over. "Are we playing or what?" I yelled.

Gun unzipped his jacket and dropped it on the bench at the far end of the court, then jogged over to us. He tried to act casual, like he didn't care, but he moved tense and unsure. Jin-woo looked from Gun to me and gave a nervous laugh. "Did I forget to mention that Chul would be here too?"

Jin-woo started for the court, but I stopped him. "It's just Gun and me for this game," I said. "Unless Gun's not up to it?"

Gun narrowed his eyes and strutted out to center like he was some kind of basketball god, overconfident because he played on the school team.

Jin-woo started backing off the court. "Yeah, I just remembered I have a chem test to study for. I'll catch you guys later."

I nodded, glad he got the hint.

"Give it up, Chul. You know you can't beat me," Gun said.

"Shut up and play." I passed him the ball. He dribbled with some showy footwork before shoulder-checking me on his way to a lay-up. "Sydney doesn't seem your type," he said, coming back to center.

I grinned at him, cut right, and snatched the ball, then breezed past for my own lay-up.

Gun retrieved and started towards his basket but stopped short and made a three pointer with just net. He turned to me, smug. "She doesn't like you. She likes me."

I retrieved the ball with a controlled dribble. "Are you sure she likes you? Your one and only date didn't end so well." I laughed. "Didn't your car get towed?"

Gun clenched his jaw and charged me. I spun the ball behind my back to my other hand.

He stopped. "We're already together," he said.

Those words hit me like a punch in the gut. The thought of Sydney being his girlfriend—no way. Even if that meant dating her myself, I would. "You're not. Not yet. And maybe Sydney is my type. Exactly my type. In fact, I think I like her." Saying it wouldn't be enough, and we both knew it. I had to make it happen. I passed him the ball.

Gun dribbled, then shot from well beyond the three-point line. We both followed the arc of the ball. It was an impossible shot, but it swooshed through, flawless. "I'm already dating her, so that's going to be a problem," he said.

Gun didn't know that I lived with Sydney. Sydney didn't either, but if I could break it to her with minimal damage, I could spend more time with her. It would give me an edge over Gun. And I *would* need an edge. Sydney couldn't see past his false charm to the slime below. I looked him square in the eye. "We'll let Sydney decide who to date." I walked off the court, shaking.

Last week in the airport, Sydney had been a nobody to me. She'd been quickly scanning the airport, shoulders tight, her hands in little fists at her side. The sun had shone behind her just as she turned. Our eyes had met, smudged makeup, messy hair, and a nervous smile. Beautiful. Now I couldn't stop thinking about her.

I should have gone to her right then, before Hyun showed up. If I had, maybe none of this would be a problem. But now I had to do something more impossible than Gun's lucky shot. I had to tell Sydney I was Loser.

15

SYDNEY

Syd,

I'm sorry that you think I dumped you in Korea, but I promise that spending the school year there won't be the end of the world. There are definitely worse fates than living in a mansion with a godmother who loves and spoils you. Make sure you don't complain or ask her to come home. It will really hurt Suni's feelings if you do.

Funny, I couldn't get you to even smile at a boy here. I'm glad you're dating. I'm sure they probably both like you. If a boy holds your hand, he's interested. Who wouldn't be? You're beautiful, smart, kind, and funny. My perfect daughter. So don't worry about how to act around them. Just be yourself.

I do have a question for you, though. Have you met Suni's son yet? I know you two didn't hit it off at first, but you should really take some time to introduce yourself. You might be surprised at how well you get along.

I miss you, but I'm so proud of you for staying there. This means more to me than I can say.

Mom

Maybe she was tired. She didn't tell me anything about work, or the beach, or a new recipe she wanted to try. Usually we talked a lot, just the small details that made up our days, gossip from the other maids at work, how bad our car sucked, what she made for dinner. I counted on hearing all that stuff. A short email felt weird. Just a quick bit of advice and she loved me?

I shrugged. Mom and I could make up for lost conversation when I went home, which might be sooner than she wanted. I still hadn't completely given up hope on leaving Korea. I'd considered emailing a friend from work. I knew Beth would lend me the money if she had it. The problem was, I didn't think she had it. She was as poor as I was.

I scrolled though my inbox. Two messages from Uncle Greg. I sent them to junk mail. Hyun knocked on my open door. "Are you ready, Sydney? We need to leave soon."

I closed my laptop and slid it into my backpack. "I'm ready when you are."

"You look very nice today," he said as I followed him out the door. "Different than before."

"Thanks." My uniform was the same, but with it, I wore cute knee-high socks, white with silver threads, and silver heeled loafers. I'd found a white leather headband that wasn't too girly, and even wore some crystal stud earrings that sparkled.

I'd wondered if Hyun told Loser to order me the clothes and decided to feel him out. "Thank you for the clothes," I said. "The maids brought everything to my room last night."

"It wasn't me." Hyun gave me a sidelong glance and smiled but said nothing further, which made me all the more curious.

I walked through the front door of Daeshim like it was just another school, like I wasn't wearing expensive shoes and carrying a leather backpack that probably cost more than our car. And it was dangerously easy. I still felt like me, normal. If I let go, even a little, then I was close to accepting this as my home. Only I didn't want to feel okay in Korea or to have ordinary days where everything was familiar. I didn't want to walk to class without looking at the map or take comfort in the idea that I had a closet full of nice clothes.

It was what my mom wanted, and what Hyun had told me I should do, but that didn't mean I had to like it. No more than I had to like the idea of Loser doing something nice for me. Mom wanted me to take the time to get to know him. But who was this guy? Most of the students I passed were laughing and talking in small groups. I only knew a few people in this school, so he could be anybody.

I stopped at my locker and opened it, staring into the dark abyss. No decorations, no cute little mirror, just an empty locker with a few books.

"Sydney."

I turned as Gun jogged up the hallway. He wore his white oxford dress shirt so tight that you could see his muscles flex as he moved.

"Hey, did you get your car back?" I asked.

He chuckled like it was no big deal. "I'm not sure why it got towed, but my dad's assistant picked it up this morning."

I looked at my shoes, a knot of guilt settling in my stomach, and I wondered again if Hyun had anything to do with it. "Yeah, that was weird."

Gun leaned closer. "Can we try again?"

"Try what?" I asked.

"Going out. Last night wasn't the best, and I want to make it up to you."

I pressed my lips into a straight line. "I kinda got grounded. I guess my godmother found out that we were at a club. It didn't go over too well." I sighed. "I have to get permission to go anywhere but school."

Gun lifted up my left hand, the hand that held my phone. "Get permission, then."

"Where do you want to go, exactly?"

"How about a movie and ice cream?"

I did want to, but the part I wasn't telling Gun was about

me needing to ask Loser. I sent a quick text and tried to sound like I wasn't asking *his* permission.

> **I'm going to text Hyun and tell him I'm going with a friend after school so he doesn't have to pick me up. We're just seeing a movie and then maybe getting ice cream.**

Loser:
No.

I texted.

> **I don't think he'll mind. It's just a few hours.**

Loser:
You're not going.
Drop it.

I texted.

Why?

After a few minutes with no reply, I put my phone away. It rankled me that I had to ask Loser. But I wasn't sure if Loser knew I was asking his permission, or if he was just saying Hyun wouldn't let me go. If he knew what Hyun had told me last night, he'd be rubbing it in my face. I turned back to Gun.

"They said no. It's probably too soon to ask."

Gun frowned his disappointment but then draped a carefully casual arm around my shoulder. "No big deal. We can go tomorrow."

I wasn't so sure, especially if Loser was in charge.

Chul tried to catch my eye when I walked into Math. I quickly headed to the back row and studiously started to read the assigned work Teacher Jang had printed on the smart board. Gun followed me in, but there were no open seats nearby. From the corner of my eye, I watched him sit on the second row. Chul sat on the fourth next to Min. He kept turning around like he was willing me to look at him. I was trying so hard to ignore Chul that I didn't notice Teacher Jang had called my name until Min started snickering.

"Excuse me. Moore. Moore," Teacher Jang snapped. "I asked you to pass out the quiz."

I jumped up. "Sorry." I hurried to the front of the room and took the stack of papers she firmly handed me.

When I started to pass them out, Gun appeared at my side. "I can help you." He reached forward. "Here, give me half."

"Sit down, Lee Gun." Teacher Jang spoke sharply. "Sydney is perfectly capable of passing out the quiz by herself. Not every girl in this school needs your romancing."

Everyone, even Gun, laughed, but Chul shifted in his seat and frowned at his shoes. Whatever bad blood was between those two had nothing to do with me, so why did I feel caught in the middle?

Near the end of class, Teacher Jang stepped into the hall, and Min was immediately out of her seat. I tried not to notice them, but how could I not? Chul was obviously trying to get my attention, and Min kept throwing me glares.

"Chul, why are you working so hard?" Min sat on his desk and trailed her fingers from the top of his shoulder down to his hand. She took the possessive girl look to a whole new level, sticking to Chul like cold ramen.

"Because we're seniors. Why aren't *you* working hard?"

"After this, we'll never escape work." She draped both arms around his shoulders and slid to his lap. I didn't want to look, but it was like turning away from a car crash. I couldn't see Chul's face until she squealed and jumped up quick. He must have shoved her off. Min somehow managed to saunter back to her seat without looking embarrassed. Something I couldn't have done.

I felt embarrassed even being near Chul, and it wasn't just that I lacked confidence. It was more than that. Chul just seemed too right. It was like when you walk next to someone and realize you've matched each other's strides without meaning to. I couldn't trust that. Or maybe I couldn't trust wanting that. I wasn't one of those girls who led a charmed life and things just worked out. I had to play it safe, no risks.

I hadn't always been this way. Sometimes I wondered what I would be like if Mom hadn't gotten sick, or if Dad hadn't died before I could remember him. Or sometimes, when I was really feeling brave, I wondered what I would have been like if Uncle Greg had been a decent human being instead of a narcissistic hemorrhoid.

I hated remembering that one therapy session. And I hated even more that I was too chicken to tell anyone. But who would I tell? Not Mom— I took care of her, not the other way around. And I was pretty sure no one else would believe that my uncle *wanted* me to be sick.

I'd been sitting on our living room floor playing with the zen sand garden my mom kept on the coffee table. I loved the way the tiny rake would smooth the sand into uniform ripples that lapped against the edge of the wood like they should just keep going on forever. The sand didn't know there were boundaries there. It didn't care that it was stuck in this tiny little garden. It didn't even know it was small. It was white sand, for crying out loud, meant for beaches and dunes you could see for miles. So it went on acting all majestic in spite of everything. The room smelled softly like sandalwood, like Mom. Uncle Greg was droning on about how there was a new therapy for PTSD he could provide at his hospital —another veiled push at in-patient care. I started humming under my breath, barely audible, but the song my mom played on the radio that morning had been stuck in my head all day. Something about those lyrics and the hypnotic flow of sand through my fingers made me let my guard down.

"Are you listening to me?"

I'd been leaning my head against the coffee table while I played in the sand. "Hmm . . . yeah, I'm listening."

It happened so fast. The wooden box flew from my fingers and exploded in a shower of glittery white against the far wall. I whipped my face up, but Uncle Greg already had me by the hair. He jerked my head back, squeezing my cheeks painfully until my mouth opened. Tiny pills flowed past my lips, choking and gagging me. He clamped his hand down on my jaw. "SWALLOW," he screamed. Bits of spittle landed on my face and tears leaked from the corners of my eyes, but he didn't let go. "You swallow that or I'm not letting you breathe."

My mouth had gone dry, and I jerked, but he held on. He smiled then, and something changed in his eyes. I could see the evil that had festered, unchecked so long in his soul. He shook me by my hair and hot pain seared my scalp. Then he dug into my lips with his fingers while holding my jaw closed with his thumb. "If you don't swallow, I'm going to make your mom take them."

I swallowed. It took two tries, and he checked my mouth after to make sure all the pills had gone down. By the time my mom came back from the grocery store, my hands tingled and my face felt numb and itchy. The garden and sand had been cleaned up and replaced on the coffee table. The room looked perfect. Uncle Greg was all nods and pats on my head when he left. I ran to the bathroom and stuck my tooth brush down my throat. The pills came up part-way dissolved.

I never found out what they were. After that, I changed during our sessions. I sat rigid in the green armchair, as far as I could get from Uncle Greg. I answered all his questions and calmly lied if the news wasn't good.

I wasn't all the way over Mom's cancer. I still had nightmares and I still ran home from school to check on her rather than hang out with friends. But *I* wasn't the sick one.

16

CHUL

I played out all the different ways of telling Sydney who I was. None of them ended well. I pulled out my phone in class and typed a text.

> **Hey, Sorry I've been such a jerk. It's because I was scared to meet you. I'm not a bad guy. We've met. More than once. Don't hate me— Chul**

The words lit my screen with an unsettling glow. My text would show up on her phone under Loser if I pushed send.

I deleted it.

SYDNEY

Robotics was my last period before lunch. I had no idea why Suni signed me up for this class. It was clearly an advanced course that carried over from last year. Everyone already had existing projects that they had worked on over the summer.

I sat down near the back and pulled out my laptop. Chul sat one row ahead, deep in conversation with a cute girl in pigtail braids.

Min and Ae-ri waltzed in a minute later and sat in two seats to my right. I sighed. Did Min have to be in *all* of my classes?

Ae-ri sneered in my direction, but I ignored her. "I don't know why Sydney is even in this class," she said loud enough for everyone to hear. "Yesterday she couldn't do anything but stare at the syllabus."

Chul turned around and looked right at me. "She's joining our team," he said.

"She is?" The girl in pigtails asked with surprise. She looked over at me but not in a mean way. "Hey, I'm Sun-he," she said with a happy bop of her head. "We do have the best robotic arm in the class." Her eyes flicked to Chul and then back to me before she tried to hide a smile. "Welcome to our group. You'll be on the winning team now."

Ae-ri scowled at Sun-he. "Only because you have Chul."

"No, I pull my weight too. My cousin helps me on weekends. He's even better than Chul with robotics," Sun-he said with a note of pride. She cocked her head. "Oh wait, Ae-ri, is that why you selected this class? Maybe you were even hoping to join the weekend tutoring sessions my cousin gives me? Too bad he already has a girlfriend."

Ae-ri's face fell.

I smiled to myself. Clearly there was a story behind Sun-he's mystery cousin. And apparently the story didn't seem to involve Ae-ri the way she wanted it to.

Sun-he sniffed and turned her cute nose up at Ae-ri. She beamed at me. "Come sit by us." I glanced at Chul, but he seemed deep in thought over some designs on his laptop. "If you're going to be on our team you need to sit with us," Sun-he said.

I changed seats, and Sun-he handed me a stack of papers. "Here, these are our plans so far. Look them over and see if there is anything you want to help with. I can hang out after class and work through lunch, if you want to stay and catch up."

Chul looked up from his work. "She's eating lunch with me."

"What?" I said.

"Lunch." Chul smiled. "Do you want to eat with me?"

I blinked, trying to break the spell that settled over me.

Chul just stared, which only made it worse. Finally, my brain kicked in. "Okay, sure." I wasn't sure.

Sun-he raised her eyebrows and hid a giggle behind her hand.

Min's face twisted into an ugly sneer, and she muttered something under her breath that I couldn't catch. I picked up the papers that Sun-he gave me and began reading over them. I had a sinking feeling that this was just the beginning with Min.

The bell rang, and I stalled while most of the class left. Chul waited patiently as I packed up. Min watched us both for a few minutes and then left without a word.

I moved slowly, nervous to be alone with him after last night. Gun didn't make me feel this nervous. He was fun and easygoing. Chul was . . . complicated.

I finished packing and Chul took my bag. I looked up to protest, but then met his eyes. I wanted to step closer, to move near enough that I could feel his body heat the way I had last night at the concert.

"I'll carry your bag." He swung the strap over his shoulder. Even the way he did that made me stop. Gun had offered to carry my bag, and I'd declined. With Chul, I didn't have a chance to. With Chul, I didn't want to say no.

"You look nice today, Sydney." He reached out and brushed the stud on my ear lobe with his thumb and forefinger. It was a quick, simple touch, but I couldn't help my flush, complete with heart flutters.

"Diamonds look right on you," he said.

I cleared my throat. I shouldn't like Chul. "They're not real."

Chul smirked, like he knew something I didn't, then held up a paper bag. "I brought you food in case you're not ready to brave the lunchroom."

"More rice?" I'd had plain rice and juice for breakfast.

"Sandwiches."

"Really? What kind of sandwich?"

"I think it's peanuts with mashed fruit."

My eyes lit up. "Peanut butter and jelly?"

Chul shrugged. "I just told our kitchen staff to make something American."

"Seriously, it's got to be peanut butter and jelly," I said, trying not to make it obvious that my mouth watered.

"Come on. We're eating outside," he said.

I should have been plotting my escape, working nights at a Korean BBQ where the owners paid me cash under the table, hoarding my money to buy a flight home. Instead, I was all gooey eyed over Chul and followed him to lunch.

I hadn't been to the back of the school yet, but there was a park-sized pavilion with cement picnic tables. A lot of students already had seats and were eating. I recognized Sun-he and the boy Chul had hung out with the day before. As we got closer, they stopped talking. Chul ignored it and motioned for me to sit down first. I did, and he sat next to me.

"You both know Sydney. You can stop staring," Chul said.

"Hey Sydney, I'm Jin-woo." He grabbed my hand, pumping it enthusiastically. He was just taller than me with stocky shoulders and a grade-school grin. Today he wore his hair combed up into a wave that reminded me of a K-pop boy band. Completely adorable.

"So . . . what do you think of Seoul so far?" Jin-woo asked.

I stretched the truth. "It's great."

Jin-woo gave Chul a curious look. "Has Chul taken you anywhere fun?"

Chul placed a canned fruit drink and a cloth-wrapped

sandwich in front of me along with a small bag of chips. "I haven't had a chance yet." He turned his gaze full-force on me. "Korea's going to grow on you."

I smiled, not sure how to take that.

"I didn't know we were going to have any new students this year," Sun-he said. But she made it more of a question than a statement and looked at me expectantly.

"Oh," I mumbled. I tried to hurry and swallow, but the peanut butter stuck in my mouth. Chul pushed my drink closer, and I took a few gulps before answering. "Yeah, it was kind of a last-minute thing. I'm going home at the end of the semester."

"That's too bad." Sun-he's eyes flicked to Chul with disappointment

"Where's home?" Jin-woo asked. "Wait. Let me guess. Iowa. No, New Jersey?"

Chul frowned and shook his head. "Dude?"

I laughed. "I live in Los Angeles."

Sun-he gave a little shriek. "I desperately want to go there." .

You couldn't help but love this girl. "Come visit me anytime. I don't live in a mansion or anything, but my mom is super nice, and she would take good care of you." Sun-he nodded vigorously but suddenly stilled and then groaned. "Yeah, I'm going to the states this summer, but with my cousin."

"She could come too," I said.

"He, not she," Chul said. "Sun-he's cousin is my best friend. He's in Pittsburg with his girlfriend now."

Jin-woo laughed. "It's funny that you both ended up having a thing for American girls."

Someone kicked Jin-woo under the table, and he jerked with a wince. Sun-he tsked and frowned over at him. She smiled at me with a look that said: *sorry Jin-woo is an idiot.*

I glanced down at my sandwich. I could feel Chul's eyes resting on me, waiting for me to say something. I took another long gulp of my drink and then shook the can back and forth. It was empty.

Chul jumped up. "Do you want another drink?"

"Sure, if it's not too much trouble."

"No trouble." He walked past our table, and the tension that felt like a boa constrictor wrapping around my ribcage eased.

Sun-he leaned closer on her elbows. "Chul usually ignores all the girls at our school, so we're just surprised that he's finally interested in someone."

"It's not like we're dating."

"You will be," Jin-woo said.

I barely knew Chul, and I wasn't sure about anything. Being around him was kind of terrifying, but now that Jin-woo had said it the idea of not dating him felt disappointing.

Athletics was the only class at Daeshim that truly scared me. At home we slacked off, ran the mile by cutting corners, and sat in the shade when the teacher wasn't watching. Not here. At Daeshim, Teacher Park called it Advanced Athletics, and it was do or die. Park was short and wiry, with a military-style buzz cut. He looked like he could be a stunt double on a martial arts movie and watched everyone with cold calculation. No one goofed off in Park's class. I knew from yesterday's "pep talk" that today was a running day.

"No excuses," Teacher Park had bellowed. "It's five kilometers. I don't care if you crawl across the finish line, but you don't go home until you finish. Got that?" he had barked. "I want all of you dressed and outside ready to run on tomorrow's bell."

I wasn't the best runner, but I wasn't awful either. Still, this was Korea. I didn't even know what an acceptable time for running five kilometers was. I entered the girls' dressing area. Everyone was changing into the spandex shorts and cotton tees that were the standard. Coach Park had given me the uniform yesterday, along with my running shoes.

A lot of the girls giggled as I walked by. I ignored them. What was their problem anyway? More bursts of laughter followed me around the corner.

The smell hit me first. Porta-potties on a hot summer day smelled better than this. Stupidly, I kept walking. Brown colored water pooled on the floor in front of my locker, and more foulness dripped from the bottom of the door. I knew without looking inside what fun surprise had been left for me. I whirled around, my face flushing in anger. Min and Ae-ri stood, bent over and laughing so hard tears streamed down their faces.

"You should do something about that smell," Min said. "I knew you were disgusting, but really, this is worse than any of us thought."

I clenched both hands into fists and gritted my teeth. My gym clothes, shoes, everything was ruined. I stormed past them without a word. I wouldn't give them a moment of satisfaction. Even if I had to run the 5K in my loafers and school uniform, I'd finish it.

17

CHUL

Sydney was too silent. The kind of silent when you know a girl has passed into the danger zone. I walked cautiously to where she stood, rigid and still in her school uniform. Red patches burned on both cheeks like warning lights on a proximity alert.

"Hey," I said, trying to sound relaxed. "You gonna change? Teacher Park doesn't let anyone off on running days."

"No, I'm running in this," she said, almost a hiss.

I nodded as scenarios of what prevented her from changing raced through my head.

Teacher Park spoke to someone on his cell phone. He looked mad, but then he always looked mad. I decided it would be safer to do my own reconnaissance rather than ask Sydney flat out. I jogged close to where he paced under the yew trees and sat down to stretch.

"No," Teacher Park said with a shake of his head. "I'm telling you, send the custodian to clean out her locker. No, she won't say what happened. I checked it myself, and I'm not touching that. Just throw it away. Throw it all away. I'll issue her a new uniform when the shipment comes in next week."

Min and Ae-Ri trotted out onto the trailhead where the girls began lining up. Ae-ri laughed and gasped for breath, while Min looked calm, careful, like a solider moving through hostile territory. She wasn't done with Sydney.

The running trail was built to blend in with the natural

environment and promote a feeling of oneness with nature. That meant the whole five kilometers were tree lined and closed off from view. Teacher Park usually gave the girls a four-minute head start. Sydney was on her own until I caught up.

Teacher Park blew his whistle and all the girls moved up to the starting line. "Okay, ladies, we're going to do this nice and clean. No whining, no stopping, and everyone finishes. Got it?"

The girls nodded, and a few of the more athletic in the group let out their whoops.

I kept eyes on Sydney. She didn't stretch, just dropped her wool blazer on the grass and unbuttoned the top button of her shirt. Her shoes were leather loafers with two-inch platform heels. I couldn't imagine her running in them. But anything I said or did at this point, would only make it worse. Teacher Park would give the class a lecture on proper footwear if I pointed out that she couldn't be expected to run. That, coupled with Min's encouragement, would be one deadly social bullet. Word would have already spread about whatever happened to her gear. Now the girls would watch and see how she handled it. She couldn't give excuses or back down if she wanted to face them again. She had to run.

"On your mark. Get set. Go!" Teacher Park blew his whistle.

Every girl in the class, Sydney included, took off running. She had strong legs and a steady pace. Even in the ridiculous shoes her foot strike was even and sure. She'd positioned herself ahead of Min, and I watched as they disappeared around the bend.

"Hey." Jin-woo bumped my shoulder. "What happened to Sydney?"

"Min happened."

Jin-woo sucked in air between his teeth. "She'll be okay? We can catch up, easy."

I nodded, knowing I could do it, and focused on warm-ups.

"Then why do you look so nervous?" Jin-woo laughed. "It's not like Min will try to kill her."

I did more sit ups.

"You guys ready?" Teacher Park yelled.

We all snapped to. "Yes, sir," we shouted in unison. He went easy on the girls, but if we even *looked* tired, we'd run ten instead of five.

"All right, then, I want to see some new records today. Pick up those feet." We lined up and waited for him to give the signal. My heart pounded. I shouldn't be nervous. Sydney would be okay.

The whistle blew, and I moved. Sunlight, trees, and shadows whipped past me. I didn't think, just let my muscles get me there. The beat of Jin-woo's footfalls crunching on the dead leaves echoed not far behind. I had to be close. Two more bends and I was passing the slowest of the girls. Sydney wasn't among them—wouldn't be at the pace she'd set. I pushed harder against the burn in my legs and lungs.

The next turn brought me to a long stretch. It was darker here. Dense trees met overhead, and I could just make out Min and Ae-ri to the side of the trail ahead. Someone yelled, the voice high and angry. Then I saw both Ae-ri and Min lunge for Sydney.

She fell and time slowed. I was too far away. My legs went heavy as my stomach threatened to heave. Sydney said something, her voice strained and angry. Twenty more meters. A rock the size of my fist whipped through the air straight at Sydney. It landed with a sickening thud.

18

SYDNEY

The rock whipped past my head and landed next to my temple. I blinked against the dust. Was Min trying to kill me? I wrapped my fingers around the jagged edge of the stone. It was solid, hard, and I was going to defend myself. I stood up, careful not to put weight on my right foot. I was pretty sure it was sprained, if not broken, from the way I'd fallen when they all but tackled me. Two against one.

Both girls watched me with identical sneers. A few of the other runners stopped with eager, curious eyes. "This is taking it too far," I growled.

Min bent down to pick up another rock, and I let mine fly, hitting her hand before she could get a grip. She screamed and clutched at her wrist.

My whole body shook. "BACK OFF."

Ae-Ri charged, and I went down hard with the first shove. A large shadow moved between us, and then Chul was kneeling over me. He helped me sit up. "Are you okay, Sydney?"

Ae-Ri did a fast retreat back to Min, and Jin-woo skidded to a stop next to us. He leaned over, bracing his hands against his thighs, and panted. "Hey, ladies."

Min's face faltered and she dropped the new rock she'd already picked up. "Sydney fell."

Chul breathed hard. "Did she now?" He started to brush dirt and leaves from my hair. "Nice of you to stop and help.

Especially, *both* of you. I've got it from here."

Min spoke quietly. "Why?"

Chul moved closer to my side and began inspecting my legs and feet. I winced when he brushed a bit of rock from my ankle. The sock was torn, and I could already see the swelling. I pushed his hands away.

Min's voice rose. "Don't ignore me. Why her?"

Chul's head snapped up. "You don't have to be so vicious."

She gasped. "What? I'm not—"

Chul stood up and loomed over Min. Trails of sweat trickled down his arms, and his voice went to ice. "She's hurt. I'm taking care of her. Do you have a problem with that?"

Ae-Ri's mouth hung open, and she tugged on Min's arm. Min didn't move. The perfect sweet smile she always showed Chul changed to a snarl. "She's not one of us."

Chul spoke quietly. "Just go."

Min turned and looked past Chul. She met my eyes. With her mask gone, only hate painted her features. She'd lost something here with Chul, and apparently, I was to blame. I'd underestimated Min. This wasn't just a catty little competition. I could see now that she'd wanted Chul for far too long. She raised her chin, and the mask returned. "I'll tell Teacher Park that Sydney needs help." And then she sprinted away. Ae-Ri stared after her stupidly for a moment and then followed.

Chul turned to Jin-woo. "Can you get our stuff and meet me at my car?"

"Got it." Jin-woo took off running.

"Where are you hurt?" Chul asked.

"I'm okay," I said and tried to stand, but the second my bad foot touched the ground, I winced.

He helped me sit back down. "Stop trying to be tough. Your ankle's swelling." He took my heel and gently wiggled the loafer off, then removed my knee-hi sock. I had to bite my lip against the pain. I was too embarrassed to meet Chul's eyes, so

I watched as more runners passed us on the trail.

"It doesn't look too bad, but you won't be able to walk." Chul scooted around so his back was facing me. "Get on and I'll carry you."

I stared at his broad shoulders. "Like a piggyback ride?"

"I guess that's what you call them in the States. Hurry and get on."

"No, I think I can walk, if you just help me a little," I said.

"Would you rather I throw you over my shoulder, or are you getting on my back? Because either way is fine with me, but you're not putting weight on that foot."

I was super conscious of my sweat-dampened shirt, but I leaned forward and locked arms around his neck. He stood up, reaching under my knees to support my legs. Then he gave a quick boost, pulling me up higher, and began to run. I was pretty sure we both looked idiotic. "Aren't we heading back?" I said, once I realized he wasn't returning to the starting point.

"No, we have to finish. Teacher Park is a little fanatical about running. Don't worry. I promise you'll still get a good time."

Chul was fast. He even passed a few of the girls. I finished my very first 5K in Korea with a time of 35:18.

Teacher Park was waiting. "Not bad, Chul. I see you picked up something extra on your run."

Chul didn't put me down. "Thank you, sir."

I wiggled to get loose. Chul tightened his grip.

"You taking Sydney home now?"

"Yes, sir."

Teacher Park smiled. He hadn't smiled once since I'd met him. "Good man. Emergencies really bring out the best in you boys."

Chul nodded and headed towards the school parking lot.

"Wait, I have a driver picking me up. You don't need to give me a ride."

"Your driver will be fine. I'm taking you home."

"I left my backpack and phone in Teacher Park's office."

"Jin-woo will have it."

I bit my lip. Maybe Loser would have pity on me and let me get a ride since I'd gotten hurt.

Jin-woo was waiting next to a midnight blue Bugatti. I almost forgot that Chul was part of the super-rich because he acted so normal.

"You okay, Sydney?" Jin-woo asked as we got close.

Chul set me down gently, and I pulled away to lean on the car while he opened the passenger door. Before I could hobble in, he swung around and scooped me up. I squeaked. Jin-woo tossed my backpack in and then stepped aside to let Chul place me in the seat. He reached past me and dropped his phone in the cupholder. I felt a little breathless. "Okay, thanks." My face burned as Chul shut the door.

Chul and Jin-woo stood outside the car talking. I fished in my backpack for my phone and quickly texted Loser.

> **I sprained my ankle in gym class. Getting a ride home.**

I pushed send. Chul's phone vibrated in his cup holder. He must have gotten a text at the same time. I waited for a reply. Nothing. I texted again.

> **I'm already on my way, so please tell Hyun not to wait for me.**

I pushed send, and again Chul's phone vibrated. I looked out the window. Chul and Jin-woo were still talking. I quickly sent one more text.

> **???**

Chul's phone vibrated, and I picked it up. There on the screen were my three question marks. The contact name was listed as *Curves*. I dropped the phone back in the cup holder like it'd burned me.

Chul's door opened, and he got in the car. He shook an instant ice pack and then leaned down and placed it on my ankle. The cold scorched with a thousand hot needles as he pressed it to my skin.

I sucked in air.

"Sorry, I bet it hurts. Let that sit there, and when I get you home, we can get it wrapped."

There were tears stinging in my eyes, but I refused to cry. "Where's home?" I asked.

Chul looked at me. "Are you all right? Do you hurt anywhere else?"

I swallowed hard. I needed to hear the words from him. "Do you know where I live? Do you know the Kim family?"

Chul narrowed his eyes and seemed to study mine more cautiously. "I know where you live."

"And do you know the Kim family?" I asked again.

He gave a simple nod.

"How?" My lips started to tremble.

He put the car in reverse before he answered. "I live there too, Sydney. I'm the guy you've been texting."

"You mean the jerk who keeps telling me to go home? You lied to me."

"I didn't lie."

"You hid the truth, and that's the same thing."

"I'm cautious. I didn't know what your motives were."

My voice rose. "My *motives*?"

"Calm down. You don't know my mother the way I do. I wasn't sure what she was up to. I had to know that she wouldn't try to force a relationship."

"What? You actually believe I would throw myself at you or something?" I gasped. "You are such a conceited, arrogant, jerk. Let me out of the car right now."

"I didn't mean it like that. You're getting too emotional."

"Stop. I'm getting out."

Chul gripped the steering wheel tighter, and a muscle jerked in his jaw, but he didn't slow the car. We were already approaching the highway.

"If you don't let me out, I'm calling the police," I said, holding up my phone.

Chul's hand flashed out and tapped my phone from the bottom. It flew straight up out of my hand. He caught it and dropped it in his lap.

"I'm taking you home," Chul said, with an edge to his voice.

"You have a real problem." Surprise and anger laced my words. "I hope you see that. Normal people don't act like this. A normal person would have just asked me why I came to Korea instead of lying and playing games." I picked up his phone out of the cup holder and threw it in the back seat. "You want to take me home? Then fine, take me home. But from here on out, don't text me, talk to me, or get anywhere near me."

We sat in angry silence for the remainder of the drive. When Chul turned onto the road for his house, I gripped the handle to open the door. But I waited as he drove around the back of the house and into an underground garage I hadn't known was there. I guess there were a lot of things I didn't know. We passed at least seven other luxury cars before Chul stopped. I threw my door open and tried to get out, but Chul was at my side before I could do more than hobble a few feet from his car. My ankle throbbed with shooting pains. I jerked away when he tried to support some of my weight with a hand around my waist.

"You're going to hurt yourself more if you don't let me help you," he said.

I leaned against the garage wall for support. The lighting was dim and the air cool. I hurt so much. I just wanted to lay down on the cement floor.

Chul sighed and folded his arms. "By now, everyone at school will know what happened between you and Min. You're definitely going to need me as a friend if you want to survive at Daeshim."

"I've taken care of myself just fine my whole life."

Chul nodded, and one corner of his mouth tugged up. "I can see you don't get it."

"What's that supposed to mean?" I imagined slapping the smirk right off his face. Maybe if I did, Suni would send me home.

"Things are different here. I'm the only person standing between you and Min, and she won't stop at just pranks."

"I'm capable of making friends and standing up to the Mins in the world. You aren't the only person who can help me. Gun was doing just fine until you showed up at that concert."

Chul's eyes went hard. "If Gun is who you want, then no one's standing in your way." He grabbed my hand and slapped my phone into my palm. "But when you can't handle the heat from Min, don't expect me to come running."

"I won't," I yelled as he walked away.

19

CHUL

I did three more sets on the bench press and then racked the bar. Jin-woo stood nearby watching. He only ever worked out with his personal trainer, but I could always count on him to spot me. He was that kind of friend, and I owed him for helping me with Sydney.

"I thought you had Min under control," he said. "What's up with her trying to smear Sydney?"

My arms shook, but I loaded on more weight, and Jin-woo moved to stand above me with a light hand on the bar. I pushed up with a grunt and then locked my arms. "Min will never be under control."

"She's been drooling over you since middle school." Jin-woo shook his head. "You'd think a girl as hot as Min would just move on already."

"She doesn't want me."

"Are you sure about that?"

"She just wants what she can't have," I said.

"Maybe if you just dated her, she'd get bored."

"If I actually agreed to even one date, her dad would be calling me son-in-law before either of us could graduate. Mr. Kang wants that Kim/Kang merger more than he wants a daughter."

"Your parents wouldn't mind. I bet they would be happy with a merger."

"I'd mind. I'm not having a wedding just to drive

business."

Jin-woo laughed. "I'm kinda scared of your parents. If I were their kid, I'd pee myself before I could say no."

"Well, you don't have to worry. Your parents are perfect."

"You know my mom micromanages me. I'd prefer parentals like yours, the kind that travel a lot."

I sighed. "They'll come home soon. They can't stay away any longer without losing face with friends." I grunted and pushed the bar up. "My mother has to introduce her goddaughter into society."

"Wonder what the Kangs will do? Min will probably flip when she sees Sydney is your family's ward." Jin-woo chuckled. "I can't wait."

"I'm more worried about Gun," I said.

"Gun can't even tie his shoelaces without Min's approval. She's the one you have to watch your six on." Jin-woo grabbed the weight bar as it started to drop and put it on the rack.

I sat up, exhausted. "Sydney trusts Gun. She'll watch out for Min, but she'll let her guard down when he's around."

"That's why she has you."

"She won't even talk to me." I snorted. "My big identity reveal didn't go over too well."   Jin-woo started laughing again. "I wish I could have seen your face when she realized it was your phone she'd been texting."

"Yeah, hilarious," I said, grabbing a towel and wiping sweat. "Thanks for spotting me. I'm heading out." I picked up my phone off the bench and unlocked the screen. I opened a new text to Sydney and quickly typed a message. She hadn't answered the last four, but what I had to say couldn't be said over a text anyway. I'd given her most of the weekend to cool down and we had Monday off. But I needed to fix things with us because come Tuesday we'd be back in school with Gun, Min, and the Universe against me. I could handle it all as long as Sydney forgave me. I kept the text simple.

**Hey, heading
home soon. Let's
talk in person.**

I knocked on her door, freshly showered and holding a bag of cheeseburgers. Sydney opened the door, then closed it in my face. But not before she smelled the food. I saw her eyes flick to the greasy paper bag.

I knocked again. "I just want to drop off dinner. Hyun's eating pig entrails if you'd rather have that."

Sydney opened the door again, slowly this time. I tried to look repentant. She folded her arms and leaned against the doorjamb.

I held the bag up. "You like cheeseburgers, right?"

Sydney reached for it, and I pulled the bag back. "Can I eat with you? There are two in here. I've even got fries and soda."

She tried to slam the door again, but I was ready with a foot inside before she could close it. "I hate eating alone," I said.

"I hate being lied to." Her voice cracked.

I looked down. I couldn't lose my cool again. "I know. I wanted to help you, but I screwed it all up. Can we please start over?"

"I shouldn't let you off this easy."

"Nothing about this feels easy to me." I noticed the moment she wavered. "Come on," I said. "We can talk over dinner."

She slipped out the door and closed it behind her but still gave me a huffy look. "I'm only coming because I'm hungry, and this doesn't mean you're forgiven."

I nodded and hid my smile. She wore ripped jeans with a pale pink T-shirt, and her feet were bare. I could see the swelling in her ankle was better but still purple. "Hyun said he wrapped your foot."

"He did, and gave me more ibuprofen."

"Good. I'm glad you can walk again." I led her up to the attic level. The rooms were all finished but smaller and mostly filled with stored furniture. It was always a little dusty because none of the staff bothered to clean this floor, but that's why I came up here. We walked to the end of the hall, and I opened the last door. The room was painted in a happy yellow, and instead of furniture, it was home to all my old school memorabilia that Hyun liked to save. It also housed my comic collection, but most importantly, this room had a balcony where you could just reach the sloping roof outside. I'd been here a thousand times, but now I was nervous. I'd never shown anyone my spot on the roof. Not even Hyun knew I came up here.

"Where are we?" Sydney asked.

"A place where we can get to the roof."

She looked around and picked up a comic lying loose on top of an open box. "You read these?"

I scratched my head and tried to think of something to say that wouldn't make me come off like a super-nerd. "More like collect them," I said, not meeting her eyes. "I like the classics. But yeah, I read them." I grabbed a heavy blanket that I kept in the closet and opened the door to the balcony. The air was welcome and fresh. I stepped out, then tossed the blanket up to the roof, followed by the bag of food.

Sydney looked nervous. "You want me to go up there?"

"It's easy. I'll help you."

She shook her head. "We could just eat in the kitchen."

"This is my favorite spot for dinner. I want you to see the view." Before she could retreat, I stood behind her and settled my hands around her waist. Sydney wasn't small, and I loved that. I tried not to think about the deep curve of her hip as I lifted. "Grab on and pull yourself up," I said. "I won't let you fall." She'd kill me if I pushed anywhere near her backside, so as she moved up, I placed my hands to support just above her knees and waited for her to climb.

After she was safely on, I jumped to grab onto the edge of the roof and let my feet dangle below, then did my normal pull-up until I was kneeling on the shingles. Sydney blinked in surprise, maybe that I'd gotten up so easily. It'd been anything but easy back when I'd been a scrawny kid trying to escape a lonely house.

I spread out the blanket for us, and we both sat down. The sun was just starting its descent. I opened the bag of what Americans call fast food. Sydney was still mad. She fidgeted and wouldn't really look at me. "It smells good," I said.

She scowled, unwrapped hers, and took a quick bite. I pulled out the fries and popped open her soda, then pushed them both towards her.

"Does it taste the same as California?"

"Almost."

She was talking to me as little as possible. I took a bite of my own food and tried to think of how to get her to let this go. I held up my burger. "I'm a fan." That earned half a smile, but she still wouldn't really meet my eyes.

"You should try spicy rice cakes sometime."

Sydney shook her head. "No spice for me. I like my food plain."

I nodded but couldn't think of more to say. After long minutes of defeated silence, I felt her looking at me. I raised my head and took her expression of pain mixed with anger full in the chest. I didn't think it would hurt that bad, but disappointing her felt like I'd just scored the winning point for the opposing team, and now I expected everyone to cheer. I'd tricked her, and she wasn't cheering.

Her voice went quiet when she asked. "If I hadn't figured it out on my own, were you going to tell me?"

I wanted to be worthy of her trust. This had to be the perfect answer, no misunderstandings. "My mother has a history of putting her own interests first. I didn't know you, and I didn't understand why you were here. I can see now that it had nothing to do with me. Once I realized this, and that you were here to stay . . . I'd already decided to introduce myself properly." I held out my hand and smiled at her. "Hi, Sydney. Welcome to the Republic of Korea. My name's Kim Chul."

She hesitated, but then her face softened, and she took my hand. "Hey, Chul, nice to meet you." She even blushed, and that, combined with the way the sun brought out the gold in her hair, made it hard to let go.

"I'm glad you planned on telling me."

It was the truth. I had planned on telling her, but I had no idea how to tell her about everything else. Tracking her every movement and hacking her accounts wasn't something she'd forgive over a cheeseburger. I didn't know how to explain that I'd done it because that was the only way I knew how to protect her. I made myself meet her eyes. "So, am I forgiven?"

"Mostly," she said, and took another bite. "But promise me that you'll be honest from here on out."

I tallied the damage in my head: emails, social media, her bank account. I'd give it all up. I could ghost out of everything I had access to. But not her phone. Tracking her location was my safety net. There were too many people who could hurt Sydney. Knowing where she was and keeping Gun from texting her let me sleep at night. "I'm not as open as you are, Sydney. I live very differently than you do."

She frowned. "What does that mean? You're either honest or you're not. Having money doesn't mean you can lie."

I rubbed the back of my neck. "This isn't a money thing. It's just me trying to protect you the best I can."

"I don't need protecting, especially if it involves lying."

It killed me, but no matter what, I couldn't give up access to her phone. "My responsibilities are different than yours."

Sydney shifted and took another bite. She wanted to let it go. I could see she was tired of fighting, and so was I. But my lame explanation sounded cryptic even to myself. "Does it make sense if I say sorry, and I'll try to be someone you can trust?"

She nodded but didn't look impressed.

I tried a different tactic. "Do you like the view?"

"Yeah, I can see why you like it up here." She gazed at the sunset. "It's the same as back home."

"What is?"

She waved her arm out. "This . . . my mom and I watch sunsets on the beach all the time. I like nights like this."

"What do you like about them?"

"You know, when the sun takes its time and doesn't rush." She almost smiled, but her eyes looked far away.

We watched in silence for a moment with me sneaking glances of her face, the way her eyelashes brushed against skin that looked like cream mixed with sunshine. I wanted to reach out and trace my thumb along her cheekbone.

She cleared her throat and I blinked, the spell broken. "Do you eat up here a lot?" she asked.

"Most of the time, unless it's raining, but I've even sat up here in the rain before."

"Why not inside with your family or Hyun?"

I shrugged, feeling uncomfortable. "It's just easier up here."

Sydney smiled. "You said you hate eating alone."

"I do hate eating alone, but as you can see, my parents don't make a lot of appearances and Hyun is usually busy for dinner. I make do up here."

Sydney nodded and looked sad. The last thing I wanted was her pity. "To be fair, I come up here even when my parents are home," I said.

"What about sharing your stories and praying together? Or what about telling someone when that day was awful and hard?"

"I don't have what you have."

"You could."

I shook my head. "My family is different from yours."

"It's okay to tell them what you need. Sometimes they don't see it on their own."

Sydney could see right through me. "What is it you think I need?" I asked.

"The same as anybody. Love."

20

SYDNEY

Hey Mom,

I had a lot of time to myself this weekend and did some thinking. You won't say it, but I know the real reason you sent me here. You want me to get my own life. So I'll stay, but with a compromise. I'll live with Suni and make friends at school, try new things (not the food), and focus on my future. But here's the compromise: I'm not doing a full year. They say it takes 29 days to form a habit. One semester should do it. When I get home, I will be a different Sydney. I won't worry, or cling, or avoid going places because I can't seem to leave you. I promise I'll figure this out, but let me come home by Christmas.

So much has happened. Do you remember Chul, the guy from the concert? Turns out, he's Suni's son. At first, I was hurt and mad. I mean, seriously—how could he keep that from me? But now I see he was just as freaked out as I was about me being here. I've decided to listen to your advice on taking the high road and forgive him. It's not like I have much of a choice. I've already made enemies, and most days at Daeshim, I feel like a Cheeto stuck in a Pringles can. If I'm going to stay here, I need a few friends.

Today is Sunday, so no school, and Monday, we have off. Lame that I'm this bored. Besides Gun and Chul, I know almost no one. Gun hasn't called or texted. I only saw him for a few minutes on Friday. I looked up his phone and email in the school directory. I'm not sure, but I'm thinking about texting him.

So, we both know that mean girls are everywhere. But Mom, there is this one student, Min, who could run circles around all the snots I knew back home. She could teach a class: Advanced Bullying. The fact that I'm friends with Chul, or maybe that I would dare breathe the expensive air at Daeshim, makes me her number one target. But don't worry. You didn't raise me to be a doormat. I'm handling her.
How are you doing? Is work still super busy? All of this would be easier if you'd email me.

Love,
Sydney

CHUL

Mother's message was clear. Don't screw up. I read the text one last time.

> **Your father and
> I will arrive
> before the party.
> We would like to
> introduce Sydney
> to the other
> families that
> night. Invitations
> have been sent,
> and I've contacted
> the staff at the
> hotel. Your only
> job is to show
> up at seven with
> Sydney ready. I'm
> assuming that
> you're taking
> proper care of her.**

My hands turned cold and clammy. I wanted to say it wasn't fear, but I was terrified. The idea of my parents seeing Sydney and me together—my mother would see it. She would know I'd fallen for her. Five more minutes on the roof last night and I would've kissed her. That couldn't happen.

I'd spent all morning playing chicken with myself. Hyun knocked on my door twice to see when I was taking Sydney shopping, but I still hadn't texted her. The dress appointment had been easy to set up. One phone call and La Monte had agreed to a rush order. We were the Kims, after all. But texting Sydney would be the Mt. Everest of glossing over what tonight would mean. My mother would expect her to look perfect, like one of us. My father would be no better. And if school had been hard on Sydney, this dinner would be killer. She would be the center of attention the entire night.

SYDNEY

I stretched on my bed and stared at my phone. No new texts, not even from Chul. Maybe I'd said too much to him on the roof last night. Maybe he felt like I was too in his business. I was glad we'd made up, but I guess that didn't mean we would hang out today. It was noon already and no plans—zero of anything going on.

I sat up straight. Why hadn't I thought of this before? A job. At home I was never bored because I worked. I grabbed the scrap of paper where I'd written Gun's info and typed in his number with a text.

Hey, this is Sydney. I'm heading out to apply for a job. I

125

> **was thinking of
> trying the COEX
> mall. Do you want
> to hang out after?**

I squeezed my eyes shut and pressed send, then I quickly read it again and waited. He texted immediately.

> **Gun:
> I'm so glad I got a
> hold of you. I tried
> texting you a
> million times but
> always got a weird
> message that it
> wasn't a working
> number. What's
> your address and
> I'll pick you up.**

I wasn't stupid. Gun coming here wasn't a good idea. I'd meet him at the mall. I texted.

> **I'm already
> heading out, but
> I can meet you
> there. Maybe we
> can get lunch.**

> **Gun:
> Why are you
> getting a job? I
> can ask if you can
> intern at my dad's
> company if you
> need money.**

There was a loud knock at my door. I opened it. Chul panted, out of breath.

"Hey," I said. "Did you just come from a jog?" He was wearing torn jeans and a grey tee, so I doubted he'd been working out.

Chul gave a stressed laugh and bent at the waist placing both hands on his thighs to catch his breath. "You just keep me on the move." He glanced at my phone, then stood up straight. "Good, you're dressed." He took my hand and pulled me out the door.

"Wait, what? Where are we going?"

"My parents are coming home today. We have a lot to do."

I twisted free. "I can't. I'm going to the mall." I spoke while walking back to my room. I grabbed shoes and a purse, but not anything Chul had purchased. He followed me into my room, which was weird. I'd never had a guy in my room before. "Also, I'm meeting a friend later."

"Who's the friend?"

"Gun."

Chul stepped in front of me and folded his arms. "Not Gun."

I pressed my lips together. "Let's not fight again. I need to get going."

Chul stepped out of my way and followed next to me as I walked down the hall. "You're walking easier today. That's too bad. I would have carried you to my car."

"Are you making fun of me?"

"No." He smiled. "I'm not."

I rolled my eyes.

"It's this way." Chul tugged me right instead of left.

By now, I knew my way to the front door. "But I—"

"I'm driving."

I paused, not sure. "You don't mind driving me?"

"We're not going to the mall."

"I am, actually." I raised my chin. "I'm going to get a job."

Chul looked pained. "You're playing with me, right? If you need money, my mother will get you your own account and dump a bunch of cash in there faster than you can say trust-fund-baby. Probably the only reason she hasn't already is because she's so busy."

My eyes went big. "You think I'd let her do that?"

Chul shrugged. "I don't see any reason why you shouldn't. If she finds out you even thought about getting a job, her hair will ignite and I'll probably get grounded."

"Seriously? Why would she care if I got a job?"

"You don't get it. My mother's responsible for you. Her way of doing that is to pay for whatever you want. It's like you're living with a famous chef but refusing their food. You getting a job would be the equivalent of eating from a vending machine."

I shook my head. "I just can't take your family's money. I already feel like I need to pay you back for all those clothes."

Chul sighed. "Okay, how about this? Help me get back in my mother's good graces, and we call it even."

"What do you mean by good graces?"

"My mother's angry because of something I did last year. She'll probably never forgive me."

"I'm sure it can't be that bad." I wanted to ask more but reined myself in.

"It was. She almost disowned me." He waved his hand dismissively. "It doesn't matter. *You,* she adores. She really wants everything to be easy for you in Korea. If I can take credit for you being happy here, she'll see me in a whole new light, like Batman-saving-Gotham-City kind of light. It will be huge with her."

"Did you just compare yourself to Batman?"

"I'm way cooler—more like X-Men level."

I laughed. "If I need to hint at you helping me adjust to life here, that's no problem."

"It's more than that. My parents will be here in three

hours, and I've got to have a whole party ready for them at our hotel. I need your help today."

"So you want me to forget about my job search and bail on Gun?"

"See, you're getting it already."

Little thorns of guilt sprang up from somewhere inside, and I grimaced. "I already told Gun I'd meet him."

"You're just going to have to tell him it's not in the cards today—or, like, ever. Don't feel too bad for Gun. He'll probably be there tonight. All the affluent families will. My parents like to show off when they're in town."

"What about Min?"

"Especially Min. The Kangs have more money than any of us, and it's just expected. No one would ever not invite them."

I wanted to stick my hand down my throat and barf whenever I thought about stupid Min and my locker. No, I wanted to stick my hand down her throat. "I don't have to go to this party, do I?"

Chul took two steps closer and grinned. "Bad news. This party is pretty much to introduce the Kims' new ward—that's you— to all their friends. So yeah, you kind of have to go."

The idea of being paraded in front of all the Kims' friends made me want to evaporate, crawl in a hole, run away, anything but be a show pony. I shoved Chul's chest. He was dangerously close.

He took a step back, but it wasn't far enough. "Come on," he said. "It won't be that bad. Just stick with me, and everything will go smoothly. The bonus is my parents will see that I'm taking good care of you."

"Are you supposed to babysit me or something?"

Chul smirked. "No, not like that. I'm your Oppa."

I knew what Oppa meant. Technically it was a term used for an older male in a position of protector, or even an older brother. But it also could be a romantic term, like calling a guy Honey. Most guys loved it when girls called them their Oppa.

"I'm not calling you Oppa."

"My mother would eat it up."

Falling for Chul would be like a goldfish deciding it could swim with a great white. And calling Chul "Oppa" would be my first suicidal dive into deep waters. I sighed. "Not gonna happen, Chul. But I'll play nice with your parents and help with whatever you need tonight."

"Disappointing, but fair," he said. "Now text Gun and give him the bad news."

"You really don't like him, do you?"

Chul's eyes went hard. "I really don't."

I sighed and smoothed my hands over the satiny material that flowed like water over my skin. "Why do I have to have a new dress? My closet is already stuffed full."

"None of them are formal enough," Chul said. "Tonight is about showing off our money. It's expected."

"If I had known this was what you meant when you said you needed my help, I would have gone with Gun. I thought we'd be setting out flowers at the hotel or something. This just puts me further in your debt."

"No, this will make my parents very, very happy."

I looked at the price again and felt sick— eight million *won*. That was close to $8,000 US dollars. "Look, my mom and I volunteer at a homeless shelter back home, and this dress could pay their food bill for a month. Seriously, I can't spend money like this."

"It's couture. Anything less will make my parents look cheap. The other dress was less expensive, if you want to get that one instead."

"The other dress was half the material too." It had been so skimpy I wouldn't even come out of the dressing room. This dress was a midnight-blue satin with gold trim at the capped sleeves. And the big plus was no crazy-low neckline. Really, it was perfect for me.

But Eight. Million. *Won.*

Chul turned to the sales associate who stood waiting. "Wrap this one up along with the shoes and have it delivered no later than four."

"Of course, Mr. Kim."

When I finished changing, I found Chul pointing out two more dresses he wanted sent back with the blue one. I tried to smile, but I knew it came out in a weird sort of grimace like someone had glued it in place but maybe with cheap glue that was starting to flake off around the edges. After two hours at the salon for nails, hair, and makeup—makeup that I'd scrub off as soon as we got home—and now trying on dresses, I was totally done. I felt like Chul was a general and I was a first-time solider he was about to send to the front lines.

"We still have to—" Chul looked at my face and stopped. "We should get food instead. Why don't I have Hyun select your jewelry? He has a good eye for stuff like that."

"Jewelry? I have lots at home."

But Chul was already texting Hyun. "No, for tonight you need a showpiece item. Nothing gaudy, maybe a simple diamond necklace and matching bracelet. You could wear the diamond studs you like, and that will be perfect."

Those studs were *real*? I leaned my back against the wall, exhausted. Somehow, I had to make Chul see what a horrible crash and burn tonight would be if he expected me to act the part of a rich heiress. "I know from your perspective it would seem like I should be happy, like this is a Cinderella moment for me or something. But it's not like that. I feel more like I've joined the circus, and no one believes me when I say I can't do the trapeze. Dressing up to be something I'm not makes me feel like a huge fake, Chul."

He took my hand, and warmth rolled along my skin. "That's one of the things I like about you. You'd shine if you showed up in jeans. All of this is because my parents are fake, not you."

I took a steadying breath and tried to pretend he

hadn't just laced our fingers together, that somehow, I would be capable of more than nerves and flutters. "I'll try not to embarrass your family."

21

CHUL

I placed a fried shrimp in Sydney's bowl while she picked at grains of rice. "It's not spicy," I said. "Just try that small piece."

"I'm not hungry."

"Do you want to go somewhere else?" I asked. "We could do cheeseburgers again."

Sydney shook her head. "No, I'm too nervous to eat. I've been counting the ways I might screw up and make your parents look bad."

There were plenty of mistakes she could make. She didn't know our culture, or my parents. But she didn't need to. I'd make sure tonight was seamless. It was one of the first times I could remember *wanting* to do what my mother demanded. I shrugged. "I don't think there's much, short of not going, that would make them look bad. Just be yourself."

Sydney dropped her chopsticks. "I don't even know what that means. Do any of us really know how to just be ourselves? We're who we *need* to be, or who someone else expects us to be."

I chewed my food, considering.

"Admit it. You wouldn't be eating lunch and shopping with me if it wasn't for your parents. You're doing what's expected. It's not you being you. It's a choice someone made for you."

I shook my head. "I'm here because you told me to eat with family."

Sydney frowned, seeming confused.

"This has nothing to do with my parents. I could have Hyun buy all your stuff and order our chef to make mac and cheese if I was doing this for them. I'm here because I want to learn from you."

"Learn what?"

"How to get along as a family. You know, eat meals together, stuff like that."

Sydney squinted at me like I was joking.

"I'm serious, I don't know how to do that in my family. I want what you and your mom have."

She smiled softly, and I could tell she was thinking about her mom. "It's not hard. You just cherish each other."

"That stuff comes naturally to you. That's who *you* are. Be yourself tonight by being that."

Sydney furrowed her brow. "Everyone knows how to love their family," she said.

Not *everyone.* I tilted my head. This was the girl who'd rather spend her dress money supporting soup kitchens. She wouldn't understand the coldness in my family. Being on my own hadn't bothered me before, but now I couldn't shake the feeling that I needed Sydney. She gave me glimpses of what real happiness felt like, and that left my heart ready to trip all over itself.

Sydney's phone buzzed on the table, and she picked it up, checking her message in her lap. My fingers itched to pick up mine and see who was texting her. But I wouldn't. She'd asked for honesty, and I needed to respect that. I signaled to the waiter. "An order of fried chicken, no spice."

"If you're ordering that for me, don't bother. I can barely stomach this rice." She spoke without looking up from her screen.

I drummed my fingers on the table. "Is that Gun?"

She met my eyes, hers full of confusion. "Yeah, he wants to know if he can pick me up for your parent's party tonight. I guess he doesn't get that the party is for me." She paused and shifted in her seat. "He thinks your parents have adopted an orphan. That's so weird. Why would he think that?"

I shrugged. "The Kims having a ward might lead people to misunderstand."

"I haven't answered him. I guess I should just tell him I'm the Kims' goddaughter and not an orphan, but it wouldn't be proper if he takes me there, right?"

I tried to keep my face steady before I spoke. I could feel the muscle in my jaw jump. Her eyes were trusting and so blue as she waited for my answer. I couldn't be this gone for a girl. "You should definitely show up with me and not another family. His family isn't really close to ours, but they have a certain status, so naturally they're invited."

Sydney blinked. I expected her to argue or ask why. I hoped she couldn't see what I'd been fighting all day. "Okay, I'll tell him no then."

She texted longer than I liked, then placed her phone face down on the table. It immediately buzzed with another text, and she flipped it over to look at the screen. A frown creased her brow. "What is he talking about?" She texted back and I watched with a sheen of sweat breaking out along my body.

"Can I read it?" I held out my hand.

She shrugged and handed me the phone. I scrolled up to the top of the conversation.

Gun:
Party tonight for the Kim family. They've adopted some orphan or something and want to introduce her. You know how I feel about Chul, but my parents will

expect me to be
there. Wanna go
as my date? I can
pick you up at six.
Wear something
nice.

> Sydney:
> I can't go with you
> tonight. I have to
> go with the Kims.
> It's funny but I'm
> that girl they're
> introducing to
> their friends.
> Only, I'm not an
> orphan, and they
> aren't adopting
> me. Where did
> you hear that?

Gun:
You live with the
Kims?

> Sydney:
> Yes

Gun:
When were you
going to tell me
this?

> Sydney:
> I didn't know Chul
> was their son until
> yesterday.

Gun:
Ask Chul if he's
back to hacking
again.

Syndney:
What?

Gun:
Never mind. I'll
see you tonight.

I handed the phone back to her with my stomach in knots. I really hoped she wouldn't ask me about the hacking. "I don't know where he got the idea that you're an orphan," I said. "I'm sure my parents never said that. I mean, your mom and mine are best friends."

Sydney nodded. "Yeah, I don't like him saying that. But why does he want me to ask you about hacking?"

"He knows I got arrested last year for hacking."

Sydney's mouth fell open. "You? What—" she erupted in a fit of laughter. "Did you hack something big?"

I forced a laugh and tried not to look embarrassed despite the blood rushing to my cheeks.

She quickly sobered. "Your face." She placed her hand over mine. "I'm sorry. It's not funny. It's just so unexpected, but definitely not something Gun should rub in."

"Thanks," I grumbled.

"What happened?"

I really didn't want to explain this, especially not to Sydney. I flipped my hand under hers and quickly laced our fingers together. She glanced down, and then it was her turn to blush. She tried to pull back. I held on. "This is a touchy subject for me." I nodded to our hands. "So do me this kindness."

She met my eyes and spoke with caution. "Okay, then tell me."

"Last year I was part of Seoul University's CTF team. I was their youngest member."

"Is that the thing where you do competitive hacking for awards and stuff?"

"It's more about the bragging rights than awards, but yeah." Sydney's eyes never wavered from mine. That should have scared me, but I found it helped. I swallowed. "Another well-known CTF team had hacked into a gas station as a prank. For three hours, people got free gas."

Sydney raised her eyebrows. "Really?"

I nodded. "Showing off is normal, but usually the pranks aren't that big. It's kind of an unspoken rule that if you ever get caught, it's over. Your team gets blacklisted. That's why the other team never took official credit, but we all knew who it was. They'd beaten us at the last competition, and some of the members of my team were gunning to show them what we could do. So when the challenge came, we couldn't let it go. My team wanted to top their little gas parade."

"What happened?"

"Our leader and *Sunbae* had the perfect plan. Or so he said. Nothing went right, and when the pieces started to crumble, I was the fall guy."

"Why you?"

"Everyone knew my parents would cover for me. And they did."

Sydney winced. "Is that why things with your parents aren't good?"

I nodded. "Mostly."

"What did you guys hack?"

I stared at her and licked my lips, which had gone paper-dry. "I regret it. I've wished a thousand times I could take it back."

I could see it in her face, the desire to tell me that it

wasn't my fault. It's what Hyun had said, what a lot of people said, but it didn't make me feel better. Maybe not *all* of it had been my fault, but I'd still done it. Sydney squeezed my hand and started to speak. I stopped her. "My part was small, but I knew what I was doing. No one forced me." I took a deep breath. She had to let me own this. It was the only way to fix myself, and if I knew anything, it was that I had to be better than I was to have a chance with her. "We found a way into one of the high-end talent agencies here in Seoul. They kept hidden profiles of all their top stars, real ages and weights, the medical stuff, like all the eating disorders, plastic surgeries, depression, and medications. Our *Sunbae* said we wouldn't release anything, just prove that we'd been there. It was to show off. A way to say free gas was easy. But someone released a few files. More than one career was ruined, and we got caught."

"And you took the blame for everyone?"

I didn't want her to hate me, but even more than that, I didn't want her to pity me.

"Like I said, my parents covered for me. Besides, I wasn't the victim. Two members of a boy band had all their dirt spread around the internet and got kicked out of the group."

Sydney slid her fingers out of mine and traced a slow circle on my palm. "Do you remember when we were on the roof? You said you wanted to be honest with me, but your life was more complicated than mine."

It was hard to breathe right with her caressing my hand. "Yeah."

"Is this your big secret?"

My voice cracked. "Part of it."

Sydney cocked her eyebrow. "There's more than getting arrested for illegal hacking?"

I let out a deep breath and laced our fingers back together. "There's more. I want to tell you all my secrets and not hide. But will you let me do this a little at a time? I can't change everything about myself overnight. This is me at my best right now."

She looked at me without judgment or pity, then smiled softly. "That's all I want."

22

SYDNEY

Mom,

I don't have much time. Chul is waiting for me to go into a party. I'm sitting in a bathroom stall at *their* hotel. Did you know they own a hotel? I guess I shouldn't be surprised, but seriously! You work at one. Maybe you could move here for a while and work at theirs.

But that's not why I'm writing you. Why haven't you written me back? Are you feeling okay, getting enough sleep and everything? Are you working a ton of overtime again? Maybe you've been worried about me because I was so against being here from the start. Don't be. I can do a semester. Suni and her husband have flown home, and they're going to be at the party tonight.

Chul's not as perfect as I thought. Like, he's human, and not some deity masquerading as a student. That makes me like him more.

I miss you. Please, please write me back so I can stop worrying.

Syd

CHUL

We stood side by side in one of the conference rooms off the main ballroom. My parents were out there somewhere with their guests. I'd tried twice now to walk her into the party, but each time, we ended up back here with me trying to calm Sydney down.

"You won't leave me, right?" she asked. "What am I saying? I'm just rambling. Ignore me." She laughed. "You can't stay with me the whole night."

I tucked her hand into the crook of my arm and felt her slight tremble. Her nervousness steadied mine. Made me more determined and focused. I loved who I was around Sydney. I also loved that she forgave me for getting arrested. "You won't have to be alone. I'm your date. If you so much as look in another guys' direction, I'll turn into Bruce Banner, and scary green Hulk veins will stand out on my neck."

A nervous giggle escaped her lips, and my heart beat faster.

"That won't help you with your parents," she said.

I grinned. "Probably not, so don't push me." I looked down at the top of her head. Her blonde hair had been expertly swept into an elegant updo. The makeup was gone, but if anything, it made her look prettier. The simple tear drop diamond at her throat reminded me of how I'd fumbled putting it on. Helping with a necklace should be easy— Boyfriend 101. But with Sydney, it was dangerous. When my hands had brushed the soft skin around her neck, I'd had to pull back.

Hyun poked his head around the door. "Your parents are getting annoyed. They want to know what's taking so long."

"Tell them we'll be right out." I looked down at Sydney. She stared straight ahead with her jaw locked and lips pressed to a hard line, like she was about to take a dagger to her own heart. Her grip on my arm tightened, and she raised her eyes to mine.

Part of me started to unravel.

I considered leading her out of the hotel. There was a back door that led to the service elevator. We could go to the beach, build a fire, and watch the waves all night. And my parents would never speak to me again. "You don't have to go." I couldn't stop the words from coming. Sydney had some power over me. She wasn't a naive girl from America. She wasn't a girl at all. Sydney was a mythical siren who could lure me to my death with a look. And I no longer cared.

She cleared her throat with a strangled sound. "I'm ready," she said and pulled us both forward.

23

SYDNEY

I took Chul's arm and slid closer, like we'd done this a thousand times instead of never. He was all fluid muscle, and tonight he smelled like expensive cologne. I wanted his closeness to help, to lean on him and make this party a success. I loved the way he looked at me, like I was regal, so different from who I really was. I stood up straighter in my evening gown. I'd already put on this mask. I was no longer Sydney Moore. I was the Kim's goddaughter. Everything I did would reflect on them. I took the first step, and we walked into the banquet hall.

"Is this really your hotel?" I whispered, taking in the enormity of a room packed full of monied guests. Before I could ask another stupid question, a spotlight fell on us. I blinked and started to turn away, but Chul leaned down and spoke in my ear. "Raise your head and smile. We're going up there, so follow my lead."

My stomach dropped when I saw where *up there* was. Suni and another man, who had to be Chul's father, stood arm in arm on a stage raised in front of the whole room. We walked up a short rise of stairs to stand next to the Kims. Suni beamed while the dazzling spotlight reflected off her sequined gown. Chul turned, and somehow, I moved with him until we faced the room. A full army of men with power-etched faces and women with practiced stares and red polished lips sipped from tall fluted glasses. They all waited, ready to weigh my worth. This wasn't a party; this was an execution. My knees quivered.

Chul patted my hand and leaned down again to speak in my ear. Somehow, I'd forgotten that I was holding on—no clinging —to his arm. "Take a deep breath," he said.

Chul's father spoke into a microphone, but I barely registered the words. My brain was on full stun-mode, and it seemed as if the simple acts of standing and breathing were all I could do. There was polite laughter and well-mannered clapping. Then I heard my name, and the room went quiet. All eyes rested heavily on me as every guest waited. I wasn't sure what to do until Chul took the microphone from his father. His words became my foxhole, a momentary break from the bullets ready to zip past my head. "I'm sure I speak for us all when I say: welcome to Korea, Sydney. Now let's party." Clapping erupted and I gave a little wave, complete with my bravest smile. We were walking back down the steps before I realized the battle was over.

"You okay?" Chul asked.

"No. Maybe. I'm not sure."

People began standing and moving about the room. A group of unfamiliar women approached us, but before they could get close Chul pulled me into the crowd. We wove through jewels, gowns, and laughter. Twice he changed course when someone looked eager to stop us. Waiters wearing black uniforms served drinks, and stands of flowers lined the walls. A band I hadn't noticed near the back of the room began playing what sounded like Gypsy Jazz. The whole room buzzed like a well-run hive that fed on opulence and elegance. Where I saw excess, they saw the basics. Like napkins embossed with the Kims' last name in small stacks on each table—was that something they did for every party? And an actual, full-sized, cherry-red Ferrari was on a stand in the middle of the room. How they got it up here, I couldn't guess, but that wasn't the weird part. Giant framed pictures of *me* on easels surrounded the car. I winced at some of them as we passed. They had all my baby photos and every school picture from kindergarten on up. "What's with the car? And my pictures, really?"

Chul chuckled. "You were a cute baby."

"Every baby is cute."

He stopped at my 6th grade picture. I had a goofy smile, and you could tell I'd cut my own bangs. Definitely not my best look. "I might steal this one."

I choked. "You're not taking that."

Chul smiled. "My mother will happily make me a copy."

I pulled him away. There was no winning this, and I just wanted to sit. Maybe then, I wouldn't be so close to Chul. He smelled too good. Like something you should just lean into and inhale. It made too many parts of my brain go soft and fuzzy.

Suni intercepted us before I got anywhere near a chair. "Sydney, dear." She fanned herself with a red fan that perfectly matched her dress and sighed as if relieved. "I'm so glad to see you again. You did well up there. I hope you weren't nervous. My son has been telling me how much fun you're having now that you've settled in."

It was so weird that she always called him *my son* and never Chul. This whole hidden identity trouble could have been avoided if she'd just used his name. I smiled. "Yes, Chul's been very helpful."

"Good, good," she said. "I want you to meet Jae-ho, my husband." A man turned from his conversation nearby. Now that I wasn't quaking on a stage, I had time to notice he had the same height and build as Chul. His black hair held just a touch of silver, and his carefully trimmed mustache was peppered in gray. He extended his arm and smiled. "It's so good to finally meet my goddaughter. Sydney, you are very welcome here." He patted my hand as I shook his. But his eyes went cool as he turned his attention to Chul. He nodded once. "Son," he said.

They'd been apart for so long, longer than I'd been away from my mom. But if she were suddenly here, I'd be hugging her like mad.

Chul bowed but seemed unmoved by the presence of his father. "Welcome home," he said.

"I see you're finally taking your responsibility seriously,

for once," Mr. Kim said.

I started to speak—someone needed to defend Chul. He stiffened at my side, so I stopped. Did his parents just not get him?

"I've heard good reports from the school," Suni said. "Apparently Sydney was in the top twenty-five percent of female students for the five-kilometer run on Friday."

I stifled a laugh. If she only could have seen Chul piggybacking me through the finish line. "Chul and I ran it together," I said. "I don't know how I would have survived Daeshim without him."

Mr. Kim still stared hard at Chul. "Why don't you take Sydney and begin introducing her to some of the families? People are already asking after her."

"Of course, Father." Chul gave another bow, and I added mine. He swept me past his parents, and we were again moving through the crowds. He stopped at an older man and woman. They both had silver-white hair with a look that said impropriety never dared invade their world. Every muscle in their faces stayed perfectly still, and I was reminded of expensive porcelain dolls by their serene features. Chul bowed again, so I followed.

The man's face broke with a smile. "How is my favorite grandson?"

Chul laughed. "I'm your only grandson."

The man patted him on the head affectionately. "Yes, but you're still my favorite."

Chul caught my eye and winked. "Grandfather, Grandmother," he said. "Let me introduce Sydney Moore."

I sighed. The sudden warmth in their faces made them seem human after all.

Chul's grandmother came forward. "Sydney, dear, you look just like your mother. We've missed her so much all these years. I'm so glad you've chosen to live with the Kims."

"Thank you," I said. I wanted to clarify, to tell them that I was only staying for a few months, but Chul's careful squeeze of my hand made me hold back. Maybe that's what the Kims were telling everyone, and I shouldn't contradict them. Even if it wasn't true. Instead, I said, "You remember my mom?"

"Oh, yes, we loved having Shannon stay with us. We were all sad when she went back to California for school."

"She still talks about her time in Korea and misses everyone. I will be sure to tell her how nice it was to meet you in my next email home."

"Please do that," she said. But her eyes went sad, and she took my hand. "Everything will be okay. You're part of our family now."

I laughed. Was my nervousness so obvious that she was trying to reassure me? "I'm sure tonight will go well."

Grandmother opened her mouth as if to respond but closed it with a frown.

"Don't let us hold you up," Grandfather said. "Everyone wants to meet this beautiful young lady. And Chul, you take excellent care of our Sydney now, understand?"

"I'll hardly let her out of my sight," Chul said.

I reminded myself that this whole night was all for show and I shouldn't put too much stock in his words. We bowed again.

We walked from group to group with the same formal introductions each time. People stared with apparent awe and curiosity, but nothing about me in their world would be permanent. I was the first snow, melting before it touched. I'd be forgotten by morning. Still, I remained poised throughout, until we came to Mr. and Mrs. Kang and Min.

Stupid Min.

She was twisted in her seat, laughing with a woman sitting at the next table, her back to us. She stiffened and turned when Chul spoke.

"Mr. and Mrs. Kang, I'd like to introduce my mother's goddaughter, Sydney Moore."

Min looked at my hand tucked into the crook of his arm and rolled her eyes. But there was no hiding that her face flushed a deep red and her nostrils flared. Min's mom noticed and took her daughters hand, seeming to lean closer.

The moment was every revenge movie rolled into one, only a hundred times better. She couldn't hide her anger, and I just let her drown in it. Waves of jealousy washed over her. I knew she would make me pay later, but I didn't care. Min was a loaded gun. I'd bleed either way, so I might as well enjoy the moment. "Min, it's so nice to see you again," I said. "Mrs. Kang, your daughter is so attentive to me in school." She didn't like me being escorted on Chul's arm any more than her daughter did. Which only encouraged me. "It's like fate that she's in every one of my classes. Of course, my Oppa is too," I said, squeezing Chul's arm and leaning into him. "So we all have a good time together." My high school drama teacher would have been moved to tears.

Chul played along. He tucked a few locks of hair behind my ear and let his fingers trail down my neck before taking my hand, giving it a quick kiss, and then placed it back around his arm. He did it so naturally, like we were both comfortable with touching each other. Like we were a real couple. "Sydney's a breath of fresh air. That's for sure."

Min's mouth dropped open.

It was perfect.

Mr. Kang saved his daughter from the DEFCON Level-1 alarms that were likely blaring in her brain. "Now that you've introduced Miss Moore to the most important families, the others are waiting. We don't want to monopolize with our position."

Chul gave his bow, and we walked away. I wanted to do cartwheels and high-five him. I *wanted* him to touch my neck again, but I wouldn't think about that.

"You called me Oppa," he said.

"Once, just to burn Min."

"My mother was listening in. Almost the entire room listened in and watched the most powerful family in Korea converse with the son and goddaughter of the second most powerful family in Korea."

I paused and looked back over my shoulder. I hadn't noticed Suni when we spoke to the Kangs, but there she was, smiling sweetly and nodding at something Mrs. Kang said.

"Why should that matter?"

"We just established with the entire upper-class society that Kim Chul, the only son and heir of the Kim corporation, has a girlfriend."

"When you say it like that, it sounds scary. No one will think that."

He leaned down and spoke close to my ear. "You called me Oppa. You leaned into me. If you had pulled away when I touched you, then there would only be speculation. But you didn't. Your status is sealed, and my mother looks elated."

I swallowed hard and tried to move my hand off his arm. Chul gripped it tighter. "After your little face-off with Min, you need this protection, Sydney. I'm your boyfriend now, whether you like it or not."

The back of my neck warmed, followed by my face. "You're kidding, right? You have to be."

He cocked one eyebrow with a look that said he wasn't.

This couldn't be happening. I could never be Chul's girlfriend. He was the hot guy. Only Chul was way beyond normal hot guy. He was the guy with no speed limit, and I didn't even know how to drive. "I need to go to the bathroom," I said, lamely.

"It's this way." He walked me to one of the side doors and opened it. He looked like he was about to follow me out into the hall, but I put a hand up to stop him. "I'll be right back. You don't need to follow me in."

He looked doubtful for a moment, then nodded.

I walked down the hall and kept going, right past the door marked *Women*. I turned the corner, and another, until I found what I was looking for. Opposite the elevators was the door marked *Stairs*. This building had to have a roof. The party was on the thirty-fifth floor, but I'd noticed buttons for forty floors when we got in the elevator.

I took off my heels and started climbing. The air from the stairwell tasted hot and stale, but I needed to be free from a giant ballroom full of people watching my every move. The stairs ended at a heavy steel door. It wasn't locked, but I had to yank on the handle twice before it flew inwards. Fresh air blew against my skin. I sucked in a deep breath and walked onto the rooftop. There was a helipad to my left and a few benches to my right, but other than the steady hum of industrial air conditioners, the roof looked empty. I dropped my shoes and stretched up into the night sky. This was what I needed. I moved closer to the edge of the building and peered over. There was a half wall with a metal railing as a safety guard on top. I leaned over and looked down. Tiny cars and lights below dizzied my senses.

"What are you doing up here, Sydney?"

I whirled around, surprised to see Gun in a tuxedo. Before I could speak, he strode forward and closed the distance between us. A tight smile tugged at the corners of his mouth as he spoke. "I've got you alone now."

24

CHUL

It was our own stupid hotel, and I couldn't find Sydney. If she didn't show up soon, I'd have to go to security. After that, there'd be no keeping it from my father.

The ballroom pulsed with jewels and gowns, money trying to show up more money. It was all the same crowd—someone stopping me to ask about my future plans, another to beg an introduction. Everyone wanted to rub shoulders with a Kim. I just wanted Sydney.

I searched for a flash of blonde hair, her smile. I'd turn, thinking I saw her blue dress, but Sydney was a ghost. My father watched me from the table where he talked with a judge who would be running for president in the next election. His sharp eyes roamed over me, always finding inadequacies.

Tonight felt too much like when I was six and fell into the deep end of the pool. Father wouldn't save me. I was a Kim. Failure wasn't an option. *He leaned over the edge of the pool. "Kick, Chul, don't give up. It can't beat you unless you let it." I struggled, only to sink lower. His wavering image filtered down through the water and grew hazy from lack of oxygen. In the end, Hyun pulled me up. Mother cried as I sputtered. Hyun yelled and threatened to move out. My father only stared at me with those hard, glassy eyes. "Next time, don't ever stop swimming."*

The guests moving between us broke our stare-down. I quickly turned away and headed for the door. Before I could get two feet in the other direction, my mother snagged my arm.

She looked like she normally did—perfect. But tonight, it was more. She was happy.

"Son, where's Sydney? It's almost time to eat." She stepped forward and took my arm, then whispered close to my ear. "I didn't know things had progressed so much with you two. She seems to really like you."

I tried to keep the defensiveness from my voice. "I told you I'd take care of her."

"You've done well. She looks lovely tonight."

Sydney always looked hot, even in her Wonder Woman pajamas. "I took her shopping," I said.

My father stepped from behind me. I was pretty sure he could teleport. "I'd like to speak with you both for a moment."

Mother nodded. "Of course."

I groaned inwardly but followed them. He led us to the same conference room Sydney and I'd been in earlier, then closed the door. He didn't know that I'd lost her, and it was killing me to fake calm. I folded my arms and tried not to seem impatient.

He cleared his throat with an awkward look. My father never said or did anything without confidence, so I knew this was serious. "Since you and Sydney are already . . ." He rubbed the back of his neck like it pained him.

My mother nodded encouragingly, but he couldn't seem to find the words. "Together. They're a couple, Jae-ho. Just say it," she said.

My father continued. "Since you're in a relationship."

"So what if we are?" We weren't, not really, but I wanted us to be. I shrugged like none of it mattered. "You wanted me to watch out for her. It's not a big deal."

My father nodded, "Sure. It doesn't have to be anything serious. You're only eighteen."

His agreeing with me felt like a trick, like he was about to put me in checkmate. I sneered. "Wow. You know my age. You weren't here for my birthday, so I wasn't sure." His face fell and regret settled over me.

My father let out a heavy breath. "Sit down," he said, pulling out his own chair. He looked tired.

I sat, followed by Mother nervously wringing her hands. "We're sorry that we missed your birthday," she said. "I told Hyun to buy you whatever you wanted."

I wisely chose to ignore her comment. Maybe she meant well, but neither one of them seemed to get that I'd take an hour or two with my parents once in a while over a new car.

My father leaned back and laced his fingers behind his head. "Maybe you won't see this until you're older, but running an international corporation is competitive and takes most of our time. Despite that, we are still trying to be here when you need us."

I sighed. "It's fine. I get it."

"I hope you do," he said. "But I also hope that when there's a problem, we can come together as a family. And Sydney seems to have a problem."

The words *problem* and *Sydney* got my attention. I tried for control, to stamp down my temper and not make it all about me. Hyun's advice banged around in my head. *Your parents love you. They just aren't perfect.* Maybe my father really did feel bad about being gone all the time. "Okay, then." I swallowed the lump in my throat along with half my pride. "We're here together. So what's the problem with Sydney?" I asked.

"It's not really a problem," Mother said.

My father raised both eyebrows. "It most definitely is, but with Chul around it might be an easy fix."

I needed to look for Sydney, not play guessing games. "Spell it out for me."

"You've fallen for her," he said.

I sat up straighter. "No."

My father smiled, a little wolfish. It galled me that he was right. We both knew I was gone over Sydney. "It's not a bad thing," he said. "But she's here permanently."

"I think she plans to go home after Christmas, not live

here forever." But even as I spoke the words, part of me crumbled at the idea of Sydney leaving. If she went back home, I might just follow her.

"Shannon needs her to live here now," he said. "She's having difficulties in the States."

"What kind of difficulties?" I watched him closely. This was a big secret. I could tell by the way his eyes flicked down. It couldn't be money, or they'd already have taken care of it.

"We are not at liberty to disclose their family business," he said.

"Are you at liberty to disclose it to *her*? Neither one of us know why she's here, and it's not fair to keep both of us in the dark."

My parent's exchanged a look, and my mother nodded. "Someone has threatened Sydney," he said. "Shannon has tried to protect her, but she finally decided to send her here."

My stomach twisted at the thought. "Who is it?"

"It's her uncle," my mother said. "Shannon isn't sure, but she thinks he has a mental illness, something called Munchausen syndrome by proxy."

I wrinkled my brow. "Never heard of that one. What is it?"

My father cleared his throat. "It's very rare. Usually it's a parent, but sometimes a caregiver will purposely try to make a child sick. They make up symptoms, and frequently use drugs or poison to create symptoms. I talked with our own doctor, and it can be a serious mental illness. They have documented cases where children have died when their caregiver had Munchausen syndrome by proxy."

Fear, hot and sharp, burrowed like a piece of shrapnel somewhere under my left ribcage. I folded my arms, tight against myself. "And you think her uncle did this to Sydney?"

"Shannon isn't sure, she just began to suspect," he said. "But she's here, so Greg Moore can't get close to her."

"Why would he do that, though? That's his niece."

My father shrugged. "Her uncle was her therapist after

her mom got cancer. I'm sure at first, she did need therapy, but Greg probably couldn't let go. Maybe Sydney being sick gave him some kind of power or control, and some people are pulled to that."

I raked my hands through my hair. "Did Sydney ever mention anything dangerous, or this Greg guy trying to hurt her? Did he, like, molest her? She would have said something to her mother, right?" My voice shook and my face warmed. "What exactly did he do to her?"

My father placed a hand over mine. "Shannon doesn't think he went that far. There was no evidence of sexual abuse, and Sydney never had any injuries. It was emotional abuse. Greg systematically exaggerated Sydney's mental condition. Whenever she showed signs of getting better, he claimed she was worsening. Over time, Shannon noticed that Greg became more aggressive with suggesting drugs and the number of appointments she needed. Shannon always put him off, but he got bolder."

My mother let out a shaky sigh. "Shannon tried to talk with him about Sydney not needing therapy anymore. He turned into a madman and became completely irrational. He even fabricated evidence that Shannon was an unfit parent and threatened to try to take Sydney away if she didn't agree to hospitalize her. It scared Shannon so much that she called me. That same day, Sydney was packed and on the plane."

"So, great. She's here and safe," I said. "Now let's put Greg behind bars where he belongs."

My father smiled at me, and I knew we were having one of those rare moments when we agreed. He wouldn't let Greg off that easy. "I hired a private investigator," he said. "Greg has done nothing illegal since Sydney has been here, but we're watching him."

"He can't get anywhere near her, ever again," I said. My words reassured me, but my hands still shook under the table. I took a deep breath. I needed to be smart about this and stay calm.

Mother got tears in her eyes. "Please don't say anything to her. She doesn't do well with stress. When Shannon got sick, she was so little, with no one to care for her. I should have gone to the States and taken her then, but Shannon insisted they were okay."

I hadn't considered what Sydney's life must have been like when her mom had cancer. "I won't say anything for now, but you should tell her soon. Sydney is homesick and deserves to know why she's here."

"I'll tell her when the time is right," she said. "But I don't want to say anything that would alarm her more. She already wants to go home, and I need her to stay at least until she turns eighteen in the summer." My mother gave me a pleading look. "You could be the reason she wants to stay. She already likes you."

I wasn't so sure. I'd grown on Sydney, but as far as her falling for me, that was about as easy as trying to balance on a highwire during a tornado. Still, I wouldn't tell my parents that. I'd fight to win her heart, and tonight was a big step forward. "She's still going to want to go home eventually."

My mother fluttered her hands to her throat. "I'll tell her soon, but first, we need you to understand your part."

My parents could see that I liked Sydney, just not how much. If Sydney was in danger, I'd do whatever it took to protect her. "I know my part. I'll take care of her."

"I don't think you completely understand what that entails," Father said.

I ground my teeth. "What more can I do?"

"Do you remember when Mr. Kang offered us a merger if we would arrange for you and Min to marry?" Mother said. "He really liked the idea of you as his son-in-law."

My father scoffed. "He still does."

I shuddered. "I'll never marry Min."

"That's why we didn't agree to the merger," he said. "It was clear that you didn't have feelings for her."

"Thanks, I guess, for not forcing us to marry." I snorted.

"Min is heartless, but what does that have to do with Sydney?"

My Mother took my hand between her small ones. "We would never force a relationship on you with Min, but you do like Sydney."

Fear and hope twisted inside me. "What are you saying?"

My father leaned closer. "Shannon asked us to adopt Sydney. But now that we see you like each other, it might be wise to change plans."

"Adoption is kind of extreme." I pulled my hand away from my mother and shook my head. "She can't be my sister."

My mother laughed and twisted her wedding ring. "There are other ways to join a family."

I stared. They were serious.

My father continued. "If you're not sure about dating her, then back down now and we'll play tonight off as a misunderstanding between you two."

"There's no misunderstanding." The words left my mouth as this little mutinous part of my brain took the wheel, laughing manically and speeding into an unknown future.

"There will be no erasing this after tonight. If you're serious about Sydney, then I'm cancelling the adoption." My father spoke the words with the same command he would use to close a business transaction.

"Give him time to think on it," Mother said. "You shouldn't force his decision so quickly, Jae-ho. This is exactly the reason you both fight."

"I don't need time." It all seemed so childish suddenly, this part of me that always had to push back and refuse. My parents were calculating, and who knew what they were really planning. But if this was them winning, it didn't feel wrong. I only knew that the idea of losing Sydney made my chest go tight. I met my father with a level gaze. "I'm sure about her, but what if that's not what she wants? She's only seventeen."

"I can't help you there. I'm cancelling the adoption papers, but you'll need to convince her to stay. Are you up for it?"

I took a deep breath. Now that I'd made up my mind, I couldn't see us *not* together. "I am, actually."

My father smiled and clapped me on the shoulder. "Good man."

My mother flushed and smiled up at him. I hadn't seen her this happy in a long time. Maybe never.

I bowed. "If you'll excuse me, I'll go retrieve Sydney for the meal now."

My mother stopped me with a hand on my arm. "Son."

"Yes?"

But then she teared up again. I wondered if she'd had too much champagne. Words seemed to fail her, and my father stepped in. "What your mother means to say, is that you taking care of Sydney makes us both proud."

That was as close to a compliment as I'd ever gotten from the man. "Thank you." I shifted, uncomfortably, then bowed again and left.

I headed to the elevators. Security was on the main floor, and from there I'd have access to every camera in the hotel.

Finding her would be the easy part. Figuring out what to do after that, made me sweat.

25

SYDNEY

"You're here," I said. Gun took a long drag on a cigarette and stepped close. It burned red and made his eyes glitter in the shadows. "I didn't see you at the party."

"I saw you." He blew smoke out of the side of his mouth. "Hanging on Chul's arm." He smiled, but it was all ice. "And now you're here alone? I thought you'd be mingling with the rest of them."

The acrid smell of his cigarette made my stomach queasy, and I swallowed against my dry throat. I didn't like this new side of Gun, the smoking and angry looks he slanted my way. "I'm getting some air." It was lame, but I wasn't about to say I'd come up to avoid freaking out over Chul and the Oppa thing.

Gun took another puff on his cigarette and looked at me like he knew what I was really doing—hiding. "You smoke?" He held his cigarette out.

I shook my head. "No. Definitely no." I hated that he did.

"I was surprised when I read your text," Gun said. "Why didn't you tell me sooner that you lived with the Kims? I feel like such an idiot." His voice held a hint of hurt.

I looked down at my bare feet with a nervous laugh. "I was shocked, too. I didn't find out who Chul was until recently."

"You were shocked? Is that all? The guy played you the whole time." He took another long drag. "Then you walk in all smiles and wrapped around his arm, like a bow on a box."

There was no way to justify what Chul had done. But remembering his eyes when he'd said he was sorry got my defenses up. None of this was Gun's business anyway. "I was mad and hurt, but he apologized."

Gun snarled. "And you just forgave him?"

"None of it was easy," I snapped. "He's embarrassed about it now, but everyone deserves a second chance. Do you really want to fight over this?" A gust of wind whipped a loose lock of hair around my face.

He reached out to tuck it behind my ear and I pulled back. "No, but you don't have to put up with him, you know."

"Chul won't be a problem."

"You live with him. And he's a player."

I hadn't flat out asked Chul about his past love life, and I wasn't going to. I shrugged like it didn't bother me. It must have been my imagination, but the lights around us seemed to dim. "Chul can do what he wants. We're not together, so I don't keep track of the girls he likes."

"That's good to hear." He took a step closer. "But what about us? I like you a lot. I thought you liked me, too."

I tried to keep my voice light. "We can still hang out."

"I don't want to hang out. You don't have to be with him." He spoke softly and took my hand in his. "Come with me tonight."

"In the middle of a party? Where would we go?"

"Anywhere you want. I have an apartment my parents don't know about. It's close to school, and you could stay there. You said earlier that you were looking for a job. You won't need to. I can buy you whatever you want."

If his words didn't make his intentions clear, the way his eyes roamed over my body did. It left me cold. I was poor, but I had standards and morals. I clenched my jaw and jerked my hand back. "I'm not doing that."

Rage flashed in his eyes. He quickly tucked it away, but I'd read it there. No one knew I was up here. This was nothing like being alone with Chul on his roof yesterday. I looked around with the hope that some other guests would appear. There were only a few empty benches. Everything felt far away and removed, with just the hum of air conditioners and the sounds of the city far below us.

Gun flicked his cigarette to the ground and pressed the heel of his shoe into the ember. "There's another thing you're not considering. Min's been in love with Chul since forever. You living with him will bring out her worst. That alone should be a reason for you to leave the Kims."

"I'm not afraid of Min."

He cocked his head with a smirk. "You should be. She's already stolen your school records. She knows your weaknesses now."

"What, that I'm a straight-A student?"

"I heard there were more than grades in those files."

"Please, I'm an honor student. What more could there be?"

"There's a rumor that you're some kind of psycho."

I jerked. "What did you say?"

"Min's got your medical history."

It couldn't be. My mom wouldn't share that. It was too private, too embarrassing—all the meds I used to be on, the breakdowns when I was younger. "I don't know what you've heard, but I'm not a psycho, so don't call me that."

Gun held his hands up in defense. "I'm just saying what I heard. I've never thought that."

I sighed. As if Min wasn't bad enough before. Why was everything so hard here?

"I can help you, Sydney."

"Listen, Gun." I tried to side-step and put distance between us, but he mimicked my move, and somehow, he ended up a fraction closer. The wind turned biting at my back, a reminder that the edge of the half wall and a two-foot railing were the only thing that stood between me and . . . air. I bit my lip against the urge to move away closer to the door. Gun seemed angry and worked up. "I'm staying with the Kims for a short time, and then I go home. It's not like I'm making life-changing decisions here."

"Don't be so sure. The Kims threw this party for a reason."

"They're trying to make me feel welcome."

"Parties like this are announcements," he said. "They just claimed you as one of their own."

"I'm their goddaughter."

"No." Gun jerked his head. "I saw the way his mother looked at you, his father too. I don't know what it is, but they want something from you."

"You're being paranoid."

"You're being naïve. People like us always have motivations."

"What's yours, then? Do you really like me, or is this just about getting back at Chul?"

"I just offered to take care of you. Is that not proof enough that I like you?"

"It's insulting. I can take care of myself. I don't need money from some guy I barely know."

Gun flew at me, and with one swift motion he pinned me to the half wall with his arm against my collar bone.

"Listen to me. I'm not just some guy. I'm trying to shield you from the Kims. Why do you keep turning me down?"

The cold metal of the safety rail dug into my shoulder. For a second, the lights around me spun, and then fear stoked my stunned brain.

I slammed my fist into his windpipe, and he stumbled back, clutching at his throat and coughing.

Twenty feet away, the door to the stairs waited for me. I could see my high-heeled pumps on the ground where I'd dropped them earlier.

I ran.

"Stop," he yelled.

I scooped up a shoe with one hand then pushed the door

open with the other. I stumbled into the stairwell, and with shaking hands I grasped the heel and shoved the toe under the door like a wedge. It wouldn't hold forever, but Gun would have to push hard to dislodge it.

I hiked up my dress and flew down the stairs. The slap of my bare feet on painted cement echoed as adrenaline sped me on. Only three more levels left, and I was panting. The door crashed open above me. I stopped to look up. Gun vaulted over the rail and landed onto the stairs of the next floor like it was nothing. "Sydney, WAIT!" he yelled.

I kept moving. No way was I getting anywhere near that lunatic. As I ran, I looked down the stairwell and caught glimpses of the number thirty-five painted in black above the door that would lead me back to the party, back to safety. I was close, one more floor to go. His shoes echoed on the stairs directly behind me, but I'd reached the door. My heart raced as my hand found the handle. I ran into the hall.

Chul waited for the elevator and turned in surprise. Soft piano music played from speakers somewhere in the ceiling. I slowed to a walk and tried to control my breathing, but he studied me as I approached. "What's wrong? Are you okay?"

I might have fooled him into thinking I wasn't running away, but then Gun burst through the door. In two quick strides Chul pulled me behind him.

Gun skidded to a stop when he saw us together. His face twisted in anger. "Sydney, you're misunderstanding."

Chul took another step forward. "Stay away from her."

Gun barked out a laugh. "You're the one who should stay away. Why do you think she was hiding on the roof? She wanted to get away from the control-freak creep who pretended to be someone else at school."

Chul's hands fisted at his side, and his muscles tensed.

I pulled on his arm. "Let's just go." If this went bad, and it could go very, very bad, Chul's parents would probably blame him.

Gun narrowed his eyes at Chul. "You've lied and

manipulated her."

Chul shook me off and stormed forward. I slipped in front of him and wrapped my arms around his waist. "Stop." Chul's chest heaved up and down in angry huffs. I looked up at him, but he only glared at Gun. "Don't," I whispered.

He lowered his eyes and I stepped back, hesitant.

Chul studied me from head to toe, noting my bare feet. I tried to calm myself and not look so panicked. He took my hand and turned back towards the banquet hall.

"He's going to get sick of you, Sydney," Gun called out. "And when he does, he'll dump you like all the other girls."

Chul didn't stop walking, and for that I was grateful. My arms and legs quivered from adrenaline, but I kept moving.

We passed a few guests in the hallway, and Chul nodded when appropriate. When we reached the banquet doors, he stopped and lowered his voice. "What happened?"

"I went to the roof."

"To meet Gun?"

"No, I was nervous from the whole Oppa thing. I only wanted some time alone. I didn't know he was up there too."

Chul seemed too quiet next to my still-trembling limbs. His voice had gone gentle and honey smooth. I hoped I didn't look like a wild animal that needed calming. I felt like one. I tried to shake off the trapped, smothered feeling Gun had left.

"Did he touch you?"

"He didn't hurt me. He just got too close, so I left."

"Where are your shoes?"

I winced. "They're probably ruined. I shoved one under the door to the roof to keep him from following me. I'm sure it didn't survive."

Chul's hand flexed in mine. "So he *was* chasing you."

"I said following, not chasing. There's a difference, you know." I tried for a smile. "Are the shoes that big a deal? Don't all the cool girls ruin haute-couture shoes now and then?"

He let out a long breath. The kind that said he was trying to be patient. "I'm going to deal with Gun in my own way. For now, just do your best to stay away from the guy."

"This is not your problem. *I* will deal with Gun. He just needs time to cool off."

"That's not what Gun needs." Chul pressed his lips into a hard line. "Look. We have to go back in. My mother's going to start freaking out if we don't show up soon. They expect me to make this night perfect, remember?"

I did remember. And I knew I'd promised to help Chul look good with them, but I was more worried about what Chul had meant when he'd said he would deal with Gun in his own way. "How about I go smooth things over and play the perfect goddaughter? In return you promise not to fight with Gun."

"No deal, Sydney. Maybe if you promise something more substantial, I'll say yes, though."

"Like what?"

"Promise to be my girlfriend, and I won't fight with Gun."

"What? No."

"Gun and I trained at the same dojo. He's really good at Hapkido. If I don't make it, you can have my comic book collection."

"Don't be ridiculous," I said.

"I'm not. I've seen Gun fight. I'm sure we'll both get at least a few broken bones."

I stared at him. He was serious. "How about we just tell everyone we're together at school, but at home we keep our distance."

"No. I don't fake date." Chul leaned against the wall and managed to look bored. "The dinner has already started. I can go in and tell them what happened instead, if that's what you want."

"No."

"I need you to make a decision," he said.

I couldn't believe he was pushing things this far. "What will your parents say if we start dating?"

"They already think we're together since you blatantly

called me Oppa in front of their guests."

My face warmed, and I had to look down. "How many girls have called you that?" Gun had said Chul was a player, and I wanted to believe he was lying, but girls clearly liked Chul. I could see it on their faces as we walked down the halls at school, and I could see it here at the party. Chul was the guy who would never have a problem getting a girl.

"If you mean have I had a girlfriend before, the answer is yes, I had one, but don't be intimated by that."

"I'm not. Just wondering."

"What about you?"

"That's none of your business."

"I'm only asking the same thing you asked me."

"It's still none of your business," I snapped.

"Okay." Chul held up both hands. "Will you be my girlfriend, though?"

I thought about it. There were a lot of things that would be easier as his girlfriend and a lot that would be harder. But the real reason I wanted to say yes was much simpler. I liked Chul. "Fine," I mumbled.

Chul leaned closer. "What was that?"

"Okay. We can date."

"Not just a few dates. You're my girlfriend."

"If that means physical stuff, then no. I'm not casual about sex."

"I'm not either. I've never had sex," he said.

I opened my mouth but couldn't think of anything to say to that. I mean, I was relieved, but I probably sounded crazy. Why did I have to bring that up?

"I'll never try to make you uncomfortable. But we can hold hands, right?"

I nodded, but my brain felt scrambled.

Chul seemed to study me. "I don't want you to be scared or nervous. We already spend a lot of time together, and the way I treat you isn't going to change."

He was right. I didn't need to make a big deal of this.

"Okay, I'm your girlfriend."

"Thank you." He leaned in close, too close. Our lips were a breath away. My face went hot. What was he doing? He was just looking at me and . . . waiting.

"What?" I whispered, barely moving my lips.

He cocked an eyebrow. "I just wondered. But no, I can see the answer is no." Then he raised his head to press his lips against my forehead before stepping away. "We'll be joining my parents at their table with another family, so you need to be ready."

"Um." I couldn't even look up. My face still burned.

He took my hand again, and it helped. I raised my eyes and met his. Chul made my heart race and my face burn, but he also made me feel safe. I smiled reassuringly, and he opened the door.

The room was a quiet hum of talking and the gentle chink of china as people ate. His parents were seated at a round table in the middle of the room. There were two empty seats waiting for us. Suni waved us over but not before frowning at my bare feet.

Everyone nodded and greeted me as we entered. A few couples even stood and bowed as we passed. I was part of the inner circle now. I wondered if there had been some kind of hidden silent test. Maybe it was like with CIA agents on TV. Their final trial is to fool a room full of Russians into thinking they were born and raised in the motherland. Had I fooled these people with their billions upon billions of *won* into thinking I was one of them? Or maybe just the Kims claiming me was all it took, a nod from the king and queen.

Chul held the seat out for me at his parents' table, but I almost tripped and fell into the chair when I realized the Kangs were seated there as well. Mr. Kang sat to my right, next to Mrs. Kang and Min. Chul took the seat on my left. I tried to look respectable, or at least not look like I'd just run down five flights of stairs and broken up a testosterone match.

Waiters brought us warm plates of what looked like

grilled octopus. Long, fat tentacles lined with pink and white suckers curled on my plate. Breathing through my mouth, I tried not to smell the food as I pushed my plate away and instead, focused hard on my small bowl of rice.

"Are you feeling better now, Sydney?" Mrs. Kang asked. "We were all worried when you were gone for so long. And what happened to your shoes?" She smiled sweetly, but her eyes glared flat and snake-like.

"Chul, you must have bought her the wrong size," Suni said quickly. "They probably hurt your feet, dear."

"They were the right size. I'm just not used to high heels."

Mrs. Kang smiled. "I hope you will become accustomed to the proper way of things soon. But then you *are* an American. Maybe running about with bare feet is acceptable there."

Mr. Kang frowned at his wife and whispered something I couldn't hear. She lowered her head but not before casting a barbed look in Suni's direction.

Min placed a hand over her mother's. "Sydney met Gun on the roof. She was disappointed not to see him at the party. Right, Sydney?"

All eyes went to me.

Oh, Min was good. She made it sound like we'd been meeting for a clandestine affair. But how had she known that I was on the roof with Gun in the first place? "Chul found Gun for me," I said with just enough emphasis on Chul's name to let everyone know where I stood. "He was worried about Gun, too."

"He's not going to make it tonight," Chul said smoothly. "He had a family emergency,"

"Who says?" Gun appeared behind me and pulled up a chair in the too small space between me and Mr. Kang. "Crisis averted, Chul. I'm here now." He placed his big hand on my shoulder and gave a squeeze. From the corner of my eye, I saw Chul's face twitch.

Mr. Kim motioned for one of the waiters, who immediately brought a place setting for Gun.

Mr. Kang patted him on the back with clear fondness. "We haven't seen you around as much lately."

"School, sir. I'm trying to focus on my grades."

Mr. Kang nodded with approval. "You've always been a steady kid."

Gun was all humble smiles. It made me sick. "I don't want to disappoint anyone," he said. "My parents expect me to grow our company."

"Where do you plan to go to school?" Suni asked.

"Somewhere in the States. I'm still doing applications." Gun smiled at Chul. "Who knows, I may even end up at the same university as Sydney when she goes back. I don't want her to be lonely." He slipped his hand under the table to my leg and looked at me with innocent eyes.

I jerked my knee up, smashing Gun's hand into the bottom of the table. The dishes closest to us clattered. "Sorry," I said. "The table is crowded."

Chul titled his head just a fraction, and the twitching in his face got worse.

Suni frowned in Gun's direction, then cleared her throat. "Sydney's going to Seoul National after high school. I already submitted her application, and she's been accepted. Chul's going there too, so she won't be lonely. I'm buying them a small apartment near campus."

My mouth dropped open. "What?"

"You shouldn't have ruined the surprise," Mr. Kim said. He looked at me with a touch of concern. "We wanted to tell you later, but Suni is excited that you and Chul will go to the same school."

I swallowed. "I, uhhh, that *is* a surprise." What was up with these people? And buying an apartment near campus? Was she thinking we'd live together, too? It was one thing to live in a crazy-big mansion with servants and Chul having his own wing, but an apartment was a hard pass. I caught Chul shaking his head at his mother. After that he didn't speak, just stared hard at his plate.

Mr. Kang raised his glass to the Kims with a look of admiration. "Things are looking solid for Chul these days. We should take note and start planning for Min instead of letting her run around with her silly friends."

Min had been quiet during the whole conversation, but now, she spoke. "Are you sure this is what Chul wants?" Her face flushed, and her eyes glistened. "It's not like we're in the Joseon era and need parents to arrange our lives."

Mr. Kang laughed. "None of you know what you want."

Min stood abruptly. Her mother clutched at her hand, but she shook her off. "Excuse me, I'm sorry. I need to go make a phone call." She bowed to both sets of parents and walked away.

Gun stood up. "Don't worry." His eyes flicked nervously after Min. "I'll check on her." He bowed and followed.

I snuck a look at Chul and noticed sweat along his brow. He clenched his teeth, and I could only imagine how unhappy and trapped he felt. For once I had to agree with Min. Chul's parents should let him choose what he wanted. Suni could brag about Chul and me going off to school together all night. But in the end, it wouldn't change that I would do what *I* wanted. The sad truth was, I wasn't so sure Chul had that freedom.

26

CHUL

My parents wanted to mold Sydney to be like them. But they didn't get it. Sydney wasn't someone you could change because she didn't care about money or schools or connections. She cared about people. And that girl's number one was her mom. Weird, yes—to like your mom that much. But that was Syd. Only with all of Sydney's unconditional love for her mom, she was about to get burned. Shannon wasn't perfect. She'd sent her daughter here completely blind—no explanation, no honesty—and Sydney couldn't seem to grasp that her mom would lie. I could feel it like a burr scratching at my heart. Sydney's mom was about to hurt her. And there was nothing I could do.

SYDNEY

Chul walked with me to the elevator after the party started winding down. There were a few guests left, but his parents had waved us off, saying we could head home.

The tired shuffle of my feet along the hotel carpet reminded me of my last appointment with Uncle Greg. His new office was on the top floor of a business complex with a corner view. Neither the creamy soft leather of his sofa nor the paintings of ocean tides helped me relax. With Uncle Greg, I was always on edge.

"*Sydney,*" *he said.* "*Your PTSD is getting worse. You won't get better without treatment at my hospital. You know this, so why put it off?*"

I glared at him. "*I visit you every week for treatment. What teenager doesn't get stressed sometimes?*" *I shook my head.* "*Look, I have a few friends now, a part-time job, good grades, and I've already started looking at colleges. What more do you want?*"

He smiled at me like I was a little kid crying over what she couldn't have. With Uncle Greg, none of my progress counted. "*You need to be admitted. I can give you round the clock care then.*"

"*You act like I need to be spoon fed and on IVs.*"

"*That can be arranged.*"

I clamped my mouth shut and counted to ten in my head. "*Uncle Greg, you need to understand that I'm happy. I have Mom, and we are doing great.*"

"*See, that right there isn't healthy, Sydney. Your obsessive behavior with your mom is part of your condition. To fix you, I need to separate you from your object of obsession.*"

"*Stop it, Greg.*" *I said through gritted teeth.*

"*I've asked you to call me Uncle Greg,*" *he snapped.* "*I am your only living family.*"

"*Except my MOM.*" *My voice shook. He wasn't the only one who could get angry.* "*Why do you act like she isn't my family? She is everything to me.*"

Greg leaned forward in his chair, and the sour smell of tuna fish wafted from his mouth. "*I'm the only one who can help you get better. Your mom couldn't take care of you or your dad. He left our family because of her, and now he's dead.*"

"Are you tired Sydney?" Chul touched my shoulder. "What's wrong?" he asked. I blinked and realized I'd been lost in bad memories. I hated that I still thought of Greg. Mom may have pushed me into coming here against my will, but being away from home did make me feel stronger. When I got back, the first thing I would do would be to tell him I was done with his stupid therapy sessions. "I'm fine, just thinking about how different life is here with your family."

"I bet you're freaked out by what my mother said. You know, about us going to college and living together."

I laughed. "I should be, but I'm not. I think your mom just likes to plan people's lives. I'm going home at Christmas. She might be disappointed, but I am leaving."

Chul didn't say anything. His mother was a touchy subject, so maybe I offended him. I smiled brightly. "I emailed my mom some pictures of the party. I wish she could have been here with me. She likes parties more than I do. I'm hoping she can come out for a visit. I'd like you to meet her." Chul nodded but didn't say more as we waited for the elevator. When we got in, he took my hand in his. A wave of nerves rushed up my arm, straight to my heart. I didn't want to pull away. In that moment I wanted to hold his hand forever. I shook myself. This was exactly why liking Chul was dangerous.

The elevator started moving up instead of down. "Where are we going?"

"To the penthouse suite. I had Hyun bring us some clothes."

I shifted in my bare feet. Was he serious? I wasn't going into a hotel room alone with him. "I don't mind changing when we get back to your house."

He looked down at me and smirked like he could read my mind. "It's always reserved for us. My grandmother usually gets tired early and ends up camping out there for the night whenever there's a big party. I bet Hyun's up there with them right now watching TV. Don't worry . . . too much."

I looked away. "I'm not."

"He brought you shoes. I didn't think you'd want me to carry you again. But I can, if you want."

"No," I said quickly. "I'm good with getting shoes." The elevator stopped, and we walked to double doors. He only let go of my hand to enter a code on the lock and open the door for me.

"What episode are you on?" Chul called out as soon as we

entered.

Hyun and Chul's grandparents all sat on a leather sofa holding chopsticks over bowls. It smelled like noodles, something I was starting to associate with comfort these days. A giant screen took up most of the wall opposite the couch. No one looked away, but Chul's grandmother waved her chopsticks at us. "Shh, we can't miss this part."

"They love American crime shows," Chul said.

"Really?" I asked, surprised.

"They're nuts over them. They watch with Korean subtitles."

Chul's grandmother looked up. "Oh, Sydney, you're here."

"Stay and watch the show with us," Chul's grandfather said.

"We just came to change. Sorry, can't stay." Chul pointed me to one of the bedroom doors off the main room. "Hurry. I want to take you somewhere before it gets too late."

"It's already after eleven."

"I thought you weren't tired."

I wasn't tired, just nervous. I bit my lip and hesitated. Being Chul's girlfriend—anyone's girlfriend—was new territory, and I didn't know the rules. But I didn't want the night to end. Not yet. "As long as your parents don't mind us being out so late. We don't have a curfew?"

He looked at me blankly like he didn't know what the word meant.

"You know, like do we have to be back at the house by a certain time?"

"My parents don't use curfews," he said.

"Okay." I shrugged and walked into the bedroom. It made sense. Chul didn't have a curfew because who would be around to enforce it?

There were three separate outfits laid out on a king-sized bed covered with enough poufy white bedding that I could have been in a bridal suite. Sets of shoes were neatly arranged on the floor near an oversized white velvet tufted chair.

I grabbed the clothes closest to me—jeans, a soft pale green shirt and white shoes. None of it was from the stuff in my closet. I just couldn't get used to how they blew through money like the world was their own personal all-you-can-eat buffet. Chul, at least, didn't show it off. He treated his fortune matter-of-factly. If he ever lost all his money, I was pretty sure he'd shrug and make some more. I quickly changed clothes and pulled the pins from my updo, letting my hair shake free.

When I came out, he'd already changed. Chul was just as distracting in jeans and a black leather jacket as he'd been in a tux. He held out an identical jacket for me.

"What's this for?" I asked.

"We're taking my bike. It will protect you from the wind."

"I've never been on a motorcycle before."

Chul moved to stand at my back and held open the jacket for me to slip on. "It's easy. You just have to hold on."

I hesitated. Even if I got past my fear of getting on a bike, there was still wrapping my arms around Chul. If just holding his hand turned me into a lovesick mess, then I didn't trust myself to not turn into a pile of senseless goo.

I slipped into the coat, and he leaned down to whisper in my ear. "Trust me." He turned to his grandparents who were still entranced by heat-packing Americans. "We're leaving now."

Both grandparents stood and Hyun paused the show. "Where are you taking Sydney this late at night?" Grandfather asked.

"Chul's taking her to Namsan Tower," Hyun said.

Chul nodded. "Sydney hasn't seen any of the sights in Korea yet."

"Really? I've always wanted to go," I said.

"Oh, Namsan is so romantic with all the lights. Are you putting a lock on?" Grandmother asked.

I knew about the locks at Namsan Tower. Couples would go there and put on a "padlock of love." It was supposed to symbolize that their love would last forever, but lots of tourists just went to Namsan for the view. My face warmed, and I wished Grandmother hadn't felt the need to bring up the locks.

"Not tonight," Chul said.

Grandmother looked disappointed. "You need to take her and put on a lock soon. It's good luck in our family. Your father did one for your mother." She stepped forward and took my hands in hers. "I'm so glad you'll be joining our family, dear."

"Um . . ." I paused, panic warring with confusion. Did these people not get what the word visit meant?

Chul took my arm, pulling me back. "We've got to get going. Goodnight, Grandmother, Grandfather. Hyun, I'll see you at the house." We walked quickly to the door. Once we reached the safety of the hallway he relaxed. "She really likes you."

"She barely knows me. She can't like me that much."

Chul cleared his throat. "My family has a soft spot for your mom. That extends to you."

I nodded but still felt uncomfortable. I didn't want to sound ungrateful, but I'd started to think that maybe I should talk with Suni and make myself clear so people wouldn't misunderstand me.

We rode the elevator down to the lobby and then exited through glass revolving doors. A shiny sleek bullet bike sat at the curb. Everything on it looked custom, from the green and black paint job, to the polished exhaust pipe.

Chul handed me a helmet before putting on his own and straddling his bike. He started the ignition, and the throttle sounded with a deep rumble.

I took a step back.

"Get on. It's perfectly safe."

I laughed nervously. I looked like an idiot just standing there, trembling like a little kid afraid to go on the rollercoaster. He watched me intently, which was almost worse. Finally, I climbed on the back and slapped my visor down.

"You need to hold onto me."

"I am. I'm holding your jacket," I said.

Chul grabbed my hands, wrapping them around his waist.

I leaned against him. There was no fighting the feel of his solid strength supporting mine. Chul was lean and sleek, and I could feel the cords of muscle under his jacket. He revved the engine once, and I held on tighter. Then we started to move. Lights blurred past me in a rush of colors. Muffled rumbles and the vibration of the bike overwhelmed my senses until all I could feel was cool against my legs. The rest of me stayed warm as I pressed tight against his back. I closed my eyes and relaxed against him. I didn't think it was possible to feel safe flying across pavement at 60 mph, but Chul made everything easy. Each new glimpse into his life added a depth to him that I wouldn't have seen at first glance. He wasn't just some hot guy from school. He had his own hurts and insecurities and definitely a few faults, but that all added up to make his drawing power stronger. I tried to imagine the first time he'd spoken to me. I'd come out of the bathroom at school, super upset at Mom, almost ready to cry, and there he was. He'd been sitting on the floor looking careless but also like he was waiting for me. In that moment, we'd never spoken, never met, but I'd already wanted to go to him.

When he killed the engine, it was like a song cut short. He put the kickstand down before taking off his helmet. I didn't want to let go.

"Syd?"

I liked the nickname—liked the way I could feel the vibration under my fingertips as he spoke.

He tapped my hands still wrapped around him. "We're here."

"Oh," I said, embarrassed. I let go, unbuckling my

helmet, and tried not to look dreamy as I slid off.

"Were you scared?" he asked.

"Not really."

He cocked an eyebrow.

"Maybe at first. But I'd never been on a motorcycle before." I grinned. "Now I'm thinking you should lend it to me for school."

Chul got off his bike. "Is that what you want?"

"I don't have a license."

He took a step closer. "But is that what you want?"

"I want a lot of things. That doesn't mean I'll get them."

He took my hand in his. "You wanted to see Namsan Tower, and now, here you are." I smiled and looked up at where the tower met the mountain. It lit the night sky in soft hues of purple, red, and blue.

"Do you like it?" He was so close.

"It's beautiful. Like the Korean version of a colorful Eiffel Tower."

"The Eiffel Tower is bigger," he said.

"You've seen it?" I asked. "Of course you have, why would I even ask?"

Chul looked at me, his eyes dark and serious. "I'll take you to Paris if you want to go."

I should have laughed, right then. I should have made a joke and played it off. Instead, I said something stupid. "I plan on saving my first trip to Paris for my honeymoon." My voice seemed to echo in the night air.

"Are you saying you want to marry me?" He grinned. "Let me think about it. I mean, you're cute."

"Cute? I thought I was Curves." I kept saying stupid things.

Chul's eyes glittered. "You're right, and that really seals the deal for me. When should we set the date?"

Finally, I found my laugh and pulled away. I smacked his arm lightly. "You're such a dork. Seriously, we're in high school."

He shrugged and took my hand again, but I was left with the feeling that he was only half joking. "Come on," he said. "Since we can't go to Paris tonight, let's see the top of Namsan."

We walked slowly down a paved path that led to a platform and a row of dark cable cars suspended on a line that rose up the mountain. "It looks closed," I said.

"It is, but Hyun talked with the manager. One of the operators agreed to stay after for us."

"Hyun is one awesome driver," I said. "You know he goes above and beyond, right?"

"I've never considered him a driver. He's more like family to us. We don't consider Hyun staff."

"But you pay him, and he does all these errands."

"He doesn't get paid. My parents gave Hyun shares of Kim Corporation years ago. He's very well-off now. He could probably buy an island somewhere and retire if he wanted. I think he stays mostly to keep me in line."

"That's really cool. Your parents are both good people."

Chul sighed. "They're generous with others, but never seem satisfied with me."

"I bet they're happier with you than you realize," I said. "My mom told me one time that kids think it's hard to grow up, but it's harder for parents. They're growing up with you. Moms and dads don't know what they're doing, but with each mistake, they get better. Maybe your parents just aren't done growing up."

Chul shrugged. "I like that you think of the positive with them. It's easier than me being mad at them all the time. I think I'm getting tired of being mad."

A man I assumed was the operator approached us. "I have your car ready, Mr. Kim."

Chul nodded and we followed him up to the last car in the line. He opened the door, and the car automatically lit up with a soft blue light. We stepped inside and took a seat. There was a rumble as gears started grinding, and the car trembled slightly, then started moving up, up, up in a slow, steady ascent.

I looked out the window at all the glittering lights. "How long is the ride?" I asked.

Chul turned me to face him. "Long enough to kiss you."

27

CHUL

Kissing Sydney would be easy. It felt natural to move close, to turn her in my direction and tangle my fingers through her silky hair, something I'd imagined since laying eyes on her. My other hand tilted her face up to mine. She looked startled and nervous. Before she could pull away, I leaned down and touched my lips to hers. She'd never been kissed before, so I moved slow, letting my mouth linger softly.

She drew in a breath and leaned into the kiss, all softness against me. Her fingers slid up my chest and entwined around my neck. I shuddered at her touch. I'd thought I was cool and in charge, but I wasn't ready for Sydney. I was lost if she ever let me go.

SYDNEY

There was only Chul, his nearness, one hand on my face, the other sliding through my hair. His mouth came down on mine, soft at first, but with each breath we moved closer. Kissing Chul felt like waking up, like there was nothing but us and the discovery that we should have been here all along. When he pulled back, I didn't want to stop. Somehow during the kiss, I'd wrapped my arms around his neck, and I pulled his lips back down to mine. I inhaled the scent of him, reveled in the strength of his arms holding me close, in the feel of his chest rising and falling. It all felt so right, like he was perfectly familiar. I broke away, knowing that if I let this feeling go unleashed, it would be hard to stop. I leaned against his chest and tried for calm.

He threaded his hands through my hair and breathed deeply. "Your hair drives me crazy."

I didn't know what to say. Everything with Chul drove me crazy. "I think I like you."

The deep rumble of his laugh vibrated against my face. "I would hope so after kissing me like that."

My head shot up. "Like what?" I met his gaze.

His eyes were dark and fierce. He cupped my face with both hands. "Like we were made for each other."

28

SYDNEY

Mom,

I'm dying to tell you all about the party. I'm on this cloud. But not hearing from you is ruining it.

When are you going to email? I'm starting to wonder if you've been kidnapped, or maybe you ran off with a new boyfriend. Maybe said boyfriend is a prince somewhere in the Middle East, and now you're living in a palace that doesn't allow outside communication. You could have joined the circus and they only do snail mail. Am I going to get a big pack of paper letters all at once tomorrow? I even dared hope that you've been secretly saving money and haven't written because you're going to show up on the Kims' doorstep any day now to surprise me.

Mom, I'm scared. You've never ignored me like this, and I have so much to tell you. I really need your advice here.

If I don't hear from you soon, I'm going to ask Suni to let me go home for a weekend visit.

Love,
Syd

I read the email one more time before clicking the send button. I wanted to tell my mom that I'd finally kissed a boy, and that boy was Chul. But none of it seemed important next to not hearing from her.

The paranoid part of my brain wondered if this was some new therapy Greg had talked her into. He was always saying how I needed separation. But would Mom really fall for something that dumb and cut off contact? I doubted it.

In the last year, she'd gotten more firm with Greg. She'd even banned him from the house when he said the living environment was too depressing. I ended up going to his office after, which was no better, but at least he wasn't in our own personal space. My phone pinged on my bed, and I flipped it over.

> **Loser:**
> **Do you want to get**
> **breakfast?**

I bit my lip and flipped it facedown again. Chul shouldn't be any girl's first kiss. He may have ruined my chances to enjoy a kiss with anyone else ever again. The guy was just too perfect. His smell, his hands on my face. I shook myself. I could not think about him. I was going home after the semester. I might be his girlfriend, but we couldn't kiss like that again if I wanted to keep my heart safe. My phone pinged again.

> **Loser:**
> **Better idea. I'll**
> **pack us breakfast**
> **and we can eat it in**
> **the car. Let's drive**
> **to the beach today.**

I watched as another text bubble popped up. He was typing. Chul didn't understand that every kind gesture, word, every memory of us together, would haunt me when I left. He was Kim Chul. He would move on. I'd cry and pine, and mope.

And all of it would be fuel for the fire with Greg. I couldn't face him. Not until I had a plan. I texted back.

I'm not feeling great. Still tired from the party. I just want to stay in my room

29

CHUL

I flopped down on my bed with a groan. There was a ninety-nine percent chance Sydney was in her room writing another email to her mom. I couldn't read it, or I'd be lying. She hated lying.

It had taken me hours to exit out of her computer and now the temptation to hack back in settled over me. The locator on her phone was a safety thing, but anything beyond that would make me a crazy stalker at this point.

I did feel kind of crazy, though. I couldn't stop thinking about her hair, and a guy who couldn't stop thinking about a girl's hair had to be insane on some level. Maybe if it was just the hair, I wouldn't be, but I also had it bad for her lips, smile, laugh, the way she smelled.   Especially the way she smelled.

I wouldn't read it. But yeah, I was probably a crazy stalker.

Hyun knocked on my door before opening it. He carried a breakfast tray and a frown. "What happened to Sydney last night? She won't take breakfast or come out of her room."

I propped myself up on the bed and tried for the innocent look, but this was Hyun.

He put the tray down. "What did you do, Chul?"

I sat up and crossed my legs. "I took her to Namsan." I shrugged. "You know."

Hyun grumbled and picked up the tray. "If she won't eat,

you're not eating either."

I jumped off the bed and blocked Hyun at the door before he could leave.

"Move, if you don't want a beating," Hyun said.

"I don't. Hear me out first."

Hyun placed the tray on my desk but slid it out of my reach. "Okay, I'll ask again. What happened to Sydney?"

I swallowed. I knew Hyun really wouldn't beat me, but he looked terrifying. "I kissed her. That's it. Nothing too intense. She seemed to like it, but now she won't see me. I didn't know she refused breakfast."

Hyun looked at the floor and stroked his chin. "Hmm. It could be just about anything bothering her after a kiss. She liked it, she didn't like it, she thinks you didn't like it. My only advice is to find out what it is before you have a bigger problem."

"That's not much advice."

Hyun shrugged. "No two women are alike, so it's a little trial and error at this stage."

"I thought you were good at this kind of thing."

"I am. You'll never be as smooth with the ladies. Luckily, you only have Sydney to figure out."

I scoffed. "Can I eat now?"

Hyun stood, seeming satisfied and a little too happy at my predicament. "Make sure she eats something," he said, before walking out.

30

SYDNEY

I rolled over in bed with a groan and tapped the snooze button on my phone. My first thought was that Mom better have answered me. My second was that I'd kissed Chul. There'd be no avoiding him today with school. I pressed my hands against my chest to settle my heart.

I kissed Chul.

I picked my phone back up. There was one email from my friend, Beth, wondering where I'd disappeared to, and four from Greg that I moved to junk mail without reading. Nothing from Mom. I rubbed my eyes and started a text.

> **Hi Suni,**
> **Sorry to be a**
> **bother, but I'm**
> **worried that I**
> **haven't heard**
> **from my mom.**
> **Have you talked**
> **to her? She doesn't**
> **have a phone right**
> **now, but she does**
> **have email. Do**
> **you think next**
> **weekend I could**
> **fly home for a**
> **visit? I could leave**

Thursday and take
a red-eye and then
fly home Saturday.
I'd be back in
school by Monday.
I just want to
check that she is
doing okay.

Suni:
I'm sorry, with the
party yesterday I
completely forgot
to tell you. I spoke
to Shannon briefly
from a phone she
borrowed. Her
computer finally
died but she said
to tell you that
she loves you
and wants you to
wait to hear from
her. She's buying
a new one after
she gets paid. You
are welcome to
ask her what she
thinks of a short
trip in your next
email.

I stared at my phone and frowned. Suni had to be
joking. A broken computer? But then this was my mom we
were talking about. She was so analog that she still did all her
banking by hand in a little white paper register. Putting off
buying a new computer wouldn't be hard for her. And I was
pretty sure she'd never go to the library and use an unfamiliar
one.

I hated this. But here I was with a zillion dollar wardrobe, top of the line tech, and Mom was burning the candle at both ends with overtime to save for a cheap laptop. I sat up, feeling small for getting mad, and texted Suni back.

I'm glad she's okay. I'll wait to hear from her next week. If you get to talk again, tell her to find a way to call me.

**Suni:
I will for sure, sweetheart.**

I dressed in a clean uniform, blue sneakers, and white knee-highs. I put my hair up in a high ponytail and wore the stud earrings that I still preferred to think of as fake diamonds. If I could find Hyun this early, I'd convince him to drive me and disappear before Chul even got up. I grabbed my backpack and ran out the door—straight into something solid.

Warm hands grabbed my shoulders to steady me. "Hey, what's the hurry?" Chul asked.

I stared into his dark eyes, and his lips quirked up in an easy smile. He'd already showered, and his damp hair was spiky on the ends. I was too close; his scent triggered all kinds of dopamine dumps in my brain. Was I leaning closer? I retreated one step and his arms fell from my shoulders. "Hi," I said, trying not to sound breathless. "I'm just grabbing some breakfast."

"You have plenty of time. We don't have to leave for an hour."

"Oh, I was going to have Hyun drive me. I need to get there early."

Chul frowned. "Why?"

My mind raced. "Math. I need Teacher Jang to help me with the last assignment."

"I can help you with math."

"That's okay. I don't want to bother you."

"It's no bother. You're my girlfriend."

I laughed, nervously. "I know, but you don't need to help me with every little thing." I turned to walk away. Chul moved fast. His palm landed against the wall in front of me, blocking my exit.

"What's going on?" he asked.

Chul had a way with being direct. Usually I liked that, but it also made hiding from him hard. I'd agreed to be his girlfriend, and we'd kissed. There was almost no back-pedaling from here.

I turned, and Chul's other hand braced against the wall, boxing me in. He stepped in so close my back bumped against the picture behind me. "What game are we playing here, Sydney?" His voice was soft and calm.

I tried to gather my scrambled thoughts. It felt like all the blood had rushed to my head. "I just want to go to school with Hyun like before."

"You're forgetting something, though."

"I didn't forget. I agreed to be your girlfriend, but that doesn't mean things have to be serious."

"If kissing you isn't serious, then you have a different view on relationships. Everyone, including myself, thinks we're a couple. That means we drive together. I help you when you need it. Maybe that's with math. You do the same for me, like with my parents. We date, and text, and yes, I'm going to hold your hand. And absolutely I'm going to kiss you. Why are you doubting us?"

I tilted my face up to his. He was so close. Everything he said sounded awesome. Chul would be the perfect boyfriend. Except, I was going home. Time here was short, and honestly, most of living with Chul felt surreal. This world wasn't mine, so hanging out with him would always feel like pretending. I pushed hard at his chest, and he took a step back, folding his arms. "I'm leaving here in December," I said. "Maybe even sooner, so it will be hard if I get in too deep with you. I need to keep things friendly."

Chul did not look moved by any of it. My mind desperately tried to find something that would convince him that we needed to rewind. "We won't work, Chul."

"You told me lying was never okay."

I winced.

"I'll be downstairs. *I'm* taking you to school, not Hyun."

"You seem different, Sydney," Chul said, as he opened the front door to Daeshim. He held my hand firmly in his and nodded at other students who gaped as we passed.

"What? Why?" I stammered.

"I don't know, you just do. Did something happen? Maybe . . . after the party?"

I pursed my lips. "Do you want to die?"

"No, I just want you to stop ignoring me."

"I'm not ignoring you."

Chul lowered his voice as we entered the hallway so other students wouldn't hear our conversation. A few people stared at our hands laced together. "You were being so polite and distant in the car that an outsider would think we were strangers on a bus. If you don't want this to get embarrassing, then you need to relax."

How could I when Chul made me forget my own rules? It scared me to admit it, but after our kiss, I knew there needed to be more to my life than just working hard to stay close to Mom. I bit my lip. "Fine, but no PDA. We don't need to hold hands or anything. We can just be friendly, and I'll sit with you at lunch." I tried to yank my hand back.

Chul didn't miss a step and easily held on. "No. I'm

definitely holding my girlfriend's hand, but maybe I won't go so far as to kiss you in the hallway." He glanced down at me and winked.

I tried hard not to grin back at him, but it was too late for me. I was already falling down the Chul rabbit hole.

I propped my elbow on my desk and leaned my face against my hand. I could see Chul through the shop windows as he helped Sun-he cut acrylic pieces for their robotic arm. Watching Chul was quickly becoming a favorite pastime of mine. Sun-he laughed at something he said. Out of everyone at Daeshim, she was by far the most excited about Chul and me being a couple. Today she wore her hair in a cute bun with green and pink ribbons woven through. It made her look like she was barely out of grade school even though she was a sophomore. That was part of Sun-he's charm though. She was happy and loving and rocked the innocent look. Unless you were Ae-ri or Min. With those two, her mood always went dark.

I pulled out my phone and checked if Mom had written me back. My inbox was empty except for one email from Greg's office at Mountain View Behavioral Health hospital. The thought that he'd told Mom not to email me nagged at my mind again. That was exactly the kind of crap therapy he would try. I opened the email from the hospital and skimmed through.

Mountain View Behavior Health
0627 Loma Vista Blvd
Los Angeles, CA 90021

Dear Miss Moore,

I am writing to remind you of your upcoming diagnostic testing in our clinic with Dr. Gregory Moore on October 12th. Please allow 5-6 hours for the testing. You may visit our web site at MountainViewInterventions.com or call our office at (323) 555-2020 to confirm.

Sincerely,

Natalie Pormasher
Executive Assistant
N.Pormasher@mountainviewinterventions.com

Greg could throw all the fits he wanted, but I couldn't go back for more "tests" while I lived thousands of miles away. He'd probably bug Mom, though. I was sure he'd sent her a letter too. Only not a form letter from his stupid assistant. It would be one of those personal letters he liked to send that were full of scare tactics and guilt trips.

I stood up and peered through the shop windows. Most of the students were still in there. Teacher Choe was occupied with fixing someone's broken shock absorber, and Chul looked like he'd be busy until the end of class. No one seemed to notice me, so I sat back down and opened my laptop for a quick email.

Mom,

Suni told me about the computer. Bummer. You probably won't get to read this until you get the new one, but just in case you do, I wanted you to know how well I'm doing here. And if Greg is giving you a hard time, you can tell him that I'm eating and sleeping fine, making friends, and my grades are good. So don't let him guilt-trip you. You're an amazing mom, and I can't believe I'm saying this, but I'm glad you sent me on this trip. It's been really good for me.

Love you,
Sydney.

"You must really miss your mom." Min's voice came from directly over my shoulder. Her words sounded concerned, but I knew they were laced with hate.

I quickly closed my laptop, but I was sure she'd read at

least part of what I wrote. How had I been stupid enough to do anything personal with Min in the room? Chul had said she wouldn't let what happened at the party go. I believed him. From the eager way she watched me, I could tell she was the big bad wolf of revenge. If I wasn't careful, she'd find a way to hurt me, and the whole school would watch. Chul wouldn't, but she'd wait until he wasn't around. Even knowing this, I loved to egg her on.

"Yeah, sometimes I get a little homesick, but I have Chul's mom. She loves me so much. I'm like the daughter she never had. And the best part is that I get to live under the same roof as my Oppa."

Min turned bright red. I looked at her with exaggerated concern. "Are you okay, Min?" But she got my message. She'd been the unwanted houseguest, and I was the new resident. Rubbing that in a little sort of made up for the poison she and Ae-ri dished out.

Ae-ri stepped in to save face. "Since all of us here have wealthy parents, or in your case, Sydney, godparents, we like to give back to the community with our charity club. Min and I are sponsoring an event, and we really need your help. This month we've chosen something very special."

"Great, I can't wait," I said.

"Sydney won't be there," Min blurted out. "She thinks it's below her station. When the lower classes get their hooks in money, they have no compassion for those less fortunate."

A lot of the other students perked up at this, and I realized everyone in the room was listening in. Two girls to my right started whispering and shooting me dirty looks.

"Yeah, tell that to all the homeless families I served in the soup kitchen every summer," I said. "I'll definitely be there."

Min folded her arms and looked at me with a challenge. "We'll see, but I doubt you'll help, even if you do come."

"She might not even have time," Ae-ri said. "She probably needs to go see her psychiatrist."

The boy sitting in front of me turned around in his seat. I didn't know him, but he seemed nice, just a little quiet.

"You can't miss any appointments," Min said. "Remember what happened last time?"

The boy's eyes went wide.

"They're just making stuff up," I said.

Ae-ri whispered loud enough for the whole room to hear. "I heard she gets violent without her meds."

The boy got up and packed up his stuff to move seats while sneaking worried looks in my direction.

Min stopped him with a soft hand on his wrist. "No one should feel unsafe here." The boy smiled, obviously a little too caught up in Min's orbit. She let go of his wrist, and he walked away. When she turned back to me, more of the class had gathered to watch. I glanced through the shop window. Chul had his back to me, bent over his work. It was just as well. I needed to deal with Min on my own

Min folded her arms and stood tall like she was some kind of protector. "We're not going to put up with your craziness, Sydney, so watch yourself."

I swear she could smell weakness. Once she caught a trail, she'd dig until she unearthed every single skeleton in the closet. Crazy was a big one for me.

Greg loved calling me that and every other name he could come up with: nutso, certifiable, looney-toons, batty, brain-zed, head-case, schizo. And just this last year he'd started in on how I might be a bleeper, which is slang for bipolar. I'd heard them all.

I squared my shoulders and faced the room. Class wasn't over but I knew when to make my exit. "I'm not violent, and I don't see a psychiatrist. You can count me in on your charity club." I walked out of the room with my head held high. Girls like Min and Ae-ri couldn't work half as hard as I could. I had nothing to worry about.

31

CHUL

Gun leaned against my locker with his stupid shirt sleeves rolled up. He was showing off for two girls as they giggled and ran past.

"What do you want?" I asked, elbowing him aside so I could open my locker. "I'm busy."

Gun moved just barely enough for me to get the door open. "If you want to take care of Sydney, you need to control Min."

I ground my teeth. Was he ever going to bug off? "There's not much they can do now that she's my girlfriend."

"Tell me you're not that dumb, Chul." Gun shook his head. "Min does whatever she wants. Sydney being your girlfriend isn't enough. If you don't get that, then you shouldn't be with her."

I scoffed. "And you should?"

"Hate me all you want, but I really do care for her."

I glared at him, but he didn't flinch or look away.

"Look, I know what happened with my sister was my fault." Gun looked down at the floor, and a frown creased between his brows. "I regret it. That's why I don't want the same thing to happen with Sydney."

"Let me worry about her. You go ahead and keep regretting what a lame excuse for a brother you turned out to be."

"I've screwed up, but at least I'm trying to fix things. You just keep making the same mistakes over and over with Min. Do you really think you can just play house with Sydney and not expect Min to tear her apart?"

I slammed my locker shut. "I've got to go to class."

Gun pushed off the wall of lockers and turned to walk past but stopped and spoke over his shoulder. "I'll be there for her, since you can't."

I wanted to tackle him, to wipe the shiny tiled floor with his face and choke him with those words. I gripped my backpack tighter and took a deep breath to keep from losing it.

"Hey." Sun-he appeared at my side, but her carefree smile was gone. "What was that all about?"

"Nothing. Just Gun being Gun."

"I heard part of what he said. I think he might be right, though." She cleared her throat, casting nervous glances at my face.

"You think I can't take care of Sydney?"

"No." She waved her hands back and forth. "That's not what I meant at all. I just have heard some weird rumors lately, and I do think Min is up to something."

"What have you heard?"

Sun-he bit her lip and looked away.

"Tell me."

"A lot of people are saying that Sydney's some kind of mental patient, unstable. I even heard she threatened Min."

"That's rich," I said. "Most of the student body here have their therapists on speed dial."

Sun-he didn't smile. "I just know that Min has a knack for coming off as the hero in public. She can make a lot of people believe Sydney is the bad guy. Have you checked Min's social media lately? She's been hinting that someone stole her boyfriend."

I hadn't checked any of Min's accounts for a long time now. "Thanks for telling me."

Sun-he nodded. "Just be careful. I don't think there is much that Min wouldn't do, now that she knows you don't like her." She stomped her foot. "Ugh, I really hate those girls."

"It's okay, Sun-he. I'll take care of it."

Sun-he nodded, then bounded off to her next class.

I looked down the hall and saw Sydney making her way to my locker and dodging a frisbee that some idiot threw. I waved, and she smiled like she was relieved to see me. I had trouble walking straight when she did that. "Hey," I said when she got to my locker. I laced our fingers together. "Where'd you disappear to? You left class early."

"Oh, I had to go to the bathroom, and then class was over."

She was the worst liar. "Okay," I said, letting it drop. "My parents are flying in today, and they want us to eat dinner together."

Sydney beamed. "Really? Like an actual family sit-down dinner with everyone?"

I nodded, not nearly as excited as she was. "Even my father's going to be there."

"Wait." She frowned. "What are we eating? Do I have to eat what you guys eat?"

"My mother asked the chef to make something American. I think it's a pie with chicken."

"Oh, chicken pot pie? I'm sure that's it. This will be perfect, then." She looked at me expectantly. "Won't it?"

I knew she kept up this hope that I'd spend more time with my parents. I leaned down close until our noses almost touched. "With you there, it will be."

Before dinner that night, Hyun came in my room. I sat on my bed studying—or pretending to. Sydney refused to work with me any more because she said I was too distracting. I couldn't decide if I liked that or not. The idea that I distracted her just made me want to think of more ways to be distracting. But for the sake of her grades and mine, I'd agreed to three hours a night of Sydney-free homework.

Hyun cleared his throat. "Where's Sydney?"

"In her room. Probably trying to get a better grade in math than me."

"No, she's not."

I grabbed my phone and called her.

I waited and it went to voicemail. "I'll find her," I said. Hyun eyed me, but I kept up the act of confident boyfriend who could read his girlfriend's mind.

She seemed to like the library, so I checked there first. Only one small lamp lit the corner. I turned to leave, but the heavy velvet curtain next to the sofa moved. I waited for my eyes to adjust, and then I could see it, a Sydney-shaped outline behind the curtain. I crouched down and pulled the fabric back.

She startled. "You scared me."

"Why are you hiding?"

"I'm not." But she wiped at her eyes, and I could see that she'd been crying.

"Hey." I took her face in my hands. "What's wrong?" I kissed her lips, feather-soft, and then moved to kiss each eyelid. I wanted to kiss her until she never cried again. "Tell me," I said.

Sydney wrapped her arms around my neck and leaned against my shoulder. "Suni's been lying to me."

I stiffened.

"I called my mom's work. I haven't heard from her, and it's been weeks. She would have had time to buy a new computer by now, but she still won't contact me."

I sat next to her, not sure what to do. "What did her work say?"

She pulled away, and her eyes burned with anger. "They said she doesn't work there anymore. She quit the day I flew here."

Dinner started late because Sydney wanted to take a shower. I didn't blame her. Her eyes and nose had been red and puffy when we left the library.

We both sat down, but Sydney didn't say a word. I knew my mother was overly anxious about the meal, and us showing up thirty minutes late only made her more so.

My mother waved across the heavy spread of food. "What do you think, Sydney?" There was a steaming chicken pie in the middle of the table.

"It looks nice," Sydney mumbled.

My mother frowned as she scooped up a big serving and placed it on Sydney's plate. "I had Chef make this just for you. He's been watching YouTube all morning to learn the perfect technique."

Sydney snorted. "Chicken pot pie isn't supposed to be perfect. That's the beauty of it. Everything is dumped in there, you cover it in a messy dough, and then it comes out lumpy and even less perfect than when you started." She raised angry eyes to my mother, whose mouth formed a pinched line.

I noted the uniform slits in the crust, the pristine pinches along the edges of Chef's pie.

My father cleared his throat and took the serving spoon from my mother. "Let's just eat." He began dishing up plates.

"I wasn't trying for perfect," my mother spoke tersely.

Hyun and my father exchanged a look.

"I was trying to cheer you up. You've seemed worried," she said.

"I am worried," Sydney snapped.

I took a breath to speak, but my mother spoke over me.

"You shouldn't be. Focus on school and just have fun." She frosted her words with an empty smile.

"You want me to have fun?" Sydney's voice trembled. "My mom quit her freaking job. She would never do that. She's the queen of overtime."

My mother kept up her facade of sweetness and spoke softly. "Maybe she wanted a break. She could have been tired or sick of her job."

"Stop. I don't believe you anymore. Everything is glossed over, half-truths. Just tell me. What is going on?"

My mother closed her eyes and took a deep breath. "I sent Shannon money when I found out she quit her job. I've spoken to her frequently, and she is doing fine. She loves hearing about you."

"How are you talking to her? She doesn't have a phone. No landline. No computer. How?"

Suni paused and her voice went quiet. "I've been visiting Shannon between my trips to Canada."

"You've been visiting my mom and didn't tell me?" Sydney stood up, shaking with rage. "I'm going home."

"Stay right where you are." None of us could mistake the steel in my mother's voice.

"No." Sydney turned to go, but my mother spoke quickly.

"If you don't want to ruin all my careful planning, then you need to listen to me. I've finally convinced Shannon to move here," she said. "I'm going to get her next week."

32

SYDNEY

Mom,

I don't know if you're reading any of this, but Suni's leaving Friday to fly to California and bring you back here. I have so many questions. I'm still confused. Is it Greg? You haven't contacted me. You quit your job. I just don't know what to think. Are you okay? Honestly though, none of it matters if you're coming to Korea. And I can't believe I'm saying this, but I'm happy to stay if you're here. Chul has become important to me, more than I can tell you in an email. I think you just need to meet him and then I know that you'll understand how I feel. I think I love him.

Sydney

Early in the morning, the rain had started soft, barely a threat. Now it came down like it existed to wash Korea away all together. Chul and I waited with the rest of the charity club. The van that was supposed to pick us up was fifteen minutes late. Even with Chul's coat and umbrella, I stood shivering. Min and Ae-ri had been excused early to meet Min's personal driver, who was bringing a van. But with those two in charge, who knew what would happen. Maybe half their fun was making me stand in the freezing rain.

"Let's go back inside. They're not coming," Chul said.

"You know I can't back out now. Look at all the rumors

they've spread. Haven't you heard that I'm a spoiled American who lives off the Kims' money with no desire to help the less fortunate? Oh, and my favorite. I'm a seductress who stole you from the rest of the world through evil American trickery."

"None of that matters, Syd. You know I don't care, so why do you?"

"I'm not leaving," I said through chattering teeth.

Dean Nari approached the students huddled in front of us. "The girls just texted. Their driver had to get gas and should be here any minute."

Just then a white van with tinted windows pulled up to the curb. Min opened the side door holding a clipboard and stepped down onto the pavement. Ae-ri hopped out next to her. Everyone tried to push past each other to get in out of the cold.

Min threw out her arm, blocking entry. "Wait," she yelled above the rain. "I need to call your name. Only school-approved members are allowed on the field trip."

Chul grabbed my arm. "This isn't right."

"Sydney Moore," Min called first.

I tried to step forward, but Chul's grip went to iron. "Don't go. Wait until I get on first."

"Hurry up. What are you waiting for?" Ae-ri said.

The students parted and a chorus of irritated voices called out. "What's the hold up? I'm freezing."

Chul didn't let go. "Wait."

I twisted and jerked my arm away. In two steps I started climbing in. Hands pushed at my back with everyone piling in after me as Min rattled off the names. I moved to the rear and sat down quickly. Between tinted windows and the rain, it was dark inside. I craned my neck to look for Chul. I watched Min and Ae-ri get on last with satisfied smiles. He wasn't getting on. I pushed my way back to the front.

"Looks like you'll be on your own today," Min said as I passed her seat.

I could see Chul standing on the sidewalk arguing with

Dean Nari.

"I'm sorry, but your name isn't on my list." Dean Nari shook her head. "You need to go find your advisor and get a signature if you want to attend."

"Check again," Chul said. "I registered with this club last week. The same day as Sydney."

"I have no record of your registration, and again, there is no Kim Chul on my list. I can't authorize your transportation or for you to miss class."

Chul raised his head and searched for me. When our eyes met, he motioned for me to come to him.

Dean Nari turned and started to climb in, but I was in the way. "On or off, Sydney. You can't just stand here."

I hesitated. If I got off, then it would be the same as admitting the rumors were true. But if I didn't get out, I'd face the Min/Ae-ri firing squad alone. I sighed and shook my head at Chul. He was seething. Clearly this wasn't in the plan, but I couldn't help things now. I moved back to my seat in the rear and watched out the window as we started rolling. Chul had already walked away, but instead of back to the school he headed in the direction of the parking lot. He'd never get to his car in time to follow us. I hoped he wasn't so mad that he'd just go home.

I sat back in my seat feeling more defeated than I was willing to let on.

"I told you," came a familiar voice from the corner.

I turned. Gun sat unmoving across from me in the last seat on the van. Since the Kims' party, I'd avoided him—given off a cold-frost vibe. But I always felt his eyes watching me. "What are you doing here? You're not even a member of this club."

He smiled. "I'm here to help out."

I scoffed. "What, like, are you here to help Min?"

"She thinks that, but I could be helping you."

"I don't need anyone's help," I snapped. "Especially not someone who chases me down stairs like a lunatic."

He sighed. "I overreacted at the hotel. Just remember that I'm here for you when you need it."

I turned my back to him and watched the rain slide down my window for the rest of the drive. I wished it would stop. I really wished Chul was here holding my hand so I didn't feel so alone. The van slowed and turned onto a lane that wound up the mountainside. A modern white building with long horizontal windows sat at the end. Everything about the structure screamed hospital, and my eyes found the vertical sign on the side of the building that said what I'd feared: *Seoul Children's Hospital.* I shuddered.

I already knew Min had a copy of my school file and that she was the one driving the rumors. But there was one I couldn't talk about with Chul. The rumor that I was crazy, that even the shrinks in America couldn't help me hit too close to home. Whispers followed me down the halls, and just three days ago, I'd found a photoshopped picture of myself in a straitjacket taped all over my locker.

But apparently the rumors were just her first strike. This deeper cut meant she knew more. Somewhere in that file my mom must have written that I was what Greg called *"paralyzed with fear"* when I got anywhere near a hospital. He'd exaggerated it of course, but there *was* truth there. I'd certainly had my share of panic attacks sitting by my mom's bedside.

The van stopped. I waited in the back and watched as one by one, everyone climbed out with umbrellas in hand. I didn't even have that. I'd left mine when I stepped out from under the one Chul had held over me. I still wore his coat, so I flipped up the hood. Gun stood up. "Come on, Sydney, we're here."

My mouth went dry, and my legs felt rubbery when I tried to stand, but I nodded slowly. I took a few steps, then stumbled down the aisle. Gun caught me and pulled me close, closer than he needed to. "You're okay," he said softly.

Anger replaced my fear, and I pushed away hard. "I said I didn't need your help." I stood up, back straight and tugged

Chul's coat close around me. It hung oversized and warm, and it smelled like him. I was taking what comfort I could.

I walked quickly to the front and climbed out. After that, I did my best and followed the line of students through the front door of the hospital.

Dean Nari was busy passing out bags of wrapped presents to each group of students. "These are for the children you will visit today. I have you split into groups. When I call your name, please go together to visit the children on your assigned floor. We will meet at noon back in the lobby."

I accepted the bag and counted eight identically wrapped gifts. I knew exactly how it felt to be stuck here. My hours in a small, cold room, praying on hard chairs and not knowing when we would ever leave had given me hard won compassion. If nothing else, I could kind of relate to these kids. I wasn't sick, but I knew this world, knew how bad it sucked.

Min and Ae-ri watched me closely, like they were sharks hunting for the scent of blood. I smiled wide and raised both eyebrows at them.

Dean Nari called out names. "Min, Ae-ri, Gun, and Sydney, you have the second floor. These are terminal children, so be sensitive to their circumstances." I nodded, understanding the seriousness of this.

Min shoved her backpack at Gun. "Here, hold it." She turned to me and smiled, all sweetness. "Are you ready for this?"

"I'm here, aren't I?"

She stared with hardness and hate in her eyes. "Go ahead and lead, then. You should know your way around a hospital since you practically lived in one with your sick mom."

I pinched my lips together and balled my hands into fists to keep steady. Honestly, the only thing stopping me from slapping her was the Kims' good reputation. I turned away and followed the main hall until I came to a double set of elevators. We got on, and Gun pushed the button for the second floor.

The walls were bright murals of underwater seascapes, and the ceiling was painted to look like the ocean from below. Everything was made to create a sense of calm and happy, with enough whimsy for even a sick child to smile.

The doors opened and I stepped off to the familiar smells of antiseptic mixed with the subtle undercurrent of rot and infection. The tired, steady cry of discomfort came from one of the rooms down the hall.

None of it upset me. I didn't freeze in fear or even hesitate. I was here for someone else, someone sick who may not get the miracle I got with my own mom.

The nurse's station separated the two halls on that floor. I approached a woman at the desk. She had dark circles under her eyes and looked exhausted. "Excuse me," I said.

She yawned over her computer but didn't look up. "Visiting hours will end at noon so if you want to get started there are two patients in room 2188. You can start there." The woman looked up suddenly and met my eyes. "I'm sorry, I should have introduced myself, first. I'm the head nurse here. We're understaffed today, so thank you for coming and helping with these sweet darlings." She lowered her voice. "Most of them don't have much time. We try to keep things as cheerful as we can."

"I understand." I'd never considered the struggles of the nurses before. I should have been more thankful to the staff where my mom stayed. They had saved her, after all. In these buildings where Death walked the halls, there were also doctors, nurses, and therapists who worked to drive his dark shadows away. I swallowed hard, almost overcome with emotion.

I turned back to see Min and Ae-ri trailing along behind, practically holding each other in fear. Ae-ri's eyes kept darting to the room where the soft crying now rose to wails. Two nurses walked quickly to the room with worried looks and closed the door.

Gun moved past them, unconcerned, and stopped in

front of me. "Are you sure you can do this? I'm here if you need me."

I nodded, still feeling calm. "I can do the job we came to do."

Gun held an arm out to the first door. "Then, ladies first."

Min and Ae-ri still clung to each other but shuffled forward eagerly. They both watched me like I was some kind of walking apocalyptic event just waiting to happen. And the truth was, they might be right. So far, the hospital had been easy. There'd been no blood, no surgical equipment, syringes, IVs, nothing that screamed medical. But as I approached the room, I knew that could all change. I might crack, or freak out, or just start crying. Then the sharks would finally have real blood in the water. I cleared my mind and thought of what I'd felt as a small child. If my older self could have held my hand for a moment, smiled and told me it would be okay, would that have helped? I squared my shoulders and walked in.

The small boy hobbling from the bathroom rasped with effort. His thin arms and legs quivered as he reached the side of his bed and he paused to catch his breath. Long, clear tubing went from his taped wrist up to a portable IV stand that his tired-looking mother pushed behind him. Neither of them smiled. The mom half lifted her son to get him back up on his bed and then tucked a bright orange and yellow block quilt around his shoulders. His face could have been ten years old, but his body was so slight, he seemed much younger.

"Hello, we're here from Daeshim Academy." I spoke in a soft voice.

The woman turned with surprise and blinked at us where we stood in the doorway. "Oh, hello."

"Would it be okay to visit with you and your son?" I asked.

"Yes, of course. Thank you." The mother gave a slight bow and motioned for us to come in. I walked slowly into the room with Min and Ae-ri following. Gun walked next to me, looking around curiously but not uncomfortable.

I glanced over to the other end of the room where a little girl in a pink gown rubbed at sleepy eyes. Other than the two beds with a folding chair next to each, the room lacked any comforts. We stood at the end of the bed. "What's your name?" I asked.

The boy looked at his mom and tucked his chin shyly.

"My son's name is Ae-jung." Everything about the mom looked worn and frayed. I knew from experience that she'd been sleeping in that chair for more than one night. Her shirt and pants were wrinkled, and her skin and hair needed washing. Only her eyes looked alert, and in them I clearly read her silent plea for us not to pity her son.

I didn't know what Ae-jung's condition was. He had the classic signs of a stroke. The left side of his face drooped, but it had to be more than that if he was staying on this floor. Treating him like his time was short, even if it was true, was the worst thing I could do. I smiled brightly. "Hey, Ae-jung. I'm Sydney, and these are my assistants, Min, Ae-ri, and Gun. They follow me around all day and do what I say. That's why they're being so quiet, because I'm in charge, here." I cupped my hand over my mouth and whispered conspiratorially. "Don't say anything, but I didn't get them a present. Just one for you and your friend." I pointed at the sleeping girl. I heard Min's sharp intake of air behind me, but it sounded like Gun muffled a laugh.

Ae-jung snickered. I pulled out one of the gifts from the bag Dean Nari had given us. It sparkled with red foil wrapping and a sun-yellow ribbon. He gasped. "Can I open it now?" His words slurred with effort.

"Only if you promise to take your medicine after lunch," his mom said.

Ae-jung nodded.

Gun took the package from me and stepped forward to place the gift on Ae-jung's lap. "Here, let me help." He pulled a pocketknife out and cut the ribbon and tape from the foil.

Ae-jung watched Gun with the knife and then looked at me expectantly.

"It's okay," I said. "I let him have that as long as he's careful."

Gun laughed and winked at him.

Ae-jung smiled for the first time, his face lopsided and strained, but joy shined on his face. Gun stepped back and let Ae-jung peel back the wrapping. It was a new tablet. He stopped, and his hands shook. "Can I play?" he whispered, almost reverent.

His mom's eyes misted over, and she turned away, dabbing at them with a tissue. "Of course, you can play," she said. "Thank you so much for this."

"You're welcome," I said. "Gun can help set it up if you want."

"I bet you'd like to play Tenter," Gun said. "It was one of my favorites when I was your age. Let's get you started, and I can load your account with some *won*."

Ae-jung made a feeble attempt at a bounce on his bed. "Cool!"

Min and Ae-ri had stayed silent through the whole exchange, so I peeked at them from over my shoulder. They both had their backs pressed against the wall and watched Ae-jung like he was contagious or something. Idiots. They followed me when I moved to the other bed. As I got closer, I could hear the little girl's faint rasp. She lay motionless against sweat-soaked sheets except for the rapid rising and falling of her chest. Her color was dusky, and I quickly looked to her monitor, something that would tell me her numbers, but she wasn't hooked up. Her oxygen tube had been taped to her face, but she'd pulled it out of her nose and now struggled with every breath.

Min and Ae-ri moved up from behind and peered around me at the girl.

"Get a nurse, quickly," I said.

"Shut up," Min snapped. "The nurses come when they

are needed. If you're so worried about her, why don't you help?" One of them shoved me from behind, and I stumbled against the guard rails on the side of the bed. The little girl jerked awake, and her eyes went big. I reached forward with trembling hands to try and readjust her tubing. She just needed oxygen. Then she would be okay. I moved the flexible plastic to her small nose. It looked red and raw from where the cannula had rubbed. I gently guided it in and gave the girl a shaky smile. Her eyes went from wide to panicked, and she began clawing at the cannula. I tried to grab her hands, but then she immediately started a coughing fit. A trickle of blood spilled from her left nostril.

Min and Ae-ri moved to my side. "Look what you did. You're hurting her."

All my warning signs of a panic attack went off at once. My chest got tight, my heart raced, my arms pricked with cold, and I saw grey spots floating in my vision. I needed air, but fear and pain filled every muscle, every cell. I pressed my hands to my chest and focused on just getting one small breath as my face crumpled in panic. I couldn't freak out like this. No one else here would help this girl. I shut my eyes, refusing to break, and drew in air. I took slow steady breaths. I thought about everyone I loved. When I opened my eyes, I could move again.

Both Min and Ae-ri had their phones out and the little green light that said they were filming was on.

"We caught everything," Min said.

Ae-ri laughed. "You're such a freak, Sydney."

Did it really matter that they'd filmed me? Should I even care? Or was one little girl and every child in this hospital more important than what the students at Daeshim thought?

I knew the answer—had for a while now. The only way to get free of Greg and all his ridiculous therapy would be to just dive right into my fears and let go. Min didn't know it, but maybe she'd done me a favor.

I sat down on the bed and took the girl in my arms. I cradled her head while I adjusted the cannula and slid it back in each nostril. She fought me again, but this time I gently trapped her hands in my own. "Shh, It's okay. You just need to breathe, sweetie." I looked around the room for Gun, but Ae-jung sat alone playing with the tablet, and his mom had already nodded off in the corner.

"Gun's already left," Min said, still holding her phone up "It's just you alone with all the sick people."

Ae-ri snorted. "Look at Sydney's face. She's about to lose it again."

Ae-ri was right. I was about to lose it, but not over anything other than the two idiots still filming me.

The nurses had to have a call button somewhere here. I reached over gingerly, so I didn't jostle the little girl's head, and pressed the red button at the bottom of the monitor. Even if she wasn't hooked up, that should call a nurse. "Someone will be here soon," I whispered, dabbing at the blood on her nose with the corner of my shirt. I gently rocked her back and forth and began humming the same song I'd sung to my mom when she was sick. Finally, a nurse came just as the little girl nodded off. Min and Ae-ri had left. I hadn't noticed when, and I didn't care.

The nurse smiled. "Thank you," she whispered. She helped me lay her back in bed and then attached a clip onto her finger that began reading her oxygen saturation and heartbeat on the monitor. I watched the screen.

"Her numbers are never good."

"Does she have parents?" I asked.

"Her mom is here, but we sent her to sleep for a few hours in the parent rooms. You students coming to help us out today was a Godsend."

I nodded. "No one should feel alone in the hospital."

33

CHUL

I didn't need Gun's text. I knew where Sydney was. I always did.

> **Gun:**
> **Syd's in trouble.**
> **Min took a video**
> **of her at the**
> **hospital, and she's**
> **going to post it. I**
> **just dropped you a**
> **pin.**

When I pulled into the hospital parking lot, he was waiting for me. I parked and grabbed my backpack with my laptop inside. Seeing that they'd brought her to a hospital, I could guess what they'd planned. I wasn't going in there without the one weapon I had in my corner.

When I got out of the car, Gun was already jogging up to me. "I'm already in a bad mood so can we not," I said.

"I just want to talk," Gun said. "It's Min and Ae-ri, they're plotting something."

"And you? Don't tell me you're not in on this. I've seen you and Min whispering together in the halls after class."

"No." He pointed a finger at me. "I was keeping Min close to protect Sydney. I care about her."

I snorted. "If you care about her, then stop obsessing. She's taken. Don't you get that?" I knew talking to Gun was a waste of my time. The only way to calm the angry army marching around my brain was to find Sydney. "Where is she?" I asked.

Gun scowled. "Second floor. Min and Ae-ri were filming her when I left. From what I saw, she handled being *here* just fine, but I read her file. I'm sure you did, too. If they push her, who knows?"

I gripped my backpack tighter. Everything I needed was inside. It would take some time, but I'd wipe their phones so clean they wouldn't even be able to text someone without getting new SIM cards. "Anything else?" I asked.

Gun sighed. "I'm not apologizing to you."

"Good. I wouldn't accept it even if you did."

"Are you going to take care of the video? I only called you here because I know what you can do."

"You really don't."

Gun nodded but looked me square in the eye. "I'm not going to stop with Sydney."

I ground my teeth.

"I'm going to win her back," he said.

"You never had her."

"I know I'm not as rich as you, but that's going to change. Sydney's going to see how right I am for her."

I shook my head. Had I ever been this level of stupid? Gun didn't know Sydney if he thought money would help him. She never cared about that kind of thing. Just last night she'd turned down Hyun's offer to order Kobe beef. Instead, she'd surprised me with egg sandwiches on the roof.

"This is perfect," she said, taking a giant bite.

I chuckled and watched her as the sun slid lower on the horizon. I loved the happy shine in her eyes when she was content.

"If I ever buy a house, I want it to have a roof like this where I can sit and watch the sunset."

"Done," I said. "We'll start looking tomorrow."

I expected her to laugh, but the sad look she gave me made the sandwich stick in my throat. "I was joking," I said.

She smiled. "I know. It just makes me want it, though."

"Okay, then I'm not joking. I really will buy you a house."

"It's us that I want, not the house." She sighed. "Eventually, I'm going to go back to the States."

Neither one of us had talked about it. I couldn't even think about Syd leaving. I changed the subject. "What if I was too poor to buy a house?" I asked. "What if my family lost all our money? Would you still want me then?"

"We'd live with Hyun," she said.

"Hyun too, he'd lose his money first in risky investments. After that, my parent's company would go belly-up. I'd be flat broke."

She giggled. "Then I would want you even more. I'd just have to take care of us both."

"How?" I laughed. "You know I have expensive taste."

Sydney moved closer, and her sunshine smell washed over me. "Remember," she breathed into my ear. "I know how to make penniless look cool. We'd live on the beach in a tent. I'd get a job at a cafe and feed you scraps from the kitchen. You'd never even know we were poor."

I seriously loved her. And Gun didn't stand a chance. "Sydney isn't with me because of money," I said. "She's not like that."

Gun sneered at me. "Just let her know that I helped you today," he said.

SYDNEY

It felt nice to just sit in a quiet room and hold this little girl's hand. She would leave this world soon. It hurt my heart, but I knew it was true. I quietly placed one of the wrapped gifts on the side table. Her color looked better, although her breathing still rattled. I tucked the sheet around frail shoulders and kissed her forehead.

"I'm glad I got to see that."

I spun around in surprise. "Chul." He stood, leaning against the wall. "How did you get here?"

"I drove."

I rolled my eyes. "And see, I thought you'd have wanted a long walk in the rain."

Chul grinned and moved next to me until our arms touched. Having him close always made my heart beat not just faster, but harder. Like if I got anywhere near him, my heart had to work that much more to keep up.

"No, really," I said. "How did you know where I was?"

"I synced your location settings to my phone." He winced. "And Gun told me what floor you were on."

I gaped at him, but he just spoke faster. "I did it from the beginning. At first because I was afraid you would get lost, and now I do it because I don't feel like you're safe. I've wanted to tell you but . . . " He sighed. "I didn't want you to get mad."

I considered getting mad. I should have gotten mad. But something about the gesture seemed romantic. I shook my head, thinking that only Chul could make stalking romantic. I was pretty far gone on this guy, and I didn't care.

"Are you upset?" Chul asked.

I looked at him sideways and tried my hardest not to smile.

He wasn't fooled. "Can I kiss you?" Chul asked.

"No."

"I really want to kiss you right now. You look so cute when you make that face."

"If you visit the rest of the kids with me, I'll give you one kiss."

"Done." Chul grabbed my hand and pulled me out the door.

The hospital cafeteria was bright and clean with one full wall of windows. A long self-service bar steamed with bins of food

I had no intention of touching. At least until I saw they had black bean noodles. Chul had introduced me to that gloriously slurpy meal last week, and it was the first Korean food that I really liked. "I have some bad news," I said around a big messy bite that I was sure left a black smear on my cheek. I took a napkin and wiped it.

Chul tore open a foil pouch of kimchi for his rice. "Really? I have some good news."

"You go first," I said.

"You owe me a kiss."

"For what?" My face warmed.

Chul seemed to notice and raised his eyebrows. He dropped his eyes to my lips. "You said if I helped you visit the rest of the kids, I could kiss you. What's your bad news?"

I hesitated. I really didn't want Chul to see the video. But most likely it had already been loaded onto all kinds of social media. He would know about it sooner or later. "Min and Ae-ri took a video of me having a little breakdown in the hospital. It's not like I was foaming at the mouth or anything, but I had kind of a mini panic attack."

Chul chewed his rice, thoughtful. "You mean, the one where you had trouble breathing? Yeah, I already erased that from their phones."

I dropped my chopsticks. "What?"

"Gun told me about it, so I did what any good boyfriend would do and wiped their phones."

"Gun did? I thought you hated him."

"I do. But he didn't like Min and Ae-ri messing with you."

"Oh," I sighed. "I'm not mad at Gun anymore."

"You should still be mad at him."

I grinned. "Should I be mad at you, too?"

"Definitely not," he said.

"But you stole their phones."

"No, I hijacked their phones, isolated the file, and deleted it. In and out. Easy."

I held up my hand. "That's probably not legal?"

Chul shrugged. "They didn't have your permission to film you."

"But still. You shouldn't have done that."

"Do you want me to put it back?"

"Of course not. I thought you deleted it."

"I kept a copy for myself."

I choked on my water. "Why?"

"You were awesome. I mean sure, the blood and stuff freaked you out, but then you walked yourself right out of the danger zone. You went all cool and calm and helped that little girl."

I snorted. "Yeah, real impressive."

"I don't think you have PTSD," Chul said.

"You read my school records too?"

He looked away, maybe because he was embarrassed for me. "A lot of people at school know. Min posted a link on a group chat. From there, it just spread."

"I knew it." I closed my eyes and groaned.

"Most at Daeshim are afraid of Min in one way or another. They follow without question, and then there are those like Ae-ri who are happy to because they like being cruel."

It was hard to look at Chul knowing that he'd read any of it.

"But I don't think everyone believed the rumors," he said. "If anything, that file proved she'd exaggerated. Sure, it was personal, but it made you seem human. I defended you with every post, and she had nothing new. People are already losing interest."

"Is that why she did all of this? She wanted to prove that I'm crazy?"

"You're not crazy."

I rolled my eyes. "You know what I mean."

"I really don't, though. Min is a narcissistic, pathological liar. That's crazy. You, on the other hand have some normal anxiety, but honest truth, I'd say you're one of the saner people I know."

I considered it. Greg had been my therapist since I was ten. He'd told me over and over that I had PTSD, then acted like I could never really be fixed. Maybe if he'd just left me alone to begin with, I would have worked it all out. "I think watching my mom almost die will always stay with me, but after today in the hospital, and maybe even this trip to Korea, I think I'm doing good. But I don't know if everyone back home would agree with you."

Chul took my hand and laced our fingers together. "It really only matters what you think, right?"

"For now, but when I go back, I'm going to have to face Greg. He's my uncle and used to be my therapist, which makes it all the more complicated. He thinks I'll be eternally sick."

"You don't have to go back."

"I will eventually."

"Why? We could go to college together. Your mom is coming now. If she stayed . . ."

"She won't stay, but that's not why I need to go back. My uncle Greg needs setting straight, or he'll forever bug my mom."

"What exactly do you need to set straight?"

"He's kind of a controlling guy and thinks I need more therapy. My mom has a hard time standing up to him since he paid off all her hospital bills after she got better." I shrugged. "I guess we are kind of indebted to the guy. But now that I've been away for a while, I see things differently. Clearer, maybe."

Chul nodded and waited, like he wanted me to continue.

"I don't know. He's not a nice guy. I mean, he was my dad's only brother, but I never knew he existed until after my mom got sick. My dad's side never liked my mom and pretty much ghosted her after he died. When she got cancer, she was sick for a long time and none of them ever came around. It was hard on both of us, but she did get better. Then, the day my mom was discharged from the hospital, Uncle Greg showed up and started acting like I was his long-lost niece. I just think that's weird. Why then?"

Chul nodded. "It's sketchy." He paused as if to consider his next words carefully. "Has your uncle ever hurt you?"

My stomach dropped. The closest Greg had ever come was the whole pill incident. He hadn't hurt me exactly, but he'd tried to. And he was definitely a first-class loser. When he wasn't threatening me, he was coercing my mom. "Not really. But I think you'd have to meet him to get why I need to make sure he's not bugging my mom."

Chul didn't press me for more and let it drop. "I hope you stay here." He took my hand and kissed the inside of my wrist, making my brain misfire. "That's fun. I like kissing you there." He leaned down to kiss it again.

I pulled free. "That was your one kiss."

Chul hooked his foot around my chair and dragged me closer. "I'm saving that kiss for when we're alone."

I grinned and took another bite. "I don't think so," I mumbled around a mouth full of noodles.

He leaned closer. "Why not?"

I swallowed. "Because."

"Because why?" he asked. His eyes had gone all serious.

"Because I like you so much."

He smiled, but not like I expected him to. Not like he'd won. "I have something important to give you."

CHUL

A letter from her mom—like an actual paper envelope from the mail—came this morning. It was thin and light in my shirt pocket, but somehow it felt like a heavy weight. I hadn't read it, but I knew. Every instinct told me Sydney was about to get bad news.

I'd counted the days—seventy-two—since that first

time I saw her picture on my phone. The same day I ignored my mother's text to go pick her up. What had made me not want to run to her? Now I couldn't imagine not wanting Sydney. She was beautiful and smart, and I thought about her constantly. Her problems kept me up at night. I had back-up plans to my back-up plans, but I could do nothing to protect her from this letter. And then there was Greg. Just the way Sydney got pale and looked away when I'd asked about him confirmed that I couldn't ever let him be around her.

Yesterday, I'd felt like Min was Sydney's biggest problem, but now sitting in the cafeteria, my chest ached knowing what I had to do. I pulled the letter from my shirt pocket and placed it on the table between us. "This came for you in the mail this morning."

Sydney's eyes flicked down to the envelope, her mom's California address in the corner and her own name written with a flourish of cursive, front and center. Her hand reached out and pressed down hard on the smudged paper. As if somehow touching where her mom had touched, she could transport a part of her here, to this side of the world.

My stomach tightened. "Are you going to open it?" I didn't have a plan for this. I could only hope that fate would be kind to Sydney.

34

SYDNEY

Dear Sydney,

I'm sorry I haven't written. I really don't have a computer anymore, but I miss you every day. Since you left, I've spent hours thinking about how cute you were growing up. Your first day of kindergarten, learning to ride a bike, and even the time when you were four and cut all your hair off. You cried and cried but looked cute with a pixie. I have loved you from the moment I felt you move inside me. You have been my everything. Thank you for being my wonderful daughter.

Uncle Greg has been stopping by a lot. You know how he worries about you. It's best if he doesn't know you're in Korea. I understand it's hard to be apart, but you have the Kims, so please don't come here until I sort this out with him.

Love always,
Mom

I stared at my mom's familiar handwriting, willing the letters to rearrange themselves, to say something different, something normal. But they didn't change. She didn't talk about leaving to come here with Suni next week, or even how excited she was to see me. Was that all a lie too? Instead, I got that Greg was stopping by a lot. She didn't want me to come home, and Greg couldn't know I was here. It was all wrong. Really wrong. There was something she wasn't telling me.

I passed Chul the letter and watched his face as he read.

When he finished, he handed it back. He looked nervous. I didn't want to see that he was scared too. I wanted to think that I was being silly and reading too much into my mom's words. "Will you help me?" I tried to keep my voice even and calm.

He picked up my hand and laced our fingers together. "Yes."

"Do you think your mother would change her plans and fly out tonight?"

"We can ask. I know she has meetings all week, but maybe. I talked to her about flying to get your mom, and she's eager to go, excited even. Her only worry was you. My mother is just so set on . . ." He cleared his throat.

"Me, living here for all eternity?" I said.

"Not that I mind, but yes."

I shook my head. Everything felt surreal, like I was swimming underwater. My mom sounded almost afraid of Greg. I wondered if he'd gotten violent or tried to drug her like he had me. "I know she's hiding something from me."

Chul pressed his lips together and looked away. "There is one thing I could do."

"What?" I asked.

"It's definitely past the gray area."

I stared at him. Gray, black, white, I didn't care as long as it gave me answers.

"It would take some time to get access, but I could look at her bank accounts. That's usually the best place to figure out where and what a person is doing."

My jaw dropped. "I know you were part of a CTF team, but isn't a bank account way beyond your skill level?" Chul still wouldn't look at me. "Seriously, how would you even . . ."

Chul took both my hands tight in his, like he was scared. "I do know how to do that and a lot more. When you first got here, I looked at *your* bank account. It was a mistake. If you want me to suffer for it, I will, but I haven't done anything more than track your phone since the party, since I kissed you."

My heart pounded in my chest. "What did you look at?"

"Everything. It took me hours to clear my computer of all the access I had on you. I regret it, and I'm sorry."

I tried to stand up, but Chul kept a firm grip on my hands. "Please, Syd," he whispered. "I'll do whatever you want."

"Promise me you'll never do it again." Then I added. "After today." What he had done was a huge invasion of my privacy, and we'd talk about it later. But right now, fixing the problem with my mom took priority.

He frowned. "Today?"

"Today, you need to look at my mom's accounts."

Chul leaned forward and pressed his lips to mine. "I promise," he murmured.

I'd never been in Chul's room before. I peeked inside. It was mostly sparse except for one comfy-looking leather chair and a TV next to the bed. A desk in the corner was littered with tech equipment, and the bed had a pure white down comforter. I just stood there, not going in. Chul looked at me expectantly as he held the door open.

Hyun cleared his throat and I turned, surprised. He stood in the hallway and shook his head. The look he gave Chul was severe. "Keep the door open," he said.

I quickly nodded. "For sure, Hyun. I'm just . . . I'm here because Chul wants to show me something on his laptop."

"What does he want to show you?" Hyun asked, walking closer.

Chul rolled his eyes at Hyun. "You stress more than Grandmother. Seriously, you're such an old woman sometimes."

Hyun lunged forward like he was about to smack Chul on the head. Chul ducked and ran into the room. "Just remember that I'm going to be checking in on you," Hyun said.

Chul laughed.

I imagined Hyun's worry to be the way my dad would have acted if he were still alive, and for good reason.

Chul made no attempt to hide that he considered us completely together. I just wondered what his, or any of the Kims', version of that meant. It seemed more like a signed, sealed and delivered together than my own reality, where I felt barely old enough to date. But Chul's parents gave him free rein. Not Hyun. He took it upon himself to monitor every moment we were alone together in the house.

A few weeks ago, at dinner, I'd almost crawled under the table in embarrassment. Suni and Jae-ho had been on one of their rare visits home and sat talking about a supplier problem at work.

Hyun picked at his rice, looking bored, and Chul whispered something to me about going up to the roof when Suni interrupted us. "Jae-ho, do you think you could ask that friend of yours who does celebrity weddings to meet with Sydney and Chul? We should start planning for their engagement party."

I choked on my juice.

Hyun frowned. "Sydney's mom wouldn't like that."

Sydney's mom? I thought. What about I wouldn't like that?

"If they're already together, then it's only natural," Jae-ho said.

"It's natural to date first," Hyun snapped and then glared at Chul.

Chul scowled back. "We are just dating."

Jae-ho smiled at his wife. "We didn't go on more than three dates before our engagement."

My face went redder than the kimchi stew.

But it was Hyun who got mad. "Jae-ho, Shannon would be furious if she knew you were making these decisions for Sydney. She's still a teenager."

Jae-ho laughed, and Suni looked at me apologetically. Chul leaned over to whisper something to me. Hyun kicked his chair leg so hard that he almost fell over.

"Hey," Chul said.

"Eat your stew," Hyun said. "You don't need to always be whispering to Sydney."

Chul threw up his hands in innocence. "I'm a complete gentleman, even when I'm kissing her."

That's about the time I ran to my bedroom. I didn't come out for the rest of the night. Not even when Chul brought ramen to my door.

Knowing how lax Chul's parents were, it was probably not a bad idea that Hyun kept an eye on things. "Don't worry, Hyun. I promise to keep the door open," I said.

Hyun's eyes softened as he looked at me. "You're not the one who worries me, Sydney." He looked back at Chul. "I'm leaving now, but don't discount that I may have installed a camera in your room."

Chul snorted. "I'd know if you had."

Hyun shrugged and walked away.

I cleared my throat and wiped my sweaty hands down my legs as I followed Chul to his desk, noting he had some of the same equipment that we used in Robotics class. "Your room is pretty cool." I sounded lame and weird. So weird.

Chul stopped and turned around. "What's wrong?"

I froze. "Nothing."

"No, you're acting funny."

"I'm not." But my voice had gone all high.

"Don't let what Hyun said bother you. Are you nervous to be in my room?"

I swallowed and shook my head.

"You seem really nervous." Then Chul's eyes lit up like he'd just discovered a prize in his cereal box, and his smile turned knowing. "Almost like you've never been in a boy's room before."

"Stop."

Chul pointed to the door and cocked an eyebrow. "You should be nervous. I can still kiss you with it open."

I forced a laugh and tried not to fidget with my hands. He was probably kidding, but with Chul you could never tell. "So are we going to cyber spy on my mom, or what?"

Chul plopped down in his big office chair and pulled me

into his lap. Before I could respond or stand up, he stole a kiss. "You don't need to be nervous," he said.

Chul said it could take hours. I guess he was writing a program that would write a program, and it sounded like it'd take days, not hours. I flopped down on his chair and flipped through his Korean movie channel until I found a semi-decent martial arts show that I could just zone out with.

But I kept thinking about what Mom's letter had said about Greg. Usually when he gave her a hard time, it was over me. Like when she'd refused to let me participate in his medical trial for testing new PTSD drugs. He'd thrown a fit and called her daily for weeks. Maybe she'd shut down her phone and email to avoid *him*. Maybe she'd just quit her job and holed up in her apartment so she didn't have to face the harassment.

Even thinking about the weird way Mom had told me about this trip made sense now. She'd told me hours before my flight. I hadn't had time to talk about it in therapy. If Greg had gotten wind that I was leaving his care, even temporarily, he would've gone insane.

But Greg did have *my* email address. I didn't care. I never read anything he sent. I pulled out my phone and opened my junkmail folder. There were thirty-two unread emails from Gregorymindhealthmoore@gmail.com.

I started at the beginning, the day of my first missed appointment, and skimmed. It was his usual whining and finger pointing stuff. But when I got to last week's email I stopped skimming, and had to read the letter three times before it sunk in.

"Sydney," Chul's voice sounded softer than usual, and there was no playfulness to his tone. "I found something with your mom."

I looked up from my phone. Chul was kneeling in front of me with worry in his eyes. "I found something too." I spoke the words, but they sounded far away, like I wasn't in my body anymore, like maybe someone else was speaking, and I was just listening.

"I think your mom's back in the hospital, and I think she's sick."

"She's not sick," I said.

"I think she is, Syd." Chul rubbed my arms. I barely felt it.

That other person, who wasn't me, spoke the words clear and calm. "She's not sick. She's dying."

Chul went very still.

With no mercy, I spoke the words. They floated around the room to fill me with this new, terrible reality. I could only listen to myself in horror. "It's stage four lung cancer."

35

CHUL

"Should we call the Doctor and get her a sedative?" my father asked.

We all stood outside her closed door, my parents, Hyun, and myself. I'd been there the longest. She'd gone from crying, to wailing, to complete silence. The silence was the worst.

My mother shook her head. "Maybe a doctor can check her here, but I don't think we should sedate her. Especially after what Shannon told me about her uncle. I think it would do more harm than good."

My father nodded like he'd forgotten. "You're right."

My mother stepped closer to the door and knocked. "Sydney, sweetie. Please open the door. I just want to check on you. I know you don't want to talk, but we're all so worried."

Her crying started again but weaker than it had been an hour ago. I squeezed my eyes shut and leaned my forehead against the wall. I wanted to hold her, comfort her. Anything. But I couldn't fix this. "I thought you were going to bring her here. Did you know any of this?"

My mother's voice was subdued when she answered. "Shannon didn't tell me." A new wave of fresh tears glistened on her cheeks, but she quickly wiped at them. "I spoke with her doctor an hour ago, and he confirmed that she's in the cancer ward. He wouldn't tell me more because of privacy laws. I finally got a nurse to disclose that Shannon is terminal and can no longer get out of bed."

I'd never seen my mother look this defeated. "Maybe if we got her better doctors," I said. "We could fly specialists to her and—"

My father let out a heavy sigh. "The nurse said she only has days now."

"She kept it from me," my mother said. My father held her hand and stared at the floor. "Why would she do that, Jae-ho? I could have brought her here and gotten her the best medical care. She wouldn't be alone. Why would she lie to me like that? I never even knew she was sick."

Hyun's voice broke when he spoke. "She didn't want Sydney to have to watch her die."

"That's Sydney's choice," I said. "We need to take her to see her mom."

"No," my mother said softly. "When I was there last time, Shannon signed some new documents and agreed that adoption wouldn't work." She twisted her diamond ring on her finger. "But then she got really agitated and made me promise to never let Sydney go back to the States until she turns eighteen."

"What happens when she's eighteen?" I asked.

"In America, that's when you're a legal adult," Hyun said. "Shannon is probably scared that Greg will try to get custody of her."

My father nodded. "He would be her next of kin, and since he was once her doctor, he would have a strong case."

"She needs to say goodbye," I said. "It's only fair."

"I made a promise to my best friend." My mother shook her head. "I can't let Sydney go."

I stood up straighter and faced my father. "Can I have the documents Shannon signed?"

My mother sputtered. "You don't even know what she signed."

My father stared at me, his eyes hard and penetrating. We both knew what those documents were. He slowly nodded. "I have them locked in the safe. You know the code."

Sydney's crying cut off suddenly, and we all stopped to listen. I heard a few whimpers but nothing more.

My father looked at my mother. "We can't just let her go on like this."

My mother's face crumpled with pain and more tears. "What am I supposed to do? It hurts me that I'm losing Shannon, and it hurts to see Sydney fall apart, but I can't help them."

"Will she hurt herself?" My father asked.

My mother looked stricken at his words.

"All of you can go. I'll take care of Sydney," I said.

Hyun looked surprised. "What will you do?"

"Just be there for her," I said, giving her door a heavy kick. It flew inwards and bounced off the wall. I stepped inside. My mother gasped, but I shut the door and leaned against it until I heard three sets of footsteps walk away.

Sydney lay on her bed, looking like a tight ball of pain and anger. With hair plastered to her scrunched face, she barely moved and made breathing look like it hurt. I carried over her vanity chair to prop her door shut and then climbed up onto the bed next to her. I gave her the only thing I had left to offer. I wrapped her in my arms and held tight. She didn't resist, and soon I could feel the deep steady breathing of sleep.

Sydney woke a few hours before dawn. She sat up next to me and rubbed swollen eyes with a dazed look. The moon shone through the window and bathed her in soft light. I wanted to tangle my hands in her hair. I wanted to kiss her.

But I wasn't a jerk, so I handed her a bottle of water. She took it and fumbled with the lid until I opened it for her and handed it back. "Do you want to eat anything?" I asked.

She stared at me blankly. "Take me home," she whispered. "Where's Suni? She needs to send me home right now. I don't have any more time to waste."

"My mother will never agree, Syd. She promised your mom because of your uncle Greg."

Silent tears welled in her eyes and rolled down her

cheeks. "I can handle Greg, but I can't handle not saying goodbye to my mom."

I nodded and pulled her back to me. My chest ached like I'd taken a hundred hits to the sternum.

"Will you buy my ticket?"

As much as I fought with my parents, I knew they were right on this one. Their warnings, the reasoning not to take Sydney home made sense. I still couldn't say no. "I'll get you home, but I'm coming with you."

She jumped out of bed and started cramming things into a backpack. I took her hands in mine and gently turned her to look at me. "Before we go, I want you to tell me everything you know about your uncle."

36

SYDNEY

Cancer. The word had drifted in and out of my broken sleep during our flight, and now I sagged against the rental car parked at the exact hospital I swore I'd never step foot in again. Everything about the Jonsson Cancer Center looked the same: a bleak, eight-story building, ornamented with a few scrubby bushes and no trees. Even the parking lot lights glowed with that same weak yellow from seven years ago. They flickered and fought against the long night, but nothing could quite drive away the shadows in a place like this.

Chul closed the trunk and then leaned down to kiss the top of my head.

"Are you ready?"

I wasn't. Part of me wanted to give up and walk into that darkness. The other part of me wanted to run screaming through the hospital halls, right into my mom's arms, and beg her to live. I knew neither choice worked. I had to pull it together now. For the last eighteen hours, my zombified brain had followed Chul through two airports, and now that I was finally here, I didn't know what to do. I opted to lean on him just a little longer. "Can you walk me in?"

"Did you think I would leave you here alone?"

I stared up at him, wondering how I'd ended up with a guy who was willing to fly me halfway around the world while I cried all over his shoulder.

Chul ruffled my hair. "Don't look so surprised. I told you

we were sticking together."

I swallowed hard against my sandpaper throat. "Thank you."

Chul took my hand, his own warm and alive against my clammy one. "Come on, let's go in."

I followed his steady path. He talked quietly to the night security guard at the front desk before we got on an elevator. He pulled me after him when we got off on the fourth floor, and I walked in a daze until we stopped at room 4236. Dim light glowed from inside, and everything was silent.

"This is your mom's room," Chul said.

I stepped past him and made my feet move towards the solitary metal bed. It smelled like antiseptic and plastic, and the steady beep of a heart monitor sounded like a weak countdown.

"Mom."

Her eyes fluttered, but they didn't open. She looked the same, maybe just a little shrunken. I'd expected her to look like she had after months of chemo, but she still had all of her pale silky hair.

I reached out and brushed her cheek, her skin still smooth and soft. Nothing about mom here felt real. As a child, it had all seemed very real, every moment laced with fear. Tonight was like walking into a storybook where a queen lay sleeping. She looked too beautiful to die. We just had to wait for the hero to come and save her.

"You finally decided to show up."

I looked up, the spell broken. Greg's steel-grey eyes flicked over me dismissively, but I wasn't fooled. He watched my every breath, every movement. He always did.

When I was little, I'd believed the lies he told me. He'd been the adult, after all. But as I'd slowly grown up and out of my own pain, I'd started to develop a theory. My own psychoanalysis of an uncle who on the outside seemed so polished and professional. He was a well-respected psychiatrist, had even published a few articles in prominent medical journals. But Greg had cracks in his veneer. There was a part of him that became agitated whenever my dad was brought up. Whether it was jealousy or hatred for his brother, I couldn't tell, but he didn't have good feelings for his older and, apparently, more loved brother. Maybe when my dad died all that hate had to go somewhere, and it went to me. Or maybe he was just one of those broken people, too dysfunctional to do more than hide behind the shield of someone else's problems.

Before leaving California, I hadn't been entirely sure. Sometimes I'd wondered and questioned if I really was messed up in the head. Maybe what he said was true and it was just a big blind spot. But now I knew. He'd grossly exaggerated my symptoms. Here I stood in a hospital, and under the worst circumstances I could imagine, yet I was completely sane—no mental breakdown.

"Uncle Greg," I said, hiding my surprise. "I had no idea my mom was sick."

Greg got up stiffly from his chair and loomed over me. "If you were any kind of decent daughter, you would have read my emails. This is your fault."

I flinched.

"Where have you been?"

I watched from the corner of my eye as Chul entered the room. "Sydney's been staying with me." He spoke in perfect English, his face a mask of innocent politeness. But I knew him well enough to see the anger in his eyes.

"And who are you?"

Chul didn't offer his usual bow. "Sydney's boyfriend."

Greg sniffed and looked back at me. "You have time to run around with boys, but you can't answer any of my emails or even once visit your own mother?"

"I just found out she was here. And can you please lower your voice? I don't want to disturb her sleep."

Greg bellowed out a laugh that made me jump. "She won't wake up. They've got her on too many painkillers. She hasn't been conscious for days now. I'm just waiting for her to die."

My skin went cold. "How can you say that? Don't you care for her at all?"

"Of course I care. She deserves this for what she did to my family. Now, it will only be a short time before I'm your legal guardian."

"I'm almost an adult. I hardly need a guardian," I said.

He smiled, a sick kind of sneer. "But you're not well, Sydney. Someone will need to watch over you."

I clenched my jaw and fists until I could trust myself to speak without yelling. Up until that moment, I'd been willing to forgive Greg. But not this. He wasn't even human if he could speak about my mom dying like that. He was too far gone, like so gone there had to be worms crawling around in the place where his heart should be. "I'm not going to argue with you. Leave now. I'd like to spend time alone with my mom."

Greg turned and casually picked up his bag from the chair like he hadn't a care in the world. "I wouldn't want to deprive you of her last hours."

Chul stepped aside to let him pass but watched closely as he left. Chul grabbed his backpack and walked to the door. "I'm going to go get us some drinks. I'll be back soon," he said.

"Sure." I was too sickened by Greg's words to say more.

Chul looked at me with reassurance. "I won't be gone long."

CHUL

I followed Greg close enough that he knew I was there. He glanced over his shoulder and then walked faster, but I kept his pace. There was a part of me that could imagine following this sick, sadistic man out to the parking lot and dishing out a little payback for all the years he'd hurt Sydney. Soft muscles and the lax way he held himself gave him away. Greg wasn't a fighter. I waited until he got on the elevator and then took the stairs. I made it down in time to meet him when the doors opened.

He took a step back when he saw me leaning against the wall.

"Let's talk," I said.

"I have nothing to say to you," he said, obviously afraid.

"This will only take a minute."

Greg's eyes shifted to look anywhere but at me. "Stay away from Sydney. She's a very disturbed girl, and a boyfriend will only make her more unstable."

I smiled wide. I didn't need to speak, only let him see some of my pent-up rage as I tensed.

Greg coughed and quickly exited the elevator, then started for the main doors.

"I'm not done, Mr. Moore. I have a message to deliver from my family."

That stopped him. He stood with his back to me. "And who would that be?" he snarled.

"Sydney's godparents. Maybe you've heard of Mr. and Mrs. Kim."

Greg spun around.

"I can see you know who they are. Shannon probably mentioned her very wealthy best friend, Kim Suni." I shrugged. "My mother loves Sydney like her own child. Think for a minute what people as influential and wealthy as my parents will do if they think their daughter is in danger."

"Are you threatening me?"

"Not yet."

His eyes scanned the empty hallways with a paranoid fear before looking back to me. "There's security here."

I laughed, thinking about how I'd slipped the night security officer five hundred dollars so he'd go pick up food and an electric blanket for Syd when his shift ended. "I know. I'm friends with the guard," I said.

This only seemed to make him angry. "You shouldn't even be here. She's not part of your family," he spat.

"Not yet. My parents are willing to pay you two million American dollars if you detach yourself from her, forever."

I recognized the gleam of greed in Greg's eyes. I'd only known a handful of people in my life who didn't eventually bow to it. But then I saw something more. The desire driving him wasn't money. I hadn't noticed it in the hospital room with Syd, but just now, something wild flickered in his gaze. Not much could trump money, but crazy could.

I needed to tread carefully here. I had Greg cornered, and this was my one shot. "I can have the money deposited in your account by morning . . . two million dollars."

He squeezed his eyes shut tight and trembled, temptation clearly gnawing at him. When he finally opened them and looked at me, I knew I'd lost.

"That brat is the only family I have left. No amount of money could buy her from me."

"My family wants to take care of her."

Greg scoffed. "As if a kid like you could ever help a girl like Sydney. You have no idea how far in over your head you are. She's prone to complete psychological breakdowns." He almost looked delighted, like Sydney being sick gave him power. "I'm the only one capable of taking care of her," he snarled. "Shannon is the reason she's unstable, and it's my responsibility to fix her. Tell your parents my niece isn't for sale." His face had gone beet-red, and spittle formed at the corners of his mouth.

When Syd had described her uncle, I'd assumed he was just vicious. But he was way past that. This guy was completely unhinged. Money wasn't going to work. I needed to go to plan B or Syd would get hurt.

I gave him a stiff nod. The kind that politely said— screw you. "Thank you for your time then, Mr. Moore." I wasn't calling him a doctor. The man didn't deserve such a title. I spun on my heel and headed back to Sydney.

I stopped at the vending machine and bought what was supposed to be hot chocolate. While the dispenser filled a little foam cup, I unzipped my backpack and pulled out the manilla envelope my father had given me before we left. He and Hyun had driven us to the airport with a promise to not let Mother fall apart when she found out. And she would find out.

I glanced through the papers. My father had arranged it all with his lawyers. Shannon's signature was there, my parents' as well. All I needed now was for Syd to sign. Technically, she should appear in person at the US Embassy in Seoul with both documents to get them approved. But after sending these to my father, he could make a personal visit. I had no doubt he would push this through. I pulled out my phone to call home.

"Hey, I brought you some hot chocolate." I placed the cup on the small table next to Sydney's chair. "It's from the vending machine downstairs, so I can't vouch for its taste, but a little sugar might do you some good."

She turned to me, her face still pale with dark circles under both eyes. "Thanks," she said, but didn't pick it up. She stroked her mom's palm with light fingertips. Shannon didn't move or stir, but she had to know her daughter was there.

"Are you doing okay?" I asked.

She gave a small nod but didn't speak.

I wondered about the reason Sydney had always been so afraid to leave her mom. Maybe because some deep, intuitive part of her knew Shannon's life would be cut short. Like maybe all that clinginess had been Syd's way of preparing herself. Now that time was out, she could say that there were no regrets. She'd spent every moment she could with a mom that she loved.

I kissed the top of Sydney's head and pulled out both papers and a pen before sitting down next to her. "Syd, I don't want to burden you right now." I gestured to Shannon. "Your mom is way more important, but I need to overnight some legal documents to my father. The security guard is getting off his shift in a few minutes and said he'd mail this for me. I've got a way to protect you from Greg."

Syd glanced at the papers in my hand, and I held

my breath. If she started reading, I wasn't sure what would happen. She looked at me, and I only saw trust. "Your mom knows that we're here?" she asked.

"Yeah, that's what took me so long. I called home and explained the situation. She finally agreed that you need to say goodbye to your mom. Greg's going to be a problem, though, so we need to take a few legal steps. Sorry to ask this of you now." I handed her a pen. "Just sign in both highlighted boxes, and my father will take care of the rest."

She wrote her name with stiff fingers and then handed me the pen with a sad smile. "Thank you, Chul. I wouldn't have made it without you." She leaned over and brushed her lips across my cheek. Just that small gesture made my heart ache.

37

SYDNEY

My dad died before I could remember him, and that would always feel like a loss, but it was nothing like this. This hurt swelled up inside me until the pain felt like it would split my organs and bust me at the seams. And I knew that even if this unimaginable loss cracked me open, my pain wouldn't end. I would have to go on without her. Death would never be satisfied by something so small as my own suffering. Death demanded change, demanded that my entire world shift and reassemble until nothing recognizable existed for me.

The hours dragged, too long to watch her struggle, and yet I knew time was slipping away. Her heartbeats were now numbered. I didn't have long enough to say goodbye. I talked to Mom as if she could hear me. I think she could. I talked through my tears and forgot about what I would lose. Instead, I relived every happy moment I could remember. We had so many.

CHUL

I guess you love someone when you'd rather suffer yourself than let them feel even a moment of pain. And more than anything, I wanted to steal these hours from Sydney. I wanted to stand on the front line of fire, somehow protect her from the truth of mortality. But no amount of money, influence, or skill could help Sydney. I could only hold her hand and pray.

SYDNEY

"Mom, do you remember when you taught me how to ride my bike?" My tears came soft as I spoke. "Do you remember what you told me?" I needed to give her this one last thing, even if I didn't believe it myself. Mom had to know that I would be okay if she left. Her ragged breathing and pained expressions were too much. She fought for me, and I couldn't ask her to stay anymore. "I begged you to not let go of the back. I was so afraid to ride alone. But you told me that if you didn't, I wouldn't ever go fast enough to feel the wind. The way you described how it would feel in my hair and on my face made me brave enough to pedal fast, and you let go. Do you remember that I didn't fall? I yelled into the wind and let it rush past me. It felt like flying, Mom."

Mom reached out and took my hand. Her eyes fluttered open, and she slowly focused on my face. All at once she started to struggle. "Mom, it's okay. Greg already left. Don't worry." But she continued to grip my hand in panic.

Chul stood and leaned down over my mom. She looked up with wide eyes. He took her other hand in his and then moved closer to whisper in her ear. I heard him say his name and then something more that I couldn't make out. A small smile crept over Mom's face, and she gave a tiny nod. Then her eyes found mine again, and she watched me before drifting off.

CHUL

The nurse walked quietly into the room with a syringe in her hand. "It's time for more pain medicine, but she won't stay very long after I give it."

Sydney stared at her blankly from where she sat next to me. Shannon's breathing had become more ragged, making the last few hours a constant struggle.

I took Sydney's hand. "The morphine will help her pain but slow her respiratory system. Do you understand?"

She didn't answer. Her eyes welled with tears, and she dropped her forehead down on the edge of the bed.

I nodded to the nurse and then watched her screw the syringe into the capped end of the IV. I wiped at the tears streaming down my face.

SYDNEY

Three struggling gasps and then one final soft one. At 6:18 pm, Mom took her last breath. I lay down next to her and placed my hand on her chest, but I didn't feel her next to me. I turned away from the body that wasn't my mom anymore and lay on my back. I felt the tether that had bound us as mother and child stretch thin and then finally break. I closed my eyes and tried to survive the waves of pain that crashed over me.

38

SYDNEY

Our condo sat dark. I'd expected that, but I was shocked to see Mom's shell wreath, normally on our front door, replaced with plastic flowers. The three Navajo pots under the window were also missing. She'd left this world only five hours ago. How could proof of her existence already be gone?

I pulled out my key with shaking fingers, and Chul took it from me before he tried the lock. It went in but wouldn't turn. He rattled the door. "Are you sure this is the one?" he asked.

"Yes. That's my only house key."

Manic barking from inside made me jump back. Chul pulled the key out before the door swung open to reveal Greg holding Berkly, his pet Chihuahua. "Hello, Sydney. I heard from the hospital. Come in. We have a lot to discuss."

I stepped inside the doorway, followed by Chul, and knew right away that none of our stuff was here. The oak table that usually crowded our small foyer had been replaced with a black lacquered one covered in a leopard print runner.

A moment ago, I'd felt numb with loss and pain, but seeing our home violated awoke something. Maybe the stunned neurons in my brain started firing again, because everything suddenly seemed clear and sharp. I stood up straight and looked Greg square in the eye. "Did you change the lock?"

Greg put Berkley down. "Janet's living here now."

"Your stupid girlfriend?"

"She needed a place to stay," Greg said.

"That's illegal. My mom checked into the hospital—what—a week ago? You can't just give our condo away," I said, storming down the hallway to our living room. Black leather couches and more leopard print crowded the small space. The soft yellow hue Mom and I had painted the living room when we moved in had been changed to a bright lime green. "You can tell Janet to pack up and go. My mom rented this, and the lease is under her name."

"Shannon is dead, Sydney. I know you're in denial and your brain is falling apart, but this is no longer your home."

Chul had followed close on my heels, and without a word he started pulling me back to the hallway, but Greg stepped between Chul and the door. He glared. "Like I said, Sydney and I have things to discuss. But *you* should go."

Chul went rigid and I grabbed his arm. "I'm okay," I said. I could feel the violence coiled just below the surface. But if anyone was going to hit this guy, it was going to be me. "Just let me talk. I need to set my uncle straight on a few things." I stepped closer to Greg. "I know Mom passed away. Thanks for being so tactful. But I'm eighteen this summer, and I don't want you in my life anymore."

Greg frowned. "I know how emotional this is for you, and with your illness, I don't expect you to understand everything that is going on. I'm going to get you the best medical care." He placed a heavy hand on my shoulder.

Chul lunged forward and knocked his hand off. "Don't touch her," he growled.

I spun and pushed hard against Chul's chest, but he didn't move. "Please don't. I've got this."

Chul fisted both his hands but finally nodded and stepped back.

I turned to Greg. "Where's my stuff?"

"I gave it all to charity. I figured you didn't want it since you ran away and left Shannon alone on her deathbed."

Anger screamed inside me. Everything gone—our photo albums, Mom's wedding dress, Dad's old journals, my books. He'd taken everything. It was like Greg considered Mom and me to be disposable. To him, we were nothing more than cheap tissue, and he'd just taken the last one from the box with nothing more than a shrug of his shoulders. The anger pressed on my chest, making each breath tight. "You got rid of our stuff?"

"It's good that I'm here for your breakdown. I have everything in place to take care of you." Greg brushed past both of us and started to walk back to the living room. "Natalie, can you and the rest of the staff come out here? Sydney's ready to go now."

Greg's assistant walked out of the kitchen. She looked the same way she did when working at the clinic—a too tight pink dress suit, long tacky nails, and wobbly high heels. But my breath caught when two heavyset men in white uniforms followed behind her.

Chul pulled me backwards by my arm until I stood behind him. "We're leaving. Syd, get to the door."

I took one step backwards. The biggest of the men lunged for Chul, and the other pinned me before I could reach the door. The back of my head bounced off the drywall, and my left arm burned with a sharp sting. Darkness crept along my vision as a warm weight wrapped around me. I fought to push it back. I tried to twist away and yell, but only a moan escaped my lips, and then I was falling.

CHUL

The man with a short buzz-cut grabbed my neck with his left hand. He squeezed and lifted until my feet dangled a few inches off the floor. I grabbed for his hands and got a heavy punch to the side of my head. White exploded in my vision, but I could see enough to witness the other man hefting Sydney over his shoulder, Greg and Natalie following out the door. I had minutes before they got her to a car and no time to feel pain. It was either break this hold now, or Sydney was gone.

I raised my right leg and kicked down hard, connecting with his knee. At the same time, I shot my right arm straight up into the air, dropping my shoulder and turning. Then I slammed my elbow down and caught the edge of his collarbone. The man released his hold and staggered back.

I moved my feet slightly wider with my right foot forward. Both hands came up in the classic fighting stance. I tucked my elbows and moved so the front door was to my back.

Buzz Cut could hit. I was sure I had a busted ear drum.

He lunged for me, and I dodged his blow. Then I landed a solid sidekick to his chest, and he stepped back, clutching his ribs. I didn't stop but moved in close to give three quick strikes, two to the sternum, and the last to the throat. He wasn't down, only bent over. I brought my knee up and connected with his chin. It snapped his head back hard enough to bounce against the wall. He stumbled, with blood gushing from his mouth. I thought he would stop there, but he charged me. I sidestepped and followed him with a forward leg sweep that brought him crashing to the floor.

I turned and ran. He wouldn't be down long, but I didn't have time to finish the fight.

I took the steps three at a time until I made it to the cement. The parking lot had minimal lighting, but I saw a blue SUV speed out from the exit. I ran for my rental car two rows over. I slid behind the wheel, thankful I'd chosen a Dodge Charger, and backed out, then floored it to the exit. There weren't any cars, but I turned right, the way I thought the SUV had gone, and sped down the road. Two cars drove slowly ahead of me. I crossed the double yellow into the other lane and sped past them, then moved back to my lane.

The road ended at a stop sign, intersecting with a four-lane road. A quick scan and I had nothing. I turned right then wove in and out of cars, running two red lights and pushing ninety before blue and red lights flashed in my rear-view mirror and a siren sounded. I could keep looking, but I wasn't even sure this was the way they had gone. I pulled over and dialed Hyun's number, putting him on speaker. Then I put both hands on the steering wheel in plain sight.

My international permit listed me as a minor, which probably saved my life. I was sure the LA county Juvenile Hall was less of a rough crowd compared to the actual jail.

When Barry, the night shift guard, who looked like a retired wrestler, saw the dried blood caked around my ear, he got me a washcloth and bowl of water. "Here, you can clean up with this. The medical staff doesn't come until morning."

"Thanks," I muttered in English and took the water. Barry folded both arms over his barreled chest and leaned against the wall. He watched the TV at the front desk more than he watched me.

There were five bunkbeds in the room and only one empty spot, the top bunk under the window. Two boys who looked younger than me peeked out from under their blankets at the TV. Another kid lay on his back and glared at the ceiling. Everyone else seemed to be sleeping. I could see Barry wanted me to hurry up and get to bed, so I pressed the wet cloth to my throbbing ear.

Hyun had probably taken the private jet, which meant he could have left within the hour. Assuming it was the normal thirteen hours, he should be showing up tomorrow around two or three in the afternoon.

I didn't think I could wait that long. Sydney needed me. I dropped the washcloth and clenched my hands until my knuckles turned white. I shouldn't have let her go back to her house. I'd let her walk in, even when I'd seen Greg standing at the doorway.

I thought of Sydney's phone still sitting in the cup holder of the now impounded Charger. I had no way to track her, but I wasn't just going to sit here and wait.

"Hey, Barry."

"Yeah, what's up,"

"Do you have a computer?" I spoke slowly and in my best English.

"We have some in the school center."

"That works."

Barry's eyes didn't move from the TV. "It's only for homework, and it's not open."

"I need to calm myself down. The only way I know how is to do coding."

Barry looked over at me with skepticism. "Coding, huh?"

I held my hands up, innocent written all over my face. "You can come watch me if you want."

"Gee kid, that sounds like fun, but no thanks. I'm watching *M.A.S.H.* reruns."

I glanced at the TV. Two American actors dressed as doctors during the Korean War spat out a few lines.

"You should turn in like all the rest." Barry gestured to the kids in the beds.

Barry seemed like a no-nonsense guy, but he also seemed like he was the type who actually cared. I had nothing left to lose. "Sir, I just got the crap beaten out of me. I'm scared and mad, and my parents are in another country. I can sit here and talk with you, or code. But I can't sleep." This was all true, especially the scared part. I'd never been this afraid before.

Barry sighed and stood up, stretching. Then he grabbed an amazingly thick book off his desk. "Fine, I'll catch up on my Brandon Sanderson. Let's go." He led me out of the main sleeping room and down the hall past two dark doors. At the third, he swiped the card on the lanyard around his neck through the reader. The door clicked open with a beep, and the lights turned on. He gestured for me to go ahead of him. Long white tables topped with monitors and keyboards ran the length of the room. The chairs were metal and bolted to the floor, and the monitors were attached to the tables.

I turned back to Barry. "I'll work here quietly, if you want to go back to your show."

Barry gave me a look. "I'm not stupid, kid."

"It's not like there aren't bars on all the windows. I'm not going anywhere."

Barry smiled, showing two graying teeth in the front. "I'm all set to read. So either do your nerdy computer thing, or you're going to bed."

I nodded. "I'm cool with working."

Barry grunted, then settled into a metal chair and propped his feet up on the table. He thumbed through his book until he found his spot.

I sat down at one of the computers where he couldn't see my screen. He didn't appear to notice or care what I did as long as I stayed close.

Three hours later, I was in. At first glance, Greg looked squeaky clean. But after careful digging, I found discrepancies in the payroll for his clinic. They were easy to overlook, but they were frequent. Now I knew why he had employees willing to break the law for him. But what really interested me was the three mental hospitals he was affiliated with. Between the three, twelve new patients had been admitted during the night and seven of those were female. None of them went by the name Sydney Moore. The closest I found was a Sandy Clark, age twenty-one, admitted at 11:30 PM for suicide watch with dissociative identity disorder. I tried to pull up the relating medical files, but everything came up empty.

The timing matched. That was not too long after we'd gone to her condo. I tried to take comfort, knowing Hyun was on his way. My parents had said they were hiring a team to deal with this.

I closed my eyes. Losing Sydney had broken something in me, that invisible line inside my head that separated what I would and wouldn't do. I knew I'd crossed it, and I didn't care. This was all-out war, and I'd take Greg down without regard to morals or mercy. I slammed my fists into the table and yelled.

Barry jumped up. "What the . . . kid, you can't yell like that in here. I thought this was supposed to calm you down."

I swallowed hard against the burning in my throat and tried to speak, but words wouldn't come. Tears dripped on the desk in front of me, and I hung my head.

SYDNEY

"Sandy, wake up."

Tapping on my forehead, and then something cold and wet on my face.

"That's right. You're awake now."

I tried to focus my eyes, but the room spun.

"She's going to vomit. Bring me a basin."

Someone lifted my head, and I retched. The bitter taste of bile burned my throat and nose.

"That's what barbiturates do to you, Sandy. You shouldn't take things that will hurt your body."

"Here's some water, Dr. Moore."

I rolled my head to see the nurse hand him a glass. She was a heavy-set woman with straight brown hair and dark eyes.

"Thank you, Juliette," Greg said. "Here, Sandy, this will help." He supported my neck and lifted a cup to my lips.

I sipped, washing away some of the burning in my throat, and tried to speak. "Why are you doing this?"

"Do you remember taking the pills, Sandy?"

"Stop calling me that. I didn't take anything. You drugged me." I slurred my words.

"This is very typical of dissociative identity disorder. One of her identities is suicidal, but the other identities don't remember. To fill in the holes in their memories, they often create stories."

I tried to argue with him, but my mouth wouldn't work right. "Stop," I finally managed.

"It's okay, Sandy. You need to sleep."

"Stop," I said, more forceful this time.

"She's out of the danger zone now," Greg said. "Juliette, remove her IV and take her to her private room. I've written orders for her medication."

I made myself sit up and grab the water in Greg's hand. I guzzled and let the room around me come into focus. "I'm Sydney Moore, and I've been taken here against my will by you." I looked at Juliette. "He's my uncle."

Greg laughed. "Sandy, you have such the imagination. I do, in fact, have a niece, but she lives in South Korea."

"No," I mumbled.

"Make sure she gets her first dose of medication before she retires for the night." Greg sighed. "I'll be back sometime tomorrow to begin her therapy."

39

CHUL

Hyun didn't speak much when he saw me. He'd mostly let the lawyers do the talking. Now that we were alone in the hotel suite, he turned my chin from side to side and tsked at my swollen jaw, cheek, and eye. "You need ice."

I sank down on one of the sofas with a groan. Hyun had rented out the penthouse, and we had a living room, a full kitchen, and three adjoining bedrooms.

"I guarantee the other guy looks worse right about now," I grumbled.

Hyun headed to the kitchen and banged around, then came back and handed me a bag of ice. "It would have been helpful if you'd detained the man instead of getting arrested. We could have questioned him."

I rubbed my tired eyes and gingerly placed the ice on my cheek. "I lost it when they took her."

"Understandable, but you're a man now. Always think; don't just react." Hyun sat down across from me. "Your parents will be here tonight."

I sighed. "Great, how bad is it? Did they both flip?"

"They were both very worried when you were arrested."

"More like mad," I said.

He shook his head. "Your Dad said, and I quote: *Chul will do whatever it takes to get her back. Getting arrested won't faze him.* He sounded proud."

"That would be a first."

Hyun shrugged. "I also heard him bragging that you took out a bodyguard."

"It wasn't a bodyguard," I said.

"Whoever he was, he clocked you hard."

"I barely felt it."

Hyun laughed. "I bet." He seemed to watch me carefully. "What's your plan?"

Hyun had this uncanny ability to know what I was up to even before I'd figured it all out myself. "I'm going to Greg's house tonight."

"To do what?"

"Have a chat."

"Reckless driving is one thing, but torturing Greg to find Sydney will mean prison time."

"I won't get caught."

"If you find her this way, she won't want you anymore."

I flinched, taking his words like a bullet of truth. "What do you expect me to do, then?"

"We've hired a team: three in security, a few semi-reformed con artists, and one retired CIA. They have eyes on Greg, his office, home, car, phone, girlfriend, everything. When his pet Chihuahua takes a crap, they let me know. We meet with them tonight, after your parents arrive."

"So I'm just supposed to wait?"

"No." Hyun stood up and brought me my backpack. "I need security access codes and the layout of Cypress Mental Hospital. It's an underfunded state-run facility that Greg visited in the early morning hours. I want a look inside. Get me codes, and the team will handle the rest." He raised his eyebrows. "Unless that's too hard for you. They have their own specialist."

I glared at him and opened my laptop.

My mother cried when she saw me. I shifted in embarrassment

as she burst through the hotel door, sobbing, and wrapped her arms tightly around my neck. She looked exhausted with swollen, puffy eyes and a wrinkled pantsuit. It was after eleven, and I was sure both of my parents had been up for over twenty-four hours.

I patted her back. I knew she cried more for Sydney than she did for me. I was here and safe. None of us knew where Sydney was. "I'm sorry. I'll get her back."

"We should have come with you." My father looked at me grimly. "I let you down, son. Promise or no, if Sydney was that determined to say goodbye to her mom, then we should have protected both of you."

I swallowed hard, not sure who these people were who looked like my parents. "It was my job. I'll take responsibility and bring her home. I promise."

My father smiled and placed a hand on my shoulder. "I brought the documents. It's official now." He pulled out a folder and handed it to me.

I opened it up and flipped through the papers. A rush of relief at seeing her name next to the official red seal washed over me. This would give me the leverage I needed to get her back. Now I just had to find her. "Thank you." I walked to the desk in the room and placed it in the top drawer.

My mother collapsed on the sofa, and my father sank down next to her.

Hyun eyed them both. "Don't get too comfortable. We still have to meet the head of our security team. Don Harper just got here and is waiting in the lobby downstairs."

"Bring him up now," my father said. He straightened his tie and took my mother by the hand. "Are you sure you want to stay for this? You can retire and let me handle it from here."

My mother smiled sadly. "I won't sleep until we have her back."

He nodded and kissed her forehead. "All right, then."

Don Harper was a tall man. He walked with gangly arms and sharp eyes, taking in every detail as he followed Hyun into the room. He sat down on the sofa across from my parents and me with a relaxed confidence and spoke directly to my father. Hyun sat in one of the side chairs and leaned forward with his arms on his knees. He only sat like that to keep from fidgeting, which meant he was stressed.

Don cleared his throat. "Mr. and Mrs. Kim, I understand that time is crucial, so I will cut right to the chase. We started by sending in one of our operatives to pose as a visiting doctor from another facility. He placed four separate cameras in the hospital. I have both live footage and some stills to show you." He opened his laptop and logged onto his security feed. "They run on a skeleton staff after 10:00 PM. Then three more nurses roll in around six." Don pulled a stack of photos from his bag and handed them to me. "These are all of the female patients. Look through to see if anyone is Sydney."

I quickly scanned, and then slower a second time. I handed them back with a shake of my head. "Not her." I watched the live footage on his screen and waited. I wasn't sure what I was looking for. Maybe for Buzz Cut to make an appearance, or for Sydney to come wave at the camera? But I only saw one nurse drinking coffee. There were no patients.

"I have someone watching this feed," Don said. "They'll report immediately if they see anyone matching the description of your girl."

"What about Greg? Where has he been?" my father asked.

"He arrived at Cypress a few hours ago and went straight to his office."

My mother wiped tears from her eyes. "Is she not there? Maybe we should just offer Greg more money."

"He won't take money," I said.

"We do have one last place to look at Cypress."

We all stared at Don expectantly.

"One of the wings of the hospital is older and no longer in use."

"You think she could be there?" Hyun asked.

Don nodded. "It's possible. We've seen the same nurse enter that hallway twice now."

"Send your man back in," Hyun said. "The one posing as a visiting doctor."

"We are sending someone else with the morning cleaning crew to check that wing. He will put a camera in the hallway and check the rooms to make sure they are empty."

"It has been so long already." My mother started crying again.

I stood up and headed for the door. "I can't wait for tomorrow."

SYDNEY

My soul stayed with me but thin, ready to disintegrate with the storm brewing around me. I tried to remember. There was something I needed to remember. But a fuzzy haze wormed along my edges, numbing the pain and stealing memories.

Tears leaked from my eyes, but I barely noticed. Soon there would be nothing left of me to care.

Chul's face flashed somewhere on the edge of consciousness, and my world sharpened. I tried to grab on to just the tiniest bit of him. Something solid to pull me out of the ocean of numb that carried me away with each new pill.

"Sandy, it's time for your meds, sweetie." I tried to focus my eyes on the nurse leaning over my bed. Her face . . . familiar. I knew her name. Juliette.

She held the little paper cup filled with pills in one hand and propped my head up with her other. "Open up," she said in her syrup-sweet voice.

I opened obediently and waited for the little drops of oblivion that tumbled into my mouth. She helped me sip some water.

When she left, I refused to let the dark ocean of forgetting carry me away. I pictured the sunset on Chul's roof and the thrill of his motorcycle while we zipped through the streets of Seoul. My eyes fluttered around the memory of our first kiss, Chul's warm fingers lacing through mine. I grabbed onto all of him and wrenched myself up in bed.

The room spun with sickening speed. The bed was falling, or was that me? I grabbed onto the white sheet bunched around my waist and breathed deeply.

My saliva pooled thick and sticky, and I remembered why I'd sat up. I spat in my hand. Long strings clung to my chin and lips, but I spat again and again. My eyes watered as I stared at the handful of pills puddled in my hand.

The room held only a bed. There was no chair, no pictures or plants, and no window. But the ceiling above my bed had a small white air vent. I stood up on my mattress and fell back down. It took two more tries to stand before I could reach the vent. I bloodied my nail getting the vent cover unscrewed. Adrenaline and fear made me shake as I dumped the handful of pills as far down the shaft as I could reach. I replaced the cover. Already, I felt stronger. If I could fake out Juliette, then maybe tomorrow I'd be lucid enough to get out before Greg showed up.

40

SYDNEY

Uncle Greg didn't knock or give any warning. My door opened with an electronic beep, and he staggered in, laughing before sitting on the end of the bed. I stared at him, confused. His hair stuck up at odd angels, and the reek of alcohol filled the small room.

"You worked so hard." He rubbed at his red rimmed eyes. "But I'm watching you." He pointed to the small round camera in the corner of the ceiling.

I tried to keep my face calm, but tears pricked my eyes. My breathing came in shaky little gasps.

He patted my bare foot. "I know. This is hard, but I'm going to help you get better." He pulled out a syringe from his jacket coat.

I scooted back on the bed. "Please, Uncle Greg. I do want to get better, but let's do it talking and not with the drugs."

"You know most would consider you a burden. Keeping you here won't be free for me. But you're family. You're my daughter now, Sandy."

"Are you even listening to me? I don't want any more drugs," I yelled.

Confusion clouded his eyes for a moment, and then he focused on my face again. "Your dad wouldn't listen to me, even though I was older and smarter, so I guess I can't expect any different from you. But I know what you need to get better."

"You can't keep me here against my will. I want to go home."

He popped the black plastic cap off the syringe, and a tiny bead of liquid rose to the tip of the needle. "You are home, Sandy. I can fix you here."

"Stop calling me that," I said through gritted teeth. I steadied myself. He wasn't drugging me up again.

He moved closer. I didn't wait. I kicked his wrist, and the syringe flew into the air. Before he could react, I dove forward, driving my fists into his chest. We both toppled off the bed, with me landing on top and Uncle Greg's head smacking the hard tile floor. He moaned and clutched his head. I scrambled for the ID badge clipped to his breast pocket and then found his phone in his left pocket. I swiped the card through the plastic slot on a pad to the left of the door. Three lights went from red to green and then beeped once. The door clicked, and I slipped out, pulling it closed behind me. I gulped air in short pants and leaned over to brace my hands on my legs. When my breathing steadied, I looked around.

My door was the last room in a dead-end hallway. The walls echoed empty along the bare blue hall. There were no paintings or windows, just low-hanging fluorescent lights that reflected a dirty yellow floor, chipped in spots. The air smelled stale with a hint of pee that turned my already empty stomach. I shivered with cold sweat and stood up straight. I'd thought I hated hospitals before, but this place felt about as friendly as a stranger offering you a ride on a deserted road.

The passcode to Greg's phone used to be my dad's birth year. I remembered seeing him enter it during one of our sessions and wondering if it was a coincidence. I tried the numbers, hoping Greg hadn't changed anything. His phone opened to his home screen. I glanced at the time. It was 12:19 AM. Should I call the police? Should I try Chul? And what if one of the nurses heard me? I texted Chul.

**Chul, It's me.
I don't know
where I am—
some hospital but
they keep giving
me drugs. I have
Greg's phone and
I've locked him in
my room. Help if
you can.**

I checked to make sure the phone was on silent and gripped it in my hand along with the key card. I followed the hall until I came to a T. What was I doing? I had no plan. My head alternated between a dull throb and feeling like it was full of cotton. I peeked around both corners. To my left was a darkened hallway with big windows that looked into a room filled with tables and chairs. To my right was a reception area with a bright nurse's station next to a security door with a green exit sign up above. Juliette sat at the desk alone. I hoped there wasn't some beefy, sedation-packing orderly lurking somewhere close, just waiting to grab runaways like me. Maybe this late at night it was just Juliette. I walked carefully, keeping my hands in view. I didn't want to startle her. "Um . . . hi, Juliette."

Juliette's eyes jerked up from her computer screen. "Sandy," she gasped. "How did you get out of your room?"

I held up Greg's ID badge.

She narrowed her eyes, then grabbed the phone at the desk.

"Wait. Please. Before you call security, just check my file."

She paused. "My uncle doesn't have custody of me, and I'm not sick. He brought me here by force. To commit me, doesn't he need my mom's signature, or a judge, or another doctor, some kind of guardian, to agree to this? You can't just lock me up without evidence or history, right?"

Juliette hesitated.

"If you just check my records, you will know I'm not lying."

"Don't you move a muscle. You stand right there where I can see you."

I nodded. "Go ahead. Check. I won't go anywhere."

Juliette moved her mouse and then clicked a few times. She frowned, and her hands flew over the keyboard. "That's strange." She turned and opened the top drawer of a filing cabinet that took up the entire back wall. Her hands moved swiftly along the files, and then she stopped and retrieved one. She moved back to her desk. I still waited obediently while she opened the file. "It's empty. This can't be empty."

The phone vibrated in my hand, but I ignored it. I had to make sure Juliette believed me. "So I'm right? He's not following protocol or procedure. He's breaking the law." I hoped I was making sense. My head pounded, and my tongue felt thick in my mouth, like I'd swallowed glue.

"Listen to me, Juliette. My name is Sydney Moore. I'm Greg's niece, but he doesn't have custody of me. My mom died." I took a deep breath to stay calm. "I went back to our apartment, and he drugged me and brought me here. He thinks I'm sick, but I'm not.

Juliette muttered to herself and tossed the file on her desk. "Where is Dr. Moore?"

"He's in my room. He fell off the bed and hit his head." It was hard not to slur my words.

Juliette rolled her eyes. "Yeah, like I'm going to believe that."

I looked at my bare feet.

"If he's hurt, you will be in a lot of trouble. What really happened?"

"He was trying to give me another shot, and I pushed him. He's not bleeding or anything. It just knocked him out."

Juliette held her hand out to me. "Give me the badge and phone."

I gripped them tighter.

She picked up the land line and started to dial a number.

"Who are you calling?"

"Security."

"If I give these to you, will you promise to help me? Just call whoever should be in charge. Show them my files."

Juliette nodded. "I will. I give you my word that this will all get investigated, but I can't have you hurting one of our doctors."

Greg's phone started vibrating again. Juliette snatched it from my hand.

CHUL

My father rarely showed emotion, but as he turned around in the front seat, veins stuck out on his neck. "Why isn't she answering?"

"I don't know," I yelled. I stared at the screen, hands shaking, but she wasn't texting or calling me back.

"It doesn't matter. Now we know where she is." Hyun's voice was soft from the driver's seat, but the slight tremor and the fact that he drove like we were in the Indy 500 gave away his fear.

"How close are we?" my father asked.

I checked my phone. "Ten minutes, maybe less with Hyun at the wheel." I was glad we'd made my mother stay at the hotel, and even more glad that the black SUV trying to keep up with Hyun was bringing two of the lawyers my father had hired.

SYDNEY

Juliette called security anyway. When they came, I expected guns or like a mall cop uniform at least. But two guys in scrubs grabbed me painfully by both arms while Juliette ran to check on Greg. We waited at the nurse's station.

"Easy there," I said. The guy on my right gripped tighter than necessary. "I'm not going anywhere."

Neither answered me. They just acted like I was the kind of crazy that couldn't be reasoned with. We stood less than ten feet from the exit. It was locked.

If Juliette didn't keep her word, I'd be back in my room, blind with drugs. "It's not like I have superhuman strength," I said, twisting my arm. "You both outweigh me by at least a hundred pounds each." Their grips tightened.

"You're hurting me." I spoke calmly.

The guy to my left sighed. "Look, right now we're not sure how big a threat you are to others or yourself. So let's just all stand here nice and quiet until the nurse comes back."

Juliette and Greg came around the corner and words left me. I wanted to give up, right then and there, lay down on the floor and cry. I probably would have if it hadn't been for the two jerks cutting off blood flow to my arms.

Greg held an icepack to his head as he rushed to my side, playing a worried doctor. "Sydney, you must have been so scared when I fell. I'm glad you found Juliette."

Juliette stepped forward. "I thought her name was Sandy?" She glared at Greg, but he ignored her.

He looked at the orderly to my right. "She needs her meds immediately, so use the restraints if you have to, but make sure she takes them all."

"Director Perkins is on his way in," Juliette said. "I sent him her file. He wants no drugs administered until he examines the patient."

Greg spun towards her. "What? I did not give you authorization to send her file to anyone."

Juliette shrugged. "Well, he's on his way in. There is nothing I can do about it now. He was very specific that no one administer any more drugs. With what she already has in her system, I'm surprised she's standing."

"How dare you. I am her doctor, and I will not see my patient suffer." Uncle Greg's voice came out shrill and gasping. He looked to the orderlies. "Administer 10 ccs of haloperidol. Do it now."

The hallway got quiet, four sets of eyes all staring. Uncle Greg had never looked crazier. He reeked of alcohol and his shirt was untucked, but it was his eyes jerking erratically back and forth between the orderlies that sold it.

"Excuse me, Dr. Moore," Juliette snapped. "But you didn't even have her registered under the correct name. Who are you trying to hide this girl from?"

Uncle Greg ignored her. "Take her to her room. Never mind, I will do it. No one around here knows how to do their job anymore."

Both orderlies let go of my arms and stepped away. The one to my right spoke up. "We need to wait if those are the orders, Dr. Moore."

The light above the exit buzzed yellow, and Juliette ran to her desk. "Who could it be now?" She picked up the phone and spoke into the receiver, but I couldn't make out her words. She pressed a button, and the light above the door turned green.

It all happened so fast. I stepped closer to the exit. Uncle Greg lunged for me, and the orderlies went for him. Juliette started to yell, and suddenly I was falling to the floor with hands on my neck.

CHUL

I thought I knew anger before. My parents, Min, Gun, the

stupid CTF team that sold me out. But none of that compared to how I felt the night we walked into that nightmare of a hospital. What I saw replaced every thought in my head with a cold rage. I wanted to kill Greg. I wanted to crush his skull, crack each of his ribs, and beat him until he was just blood and rags. Sydney was on her back with Greg's hands wrapped around her throat. Two men were trying to pry him away.

Hyun ran for her.

I was faster.

I kicked Greg's jaw, connecting with enough speed and force to break bone. He slumped down over Sydney, and the worthless attendants rolled him over. I fell to my knees next to her, not sure if she was breathing.

Sydney gulped in air and then started coughing. She blinked rapidly with tears streaming from her eyes and reached for me. Her neck was swollen and starting to bleed from a long scratch. I scooped her up. She was light and soft and melted into my shoulder. "Are you okay?" My voice came out pleading.

"What is the meaning of this?" A tall man with deep set eyes and thick, dark hair stood in the exit doorway, his mouth in a tight line. His badge hung from his fingers as he strode to the nurse's station. He slapped his hand on the counter above the desk. "Juliette," he bellowed. "Call the police."

The nurse ran for her desk.

Sydney struggled to stand, but I pulled her back into my lap where I sat on the floor. I could tell she was drugged.

Greg sobbed a few feet away and clutched his jaw. I scooted until my back was against the wall. I wanted Sydney as far away from that psycho as I could get her.

"You're okay, Dr. Moore," one of the orderlies said while the other helped him sit up.

"Who are you people and why is Dr. Moore injured?"

Juliette rushed forward. "I'm glad you're finally here, Dr. Perkins." She bit her lip. "Dr. Moore doesn't seem to be his best self tonight. I'll leave you to investigate, but he did admit

Sydney Moore under a false name. I believe she is his niece." She handed him a paper, and he frowned down at it. "I found this information that matches what she told me."

"Hmm, so this is our patient?" he asked.

Juliette nodded. "Dr. Moore got hurt when her family arrived."

Dr. Perkins whirled on my father and Hyun. "You are not her family. Why did you assault one of my doctors?"

"No, not them," Juliette said, pointing to me. "This boy here, he was the one."

I smiled and waved.

Greg whimpered. "I think I need an ambulance."

Dr. Perkins squatted down. "You're at a hospital, Gregory. They can do scans down in the ER." He leaned closer and whispered, but I was close enough to hear. "Pull yourself together, man. You smell like booze and your lack of procedure is grounds for malpractice. Go home and shower then come back here to get examined."

My father spoke up. "I would advise against any of your staff leaving before the police arrive, Dr. Perkins."

Before the doctor could respond, the light above the exit door buzzed again. The nurse ran back to her desk and picked up the phone. "Dr. Perkins, legal representation for our patient is here." Her eyes were big as she nodded towards Sydney, still in my lap.

"No one else is allowed in until I figure out why my ward is suddenly a circus," Dr. Perkins said.

My father stepped forward and extended a business card. "I'm here to retrieve my goddaughter. She was sedated and taken against her will by Dr. Moore. And I've brought my lawyers." My father's English wasn't as good as mine, but he was passable.

The doctor frowned. "Do you have proof of this or any plan other than assaulting my staff?"

"If you would be so kind as to allow my legal team in, they have all the documentation of guardianship and proof that due process has not been followed for this patient."

Dr. Perkins scoffed. "I don't care how many fancy lawyers you have. This girl isn't leaving the hospital without a thorough evaluation from me, and then there is a waiting period after that. Sydney Moore is currently a minor with both parents deceased. You have no legal rights to this child. She will most likely stay here under our care until a court date can be arranged."

I glanced at Hyun and my father. Dr. Perkins had greatly underestimated them. My father's lip curled, and anger flashed in his eyes. "Dr. Moore will be questioned by the police before leaving this wing. My goddaughter was reported missing yesterday, and the officers covering her case are on their way here."

Hyun took over after that. He wouldn't be happy without getting a few shots in himself. "It will also be noted that you refused Sydney legal representation and access to family after her kidnapping."

Dr. Perkins snapped. "No one here kidnapped Sydney Moore, and I have not denied her access to family. You are *not* her family."

"Her name is not Sydney Moore." I spoke loud and clear. Everyone, except for Sydney who was still nestled against my neck, stared at me. "I am her legal guardian," I said.

Sydney started to stir.

"And who would you be, young man?" Dr. Perkins asked.

"Kim Chul, Sydney's husband."

SYDNEY

Everyone argued. I heard my name and Uncle Greg moaning in pain, but none of it mattered because Chul was here. He smelled so nice. I leaned harder against him, and he moved me like I weighed nothing. I wanted to tell him what had happened, and to thank him, and to cry. But not now. Now I could stop fighting. I could sink down into nothing and rest.

But then Chul spoke. He sounded angry, and his chest rumbled. I climbed back out of the heavy darkness, afraid. Only, he said something so wonderful, yet so ridiculous that I knew it was a dream. "I'm Sydney's husband."

I sat up. I didn't remember getting on Chul's lap, but there I was with my arms draped around him. I stood up dizzily and shook myself. Chul rose next to me and took my hand.

"Is this your husband, Sydney?" Another doctor was speaking to me.

"I've already explained that our lawyers have her documents. You should not be questioning her like this," Jae-ho said. How was he here? And Hyun was here too? Everyone stood, tense and angry.

The doctor held up his hand to Jae-ho and asked me again. "Sydney, is this boy married to you?"

Chul gave my hand a squeeze, like a warning, but he didn't need to. I knew we weren't married, but if it got me out of here, I had no problem being his wife. "Yes, Chul is my husband."

"And they have proof of that? You have a marriage certificate?"

Chul reached into his back pocket and pulled out a folded piece of paper. He smoothed it out before handing it to Dr. Perkins.

Dr. Perkins read it carefully and then held the paper out to me. Is this your signature, Sydney?"

And there, right next to Chul's name, was my own. The memory of signing it in the hospital flooded back.

"Is this your signature?" he asked again.

I swayed on my feet.

"I don't know what's going on or why your uncle would do what he did, but if these people are trying to force a marriage on you, I won't allow it," Dr. Perkins said.

I swallowed. My throat burned, raw from a bruised

windpipe, and my head spun. I felt Chul's hand at my back, steading me. "That's my signature," I said. "I am married to Chul. The only one forcing anything on me is my uncle, Greg Moore. He drugged me before bringing me here."

Jae-hoe beamed at me and Hyun approached, stepping past the orderlies who sat next to Greg on the floor.

"Juliette, let in Mr. Kim's visitors. We will all meet in my office." He looked at Greg. "It appears that I won't be able to help you, Dr. Moore."

41

CHUL

Two weeks after Greg went to prison, my parents had to leave. Running an international company from a hotel could only go on for so long. It didn't help that my mother was so worried watching Sydney fall apart that she couldn't work herself.

My parents stood in our hotel suite, bags packed and faces grim. Hyun was to drive them to the airport, but no one seemed to want to leave.

Hyun cleared his throat. "The kids will be fine. I'll bring them both home when Sydney is ready."

My mother teared up again. "When will that be?"

I folded my arms and stared at Sydney's closed bedroom door. At least she was leaving her room now, not often, but it wasn't just the sleeping and crying that had gone on for weeks. My mother had hired the best therapists, she'd said all the right things, even my father had tried to encourage her. Sydney refused it all.

The worst seemed to be over, but now she wouldn't talk to me. She did talk, only just dumb things like she didn't want lunch. She had a wall around not just her heart, but her mind as well. I couldn't tell if she was mad that we were married or still just sad about losing her mother. "It won't be any time soon," I said. "But I've started my online classes. Hyun's here. We'll work it out."

My father grunted at Hyun, and they both carried the luggage out into the hall where a porter waited to help them.

My mother came closer and wrapped me in a hug. For the first time I could remember, she seemed frail as I hugged her back. "Promise me that you'll watch over her," she said. "I never thought she could be this broken."

I patted her back. "I've watched her since day one."

My mother stepped back and smiled. "She's your wife now. I'm so thankful for that."

The following night, she ate with us at dinner and didn't say no when I asked for a walk. We sat side by side on the pier and watched as the sun dipped below the ocean. Sydney leaned into my coat and shivered, but I wasn't fooled by her physical closeness. She could still be distant right next to me.

"Will you talk to me?" I asked. "Be mad or sad. Yell at me or beat me, but just tell me what you're thinking."

"I'm thinking that I'm glad your parents are gone. I hated worrying them so much, and I can't cry when they're here."

I nodded like I understood, but I really didn't. She had cried. A lot. I sighed. "Anything else on your mind?"

"You lied to me. Again." Her voice was flat.

"I didn't. When?"

"You had me sign the marriage certificate and told me it was for your parents to protect me."

I ran my hand through my hair. "Oh, that."

"I get why you wanted to do it. I mean, Greg was scary, but that's not why I'm mad."

"Then why are you mad?"

"You could have told me your plan and trusted me."

"It wasn't really a trust thing. More like, I didn't have the confidence to pull it off. What would you have thought if I said, 'Hey Syd, let's get married so your mentally unbalanced uncle can't claim custody?'"

She smiled. "It does beg for a hard no."

"See?"

"Still, are you sorry that you tricked me?"

"Yes. Next time someone tries to kidnap you, I'll tell you before I make my move."

She laughed. It was a first since she'd gotten the news about her mom. It seemed like years ago instead of weeks.

Her voice dropped. "For real, though, I'm tired of being mad. I think I'll be mad at Greg for a long time, so I'll save my energy for that."

"I'm mad at Greg too, so if you want to leave it all to me, you can."

"Thanks, but you can't suffer because of me anymore."

"I did it with you, not because of you, and you'd have done the same for me."

She smiled. "If some weird uncle ever messes with you, I'll bust in like Batman and save you."

I raised my eyebrow. "You'd look cute in a bat suit. A smaller one. The bikini version."

That made her giggle, and something inside me, maybe my brain, melted. After that it was hard not to imagine her in a bikini. "So, am I really forgiven, then?"

"Yes, but I still can't wrap my head around the fact that I'm married."

I laughed. "We need to have that honeymoon in Paris."

Sydney sat up straight and pulled her hands to her lap.

I kicked myself. That was so not what she needed now. "Sorry. I can't help being an idiot lately. I won't hold you to it, the marriage, I mean. If you want an annulment, it will be like the marriage never was." I spoke the words quickly and then held my breath. I couldn't tell her that if she asked for an annulment I wouldn't recover. Syd was this invisible thread that she'd sewn through me. All of my parts held together because she was there. The thought of losing her left me airless. And the thought of staying married, of having her be my family, filled me with some kind of awesomeness that I couldn't put into words.

I took her hand again. She'd gone quiet, and I hoped that meant she was just embarrassed about my Paris comment and not considering an annulment. Marriage entailed a whole lot of things that she might not be ready for, even if I was.

She took her hand out of mine. "I can't go with you to Korea."

The cold wind bit at my skin where her hand had been. "Then I'll stay."

"Chul!" Her voice came out sharp, and she scooted away. "Don't make this harder on me than it already is."

"I'm not trying to, but why can't I stay?"

"I need to fix myself, and that will never happen if I'm leaning on you."

"You just need time. Lean on me all you want."

She hung her head. "I clung to my mom like I couldn't live a minute without her, and now she's gone. Then my uncle drugged and committed me to a psych ward. If I wasn't crazy before, I might be now."

I tried to take her hand again, but she snatched it away. "You're not crazy," I said.

"I don't know why you're still here. You don't owe me anything," she snapped.

Her words tore into my heart, sharp little daggers that twisted and severed muscle. But she hadn't demanded an annulment. I held onto that. She was asking for space. I squeezed my hands into fists. Scenarios ran through my head of how I could get her to come with me, but I stopped myself. Sydney was my wife now. This time I wouldn't push or manipulate. I'd be honest and trust her. "If that's what you want, then I'll leave. But not yet—not until I know you're ready."

SYDNEY

I surfed the hotel's movie channel and considered ordering a pizza from room service. When I woke up, both Chul and Hyun were gone with a note that said they'd be back around lunch time. But it was 2:00 and I was starting to wonder if this was just Chul's way of avoiding me. After how upset I'd gotten on the pier, I didn't blame him. I felt stupid, but it had hurt when he'd mentioned the annulment. I wasn't a book he could just check out from the library and then return. And it's not like I was one of those sappy girls who got married a week after high school graduation because they loved their boyfriend *soooo much*. That wasn't me. Circumstances had pushed us together without us choosing, but I wouldn't choose an annulment either. Apparently Chul would.

The door opened, and Hyun walked in with Chul dragging behind. He had dark circles under his eyes. I hadn't thought about him not sleeping well. A pang twinged around my heart.

"We brought lunch, beautiful." Chul deposited a brown paper bag on the kitchen counter that smelled like grease and hamburgers. He winked at me with an easy smile, like yesterday had never happened. He started pulling out thick-cut fries and a cheeseburger loaded with sauce. It smelled like heaven, and I was too hungry to feel awkward. I plopped down on a bar stool. Chul sat down next to me and gave me a plate piled high. "Do you want to swim after we eat?" he asked.

Suni had spared no expense on the hotel when they were here. We were in a penthouse suite with ocean views, three bedrooms, and a private pool. It was paid through the end of the month, but after that I had to figure out where I was going to stay.

"I don't have a swimsuit. Greg gave all my stuff away, remember?"

"I bought you more clothes today."

I gave him a sidelong look.

Chul's eyes went big with innocence. "I can't buy my wife clothes?"

"How much did you buy?"

"Not as much as Hyun. He bought you a house."

"What?" I squeaked.

Hyun shrugged. "It's just a small villa." He glared at Chul. "I told you to let me tell her."

A fry fell from my mouth. "It's not for me. You bought it as an investment or something, right?"

Chul laughed and picked up my fry from the counter.

Hyun looked insulted. "Of course, I bought it for you. It's in your name, and I've paid all the taxes for the year.

"You can't just do that," I said. "I can't be indebted to you."

Hyun cut his cheeseburger with a knife and fork. Then took a careful bite. "That's not what you need to worry about."

I didn't like that Hyun's eyes were heavy with . . . what? Fear? "Should I worry about something else?"

He took a sip of soda and looked away. "I sent an email to Suni telling her that you plan to stay in California. She won't get it right away. She's in Australia for business. But when she reads it, all of us will suffer."

I laughed nervously. "Suni won't get mad that I'm staying here. She knows my situation." I looked to Chul for assurance, but he coughed and stared hard at his food.

Hyun woke me in the middle of the night and thrust his phone against my ear. "Sydney, Sydney, are you there?" It was Suni, and her voice sounded almost shrill.

I took the phone from Hyun, waving him away, and tried to say hello, but my throat crackled.

"Hyun, for crying out loud, wake her up."

"It's me. I'm here. Sorry." I rubbed sleep from my eyes and glanced at the clock that read 3:04 AM. "Is everything okay?"

"It most certainly is not okay," she said. "What do you mean by not coming back? And Hyun said Chul plans to leave."

My brain scrambled for something to tell her, some way to explain the complicated feelings and doubts that plagued me. "Chul's already missed a lot of school and—"

"You're both doing online school," she snapped. "Don't use that as an excuse. What is going on?"

"Chul needs to go home," I said lamely.

"If he leaves, then I expect you to come with him. I don't like the idea of you out there anywhere near your uncle, even if he *is* in prison."

It was all I could do not to follow Chul back to Korea, to cling to him just as much as I had clung to my mom. And he would let me, if for no other reason than he would feel obligated. Chul didn't deserve that, and I wouldn't sink the person I loved the most.

"He's your husband, and I know it was all rather sudden, but you already liked each other. Your marriage will grow if you let it."

"Chul likes me, but he didn't have enough time to get to know me."

"He knows you enough to have followed you to California."

"That doesn't mean he should be forced to marry me. He may change his mind and not like me next year. He could meet the perfect girl five years from now and wonder how he got saddled with a penniless orphan from the States who has serious depression issues." I could hear Suni's breathing on the other end, but she remained silent, so I waited.

Finally, she spoke. "I know my son. There won't be a better girl for him. Once Chul makes up his mind, he doesn't change it. He's in love with you. If you don't feel that you could ever love him back, then I accept your decision. But can you honestly tell me you don't have feelings for him?"

I couldn't tell her that. Of course I had feelings for Chul. Strong ones. "If things are going to work with Chul, I have to heal first."

"Yes, and we can get you the best doctors and—"

"I don't need doctors. I need time. I need to come to grips with the horrible things that happened, and I need to do it on my own. But even more than that, I need this to be a choice for Chul. I can't keep him when he married me just to protect me."

Suni sighed. "Sydney, did you know that the papers you signed also had your mother's signature?" She let that hang there for a few torturous seconds. "The night of your party, I had our lawyers draw up papers. They weren't adoption papers, like she originally wanted, but something a lot easier— marriage documents. Do you know why I did that?"

"No."

"That was the day I saw Chul watching you. I knew he wouldn't understand how he felt until later. He was always so defiant, but my son loved you from the beginning."

CHUL

I didn't know that I could feel the way I did about Sydney. Love wasn't a word I would use to describe it. That seemed too ordinary, something that happened every day. What I felt for Syd was so big and wide, I couldn't hold it all. Loving her hurt. And at this point, I was pretty sure if she died, I'd cease to exist.

I got my parents now. They loved each other, and it kinda eclipsed everything else. Maybe that's why I felt unimportant to them. Because when I pushed them away, they pulled together. Good for them, and good for me that I'd finally grown up enough to appreciate that.

42

SYDNEY

After we moved into the house, Hyun started buying furniture and cooking meals. He said my mom's ghost had told him to stay and be my temporary guardian. I told him he was full of crap.

School took up most of my time and Chul's. We both had a lot of catch-up from the days we missed. It was what I needed —routine and work to keep my mind off all the bad that had happened.

But as Chul's departure date got closer, I found myself crying more. I needed to let him have a chance at a real life, at normal. I had to fight myself to keep from wondering what it would be like if he stayed. Would we graduate and then go to college together? Would we share a room?

The night before he left, I lay on my bed, pretending to do homework. Really, I was sulking and reminding myself of all the reasons he needed to leave. All the good reasons were still there, but the selfish parts of me wanted to forget them. So what if I was clingy and a little unhinged? Chul would just deal with it. And did he really need a normal life? He was still in high school, but that's if you got technical. He could graduate early online and was rich enough to do college, or whatever he wanted. Plus, we had amazing chemistry. If we were ever alone in a room together, we couldn't stay apart. I'd find ways to touch his hands. He'd play with my hair. The next thing you know, kissing would get involved.

A loud knock saved me from my thoughts. I quickly sat up and pulled my laptop closer. "Come in," I said.

Chul opened the door and leaned against the wall, wearing a white tee shirt that made it way too obvious he lifted weights. "You're still not done?" He took a step towards me where I was sitting on the bed. "I can help you."

I jumped up and skirted around him for the door. "No, I need a break anyway." Fasting in an all-you-can-eat buffet would be easier than being married to Chul and yet . . . not having all the benefits. I walked to the kitchen. "Where's Hyun? I'm starved."

Chul followed me and leaned against the counter with a lazy smile. "He went out."

I viewed the kitchen as a sort of "Chul Safe Zone." Mostly because Hyun was frequently there. Chul smiled like he knew this. I walked with purpose to the sink and grabbed a glass like I was straight out of the desert and dying of thirst.

Chul watched me. "Do you want me to make mac 'n cheese?"

I shook my head. "I'll wait for Hyun."

"He won't be back any time soon. He told me to order take out." Chul cocked his eyebrow. "It's a good idea. We can eat Chinese and watch a movie."

I blushed. The last time we'd tried watching a movie, we'd ended up kissing. "I'm in the mood for Mexican. Let's go to that place by the mall."

Chul took my empty glass and placed it in the sink. He stood close enough that I could smell his clean soap scent and something richer that I could never identify. "I don't want to drive," he said.

"Why not?"

"I'm tired."

Chul did not look tired. I swallowed. "Okay, then I guess we order in." I reached for my phone in my back pocket. Chul took my hand, lacing our fingers together. "I'll order. Come sit with me." I started to pull away, but he held on. "Please, Syd.

I'm leaving tomorrow. It's not like I'm dangerous. Let's just relax and have dinner."

He was wrong about being dangerous, but I followed him to the brand-new overstuffed sectional Hyun had picked out for the living room. Chul sat down and pulled me next to him. "So Chinese or Mexican?"

"Pizza, extra pepperoni," I said.

He tapped on his screen for a minute and then placed his phone face down on the coffee table. Our knees touched.

Chul leaned closer. "Are you sure about tomorrow? I can still stay."

I wanted him to stay. I tried to answer but gave up when I realized I was staring at his lips.

"If I go, I'm coming back. I'll give you a week." He winked at me to let me know he wasn't serious. I'd already made him promise not to come back until I said I was ready.

"What do you mean 'if you go?' Your ticket is bought, and you go back to school on Monday. Tell Min I say hi."

He leaned closer. "What if I tell her we're married?"

"She'll assume I'm pregnant."

"You could be."

I laughed. "I really couldn't. I mean we haven't even . . ."

"I should fix that, then." He closed the already too small distance between us and brushed his lips softly against mine. My breath came faster. Kissing led to more kissing with Chul. It was never enough, and yet nothing felt like too much. It scared and thrilled me, all at once.

"We shouldn't."

Chul spoke against my mouth. "I won't do anything you don't want."

Normal thoughts fled my brain when his hands cradled my face. I let my arms slide around his neck as his lips pressed against mine. Whatever magic burned between us gathered momentum. I wanted more, his taste, his smell, his touch, that ignited something amazing and—I ripped away. "We can't."

Chul pulled back, his breathing ragged.

I gulped in air. "I want to be sure before we take this step."

He frowned. "More sure than married?"

I pushed him away and stood up. "I'm not hungry anymore. I'll see you in the morning."

We stopped at the security line that snaked with so many turns I couldn't see its end. Chul shifted his backpack and looked at me expectantly.

I kicked the toe of my boot against the floor, nervous and embarrassed. I wanted to beg him to stay. I knew what a loser that made me. I hadn't been able to bring up the annulment since that day on the pier. I was pretty sure he didn't want it, but when he left here, the girls would swarm. Absence doesn't always make the heart grow fonder, especially when you're still in high school. He so deserved me to green light him on this. I cleared my throat. "If you ever decide to send papers for me to sign, I'll sign them, no problem. I don't want you to feel obligated. You might change your mind about us being together." I stared stupidly at the scuff mark my boot had made. I couldn't say it and meet his eyes.

"What are you talking about?"

"Well, you mentioned an annulment that one day on the pier, so I just wanted to be clear that I wouldn't stand in your way, if that's what you decide."

"I thought you just needed time. We never agreed to an annulment."

I wished I could push the pause button, and the world would stop turning, letting me work out whatever stupid thing I had to do in my head before I pushed play again. But I didn't have a magic pause button and hanging onto Chul wasn't fair to him. "You said you wouldn't hold me to the marriage. So I thought . . ."

All the agony we couldn't speak about, all the bad things that happened, filled the space between us. "Go on," he said.

"I thought that was maybe your way of letting me down

easy, but either way, I just want you to feel free. I don't want you to feel trapped."

Chul closed his eyes, and when he opened them to speak his voice cracked. He swallowed hard and tried again. His eyes glistened, and his eyelashes stuck together, like he was hanging on so hard he wouldn't even let the tears fall. "I need us to be together. If you want time, take it. But I'm the guy taking you to Paris."

I braved a smile that I knew came out sad. We were too young. He would change, and when he did, he had to be free to send the papers if he wanted out. I couldn't bear a sappy goodbye with empty promises if he moved on. "You're going to miss your flight."

"Promise me we'll be together."

"When I get my head on straight, if you're still interested, I'll be around." It was the best I could do, and it cost me. I would always want Chul. I loved him. But I rarely got what I wanted.

Chul dropped his bag and his arms slid around me, pulling me close. He looked down into my eyes, and I saw something there that trumped all my realism and the we're-too-young-arguments. His lips crushed to mine, desperate. But it wasn't a goodbye kiss, more like a pledge, his guarantee that this wasn't the end.

When he let me go, I stumbled and caught his hand to right myself. He touched my face and whispered, "I love you." Then it was over, and he entered the security line without looking back.

43

CHUL

After the first week of her not answering my texts or calls, I tried Hyun. He answered on the first ring.

"Hello, Chul."

"Is Sydney there?"

He sighed. "She's in her room."

"I'm just wondering why she's refusing to answer her phone."

"She put it in the microwave."

"What?" I yelled.

"It started a small fire."

"Let me talk to her," I said.

"I doubt she'll talk. She barely talks to me. She's back to all the crying again." He paused. "We need to let her."

I breathed hard. "I can't just let her suffer."

"I know a way you can help her."

"How?" I asked.

"Send her videos."

I snorted. "Videos? Why am I even asking you? You're past forty."

I could almost hear the smile in his voice. "I understand women, and you don't. Not yet."

It was true. Hyun seemed to speak whatever secret language girls used. He didn't have amazing looks or the best body, but the women always noticed him. When I was fourteen, he stole the girlfriend of a prominent plastic surgeon after just one conversation. "Fine, I'm listening. What do I say in a dumb video? *Hi, Syd, I miss you, come home soon?*"

Hyun scoffed his don't-be-an-idiot scoff. "First, you should send her one every day. She needs to realize that you aren't going anywhere. After enough time, she'll see that you're waiting and not moving on."

"Easy enough," I said.

"Second, you need to understand why she melted her phone."

"I'm guessing it's not because she wants a newer model."

"She's afraid that if she talks to you, she'll beg you to come back."

"I want to go back," I said.

"She knows that, but what she needs instead is to know that you married her for more than just a quick fix to a problem."

"I've told her how I feel. I've told her a million times."

"You think just telling a girl works?" Hyun laughed. "You need to sell it. Woo her, be gentle and romantic. Send videos where you confide and confess in all different ways. Let her know that you are missing her. And most importantly, that you will never stop."

I sent a video every day. Hyun was dumb, but I still sent one.

Every day.

I taught myself guitar. Girls supposedly liked love songs. I tried poetry. It was easy to write when I thought about her. I told her how school was going. Min had a serious boyfriend, such a relief. I made fun of the teachers and told her how I had straight A's. Grades weren't hard because I never left my room. I did one video where I read Pride and Prejudice cliff notes and gave commentary. I let my mother and grandmother watch it first. I wasn't sure. They both laughed until they cried, so I sent it.

My father recommended naming a star after her. You literally buy a star and they send you a certificate. It was lame, but I did it, and then had a telescope shipped to her house with the official certificate.

For Valentine's Day, I took her on a video date where I went to Namsan Tower again and talked the whole time like she was right there with me. I even put on a lock with our names on it.

When spring came and the weather warmed, I cooked a meal and ate it on the roof with the sun setting.

Most days, I just talked. It felt weird at first, but then I got the flow and relaxed. I told her stories about my childhood. I confided that I'd finally manned up and told my dad thank you for bailing me out of jail when I got arrested for hacking.

A few weeks before graduation, I cried while trying to talk about our future plans together. I think it was because I wanted it so badly.

After that, I started sleeping all the time. My mother called in two different doctors, but they both said the same thing. "Too much pressure on young kids these days." They prescribed anti-depressants, anti-anxiety meds, and just to be safe, anti-psychotics. I flushed them all.

Maybe I was depressed, or maybe I just missed my wife. Sometimes I dreamed about Sydney. I wished they'd been R-rated dreams, something I could enjoy, but they never were. She always had her back to me, or she was walking away. I'd yell and scream at her to stop, but she never did.

I think this is when the videos started getting weird. I'd just ramble a lot, and a few times I fell asleep during the video. I sent it all, but she never responded. Hyun said she'd sit for hours with her laptop and watch my videos over and over, but she never said anything.

I called Hyun again.

"Hello."

"Is Sydney there?"

"Yes." Hyun sounded tired.

"What's she doing?"

"Hang on." I heard him walk to another room.

"She's watching your latest video. She's watched it eight times already. She finishes it and then starts pacing. She wants me to fly home and check on you."

"You told her no, right?"

"I said she could check on you herself."

I smiled. At least she was worried.

SYDNEY

Hyun was making breakfast when I came out of my room, showered and ready to go. "Can I get the keys to the car?"

"No."

"Why?" I asked, annoyed.

"Because you just barely got your license, and it's a Mercedes."

"You told me if I got my license, I could have the car. Now I can't drive it because it's too expensive?"

He frowned down at the eggs frying in the skillet. "I thought you'd be a better driver when you got your license. Are you sure you passed the test?"

I glared at him. "The instructor said I did very well."

Hyun looked up and raised both eyebrows. "He was being nice."

"Didn't Chul buy that car for *me*?"

"Yes, and he told me not to let you drive it until you were safe."

"I'm perfectly safe."

He slid two eggs onto a plate piled high with fluffy pancakes and placed it in front of me. "Where do you plan on going?"

I bit my lip. Hyun told Chul everything. And Chul was a mess. "You don't have to know where I'm going. I have a license, and I've graduated."

"You're not yet eighteen."

I rolled my eyes. "Two months, Hyun."

"Tell me, or you're not going anywhere," he said firmly.

"I'm going to the state prison."

Hyun stilled. "You're going to go see your uncle?"

I nodded.

"Is that really necessary?"

"It is if I'm going to stop sleeping with the light on."

Hyun's voice went soft. "You don't actually have to see him to face your demons."

"I think you know that I'm out of time," I said. "I've had to watch Chul suffer all year, and I can't anymore. I either need to prove to myself that I can handle my issues or cut him completely free. I'd prefer to go rescue my husband at this point, thus the drastic measures."

Hyun's eyes flicked down. He knew I was right. Normally he would have argued or forbidden me from going to see Greg, but we both knew Chul was losing it. "Finish your food. I'll drive."

The prison was close to two-hours from our house, so in the end I was glad Hyun drove. He had a calming presence, even *if* he made me listen to power ballads from the 90's the whole way there. Plus, he reminded me every day how far I'd come.

I'd done more than just finish high school and get my driver's license. With every video Chul sent me, I became more determined to pull myself out of the black and gather up all my broken pieces. I'd taken myself on long walks, written letters to Mom, and listened to soothing music. When I felt strong enough, I began sewing up the tattered pieces of my heart. I read a bunch of self-help books and started a wellness journal. But more than anything, I prayed. Not the kind of prayers I'd said as a kid in the hospital, more the kind where I really talked to God. And with all that talking and pondering I got stronger.

I'd saved visiting Greg for last. I knew this was the final test. It would either scatter me again or prove that I was okay enough to be with Chul.

Hyun turned onto the road that led to visitor check in and parked near the back.

"It's just my name listed for the appointment, so you can't come with me," I said.

His eyes went big. "You didn't mention that. Reschedule."

I placed my hand on Hyun's. They were starting to age, and I could see the first signs of arthritis starting to form at his knuckles. "It will be easier for me if I do this alone. I need to face Greg, or I can't be with Chul. You understand that, I think."

He was quiet, and I waited. Finally, he said, "You'll be careful?"

"Yes."

He sighed. "Going into a place like this as a young girl can be dangerous. Just stick close to the guards and make it short with Greg."

I nodded. It was good advice. I got out of the car before I could change my mind.

Hyun lowered the window and raised his voice as I walked away. "Greg is worthless. Don't listen to anything he says."

I waved my hand over my head with an "okay" sign, but I wasn't okay. With each step away from the car, my chest got tighter. Greg still had some kind of hold over me. In my head, I knew he was wrong. I wasn't sick, and I didn't have PTSD. I was just a girl who had survived her mom getting sick and dying. I had scars but who didn't? I squared my shoulders and took three deep breaths before I entered the building.

A man with heavily graying hair and mustache sat reading a book at the desk when I walked in. "Do you have an appointment?" he asked, sitting up straighter.

I walked bravely over. "Yes, Sydney Kim. I have an appointment to see Gregory Moore."

The clerk's nametag read "Sheldon," and I wasn't sure if he was an officer, a guard, or just a receptionist. His hair matched his uniform and blurred with the rest of the room. Everything—the floor, ceiling, even the sofa and four chairs below the window, were all an unwelcoming steel-gray. The only color in the room came from a mounted television with the volume turned low and a golf channel playing.

Sheldon's fingers flew expertly over the keyboard of his very outdated desktop. He stared at the screen and then lowered his eyebrows. "Are you here alone?"

"Yes, I'm here to see my uncle."

"You need to come back with your parents," he said.

"My parents are deceased."

"Who is your guardian? I see from your appointment application that you are still a minor."

I cleared my throat. "I'm married, so technically I'm my own guardian."

He eyed me up and down, doubtful. "Do you have proof?"

Before leaving, Chul had given me my new family registry card from Korea. It listed me as Kim Sydney, married to Kim Chul, and living at his address in Korea. I'd gotten it out on nights when I needed to remind myself that it was all real. I'd never shown it to anyone, not even Hyun. I hesitated. Something about using it now seemed so final, like I was saying "I do" to Pastor Sheldon instead of just proving that I didn't need my parents to Sheldon the guard.

"Can you, or can you not, prove that you are married?" He folded his arms with an impatient look.

I bit my lip and pulled the card, along with my newly acquired driver's license, from my wallet. I placed them on the counter and smiled at Sheldon.

He took both, looking at each one carefully. "Do you have dual citizenship?"

The Kims had taken care of all the legal documents. I'd signed a bunch of papers with their lawyers before they left, but I'd been in such a haze of grief I couldn't remember. "Uh, yes."

"All right. Have a seat, and I'll get someone to escort you."

I took one of the four empty seats and stared at the floor. This was it. I steadied my breathing and went over in my head what I would say to him one last time. I wouldn't be afraid. He was in prison and couldn't hurt me.

"Are you Sydney?" A tall middle-aged officer, in a slightly darker gray uniform, stood at the doorway.

I stood up. "Yes." It came out as a squeak. I swallowed against my throat, which had gone desert-dry, and stuck both hands in my pockets to keep them from shaking.

"Follow me," he said, holding the door. We walked side by side down a long hallway, also painted gray, and I tried not to fidget with my hands. The guard had deep-set eyes, bushy eyebrows, and walked with a shuffle. But somehow, he exuded a feeling of safety, which helped. "So, your uncle, huh?"

"Yeah," I nodded.

"He's a nice enough fellow. Keeps to himself and doesn't cause trouble. He'll look good for parole when he's up."

I nodded again, not sure what to say. The guard stopped at a door. "Since you're so young, we arranged a single room. You'll be separated by a window, but this way we won't have any of the other inmates around you.

"Oh, thanks."

He opened the door and followed me inside, staying in the back of the room. Greg sat behind a window with small holes cut in the plexiglass. As soon as Greg saw me, he sat up straight and glared. Instead of sound, hate and venom seeped through the window and crawled their way to me.

Suddenly, I wasn't Sydney anymore but some form of her, only made from sand. All Greg had to do was show his face, and I crumbled into nothing. He could level me with just a stare. I took a shaky breath and tried to walk to the waiting chair on my side of the window, but my feet wouldn't work. I looked down, willing them to move.

"This is all your fault, and now you're still as broken as

ever. Can't look up. Can't talk. Can't move. And you're all alone, Sydney."

Except I wasn't. I had Chul now. And with him came a whole family that loved me. Suni and Jae-ho, Hyun, even Chul's grandparents were woven into my future. I walked forward and sat down. It wasn't graceful. Even my stomach shook, but I did it. "Hi, Greg," I managed.

His glare turned to a sneer. "Just Greg? I'm your uncle. Show some respect."

I closed my eyes against his words and leaned on my memorized speech. "I wanted to talk to you today about how I've forgiven you and—"

"Shut up. You're just as stupid as your mother. Did you trap that Korean kid into marrying you just like your mom trapped my brother?"

I reared back.

He laughed. "You didn't know that they only got married because he knocked up your mom, did you?"

I stilled. "What did you say?"

"Think about it. Why else would my brother get married as a freshman in college? He left me and our family for some tramp."

"My mom was not a tramp. And yes, I knew why they got married so young, only it wasn't as ugly as you paint it."

"You know nothing."

I gritted my teeth. I wanted to slam my chair against the plexiglass, scream, and yell and dump all the hate back on him. "I know they loved me," I croaked. "All the fear you tried pushing on me, the false diagnosis as a kid, the drugs and abuse, I survived because they loved me."

"Not enough to stay with you," he whispered. "They didn't love you enough to live."

I laughed. "That's so messed up."

"You'll always be broken, Sydney. Remember that."

I pulled my hands from my pockets and really looked at them. They weren't shaking anymore. I smiled to myself and remembered holding Chul's hands. I even remembered holding my mom's as she slipped away. Something about that felt powerful. I wasn't perfect, and maybe I would still sleep with the light on, but I was brave and smart, and I loved Chul. Nothing Greg could ever say would change that, and I think he knew. Deep down somewhere in that rotting soul of his, he understood that I knew how to love, and he didn't.

I dropped the rest of my speech, and what came out felt more right than everything I'd practiced for hours in the mirror. "I'm leaving California. I'm going to be with my husband and his family."

"You can't just leave. What about your mother? You wouldn't stay when she was sick, and now you will leave her grave, just like the ungrateful brat that you are."

"I'm taking her with me. I had her cremated. But I will be sad to leave my dad's grave. When you get out, you should go visit him. I think you need to make peace with your brother before you can find your own."

"Don't you dare mention him. He left me when I needed him the most." Greg dropped his head, breathing hard.

The guard behind me made a noise but didn't interrupt. I was thankful he had given us space. I started to stand, but Greg's head snapped up. "You're just like him. All you want to do is leave."

"I hope you figure out what went wrong in your family and find forgiveness. It's not too late to move on," I said.

"I need a way to contact you. What if I need help, or what if I get sick?"

"Don't contact me."

He looked at me with open panic. "So you're just going to cut me off?"

"You don't need me." I smiled kindly and stood up.

"Your dad wouldn't want you to do this." Heavy tears began to drip from the end of his nose. I turned to go, and he spoke in a rush. "I shouldn't have . . . I really wanted to help you. I just got lost, is all."

Before I left, I found it in myself to be gracious. "I hope you find your way back."

44

CHUL

I lay in the growing dark and tried to think of another video to send. It had to be good because it would be my last.

My mother knocked before coming in. She didn't turn on the light, but I could tell it was her. She smelled like garlic and fish. The same way she'd smelled after I'd gotten arrested for hacking. Maybe she thought that personally cooking my food would fix my problems. "Are you hungry?" she asked.

"Not really," I said.

"Can you at least try? You haven't been out of bed in two days."

"I've been trying."

She came and sat on the edge of my bed. "Have you still not heard from her?"

"I haven't."

"Should you fly out?"

"She doesn't want me there."

My mother was quiet when she spoke. "Are you giving her up?"

"No, I won't ever give her up. But I won't beg, either. I trust Sydney." I couldn't see my mother's eyes in the dim light, but I felt like she was proud.

"She's going to come around. She loves you, son."

SYDNEY

My fingers shook at the keyboard when I clicked send. It was night there. He wouldn't get it for hours.

CHUL

In my dreams, I could still smell Sydney.

SYDNEY

He would call. I made Hyun give me his phone so I could answer first.

CHUL

I opened the email on my phone, too tired to get my laptop. My inbox flooded with junk and then, there it was. One line glowed. I tapped my phone. It was short. Just a single sentence with one attachment.

I'd only go with you.

I opened the attachment to see an airline logo and quickly scrolled. It was an itinerary for two tickets to Paris.

I got out of bed.

EPILOGUE

SYDNEY and CHUL

"I didn't imagine it would be this beautiful," Sydney said. They stood staring up through the mist of early morning and watched the soft colors of dawn paint the lines along the Eiffel Tower. Chul hadn't known *any* dawn to be this beautiful, but then this was the first he'd spent with his wife.

Sydney snuggled closer and buried her hands under his shirt to press her cold fingertips against his stomach.

He sucked in air. "You're freezing, beautiful."

Sydney arched one eyebrow and smiled in that impish way he loved, that smile that she reserved just for him when they were alone. "Should I stop?" she asked and started to pull her hands back.

He captured them in his own and pressed them flat against his stomach, then leaned closer to place a kiss softly on her lips.

She closed her eyes with a sigh and felt the invisible tug of Chul's soul pulling her closer. He'd told her on the plane that he was happy, that she was his everything. Chul had confessed in every way a girl could dream. But Sydney knew that she loved him with all of that and more. Chul wasn't just her everything. Sydney knew she loved Chul with an unstoppable force that would mold and shape them together into one future. He was the other half of her story.

ACKNOWLEDGEMENTS

I'd like to thank my Korean sensitivity readers EunBin and Dasom. Your suggestions were invaluable, and I really enjoyed the fun Korean food. I must also thank my editor, Emily, who did an excellent job of adding the finishing polish. I was so fearful of edits, but you made the process painless. Special thanks to the artist, Julia Garnelo. This cover turned out better than I could have envisioned. You were so easy to work with, and I'm excited to see more from you. This book wouldn't exist without the support of my writers' group. Cindy, thank you for pushing me to publish. Without your cheering, I don't think I would have ever taken those beginning steps. Alene, you were the first to show us that it could be done and inspired us all. Brenda, your positivity and steady kindness kept me going when I felt lost. And Keri, K-pop Fridays gave birth to this book. I still remember the thrill I felt pacing on the phone in front of the library while plotting pinch points with you. Each of you are my friends and worked tirelessly to help make this a story that I love. I owe many thanks to my beta readers—Mary, you are awesome and your friendship means so much. A special shout-out to Caitlin and Heidi. You both went above and beyond when the slumps came. I owe enormous gratitude to my children. You have made me who I am, and each of you inspire my awe. Thank you, Zach, for reading All of the Chul chapters out loud so I could get the voice right. And thank you, Grace, for not waking me at two in the morning to talk when you finished your beta copy. Moms need their sleep. Peter, you have my heart and endless appreciation. Thank you for taking such good care to make the dream a reality. I couldn't have a more supportive husband. You put Gilbert to shame. And lastly, I would like to thank my readers for Falling into this world with me. I hope to share with you again.